Beautiful Shattering

GRACE COSTELLO

This one's for the broken hearted.

Chapter One

BRIGGS

I've barely made it a mile and I already want to turn back. The Texas humidity clings to my body like a second skin. The slap of my stride on the pavement mirrors the blood whooshing through my veins. I might vomit. It won't be the first time I lose the contents of my stomach in the dark morning hours, but it will be the first time I blame Dr. Thomas. He's the only reason I'm out here at five a.m.

Even though it's not actually his fault, I curse my therapist for the pathetic stitch in my side, the burn in my throat, and the battery acid taste filling my mouth. Dr. Thomas urged me to take up running because I used to do it with Jaci. He said it would be healthy to try again. But in the end, I'm the one to blame for my dusty Nikes. I still hit the weight room three times a week, but I've let my cardio endurance go, and that's on me. This "trying again bit" doesn't *feel* very healthy.

I can't take it anymore and stop at a crosswalk, panting and frowning at my surroundings as I wait for my turn. The cityscape is nothing like what Jaci and I used to enjoy on a daily basis. We'd lived out in the suburbs where the roads were quiet and sprawling fields bordered our new-build neighborhood. Almost every morning my wife would insist we lace up and run into the sunrise together. I sold that house a couple of years ago in favor of a modern condo downtown––it's closer to work and further from her memory.

The light changes and I cross the street, forcing myself to pick up the pace. No more stopping. No more being pathetic. No more feeling like a lanky sixth grader in gym class. I slow my breathing and glare at the beginnings of Austin's morning traffic. Keeping my head up and my eyes forward, I focus on drowning out the sound of the passing cars, but the more I try not to think about them, the more they seem to intrude on my thoughts, filling up my peripheral vision and demanding my attention.

I hate cars. I'd never drive if I could help it, but this is Texas, so wheels are mandatory, especially in my line of work. I've thought about hiring a driver, never touching a steering wheel again, but what would Dr. Thomas say? I can picture the graying man now, his eyes creased in concern, his frown deepening, as he poses careful questions about moving forward without running away.

A horn blares through the darkness. Brakes screech. I

freeze in panic. Where's the booming crash of metal? The dizzying smell of gasoline? The resounding silence?

Nothing.

The cars are driving away, the crisis is averted, and the commuters are back on track.

That's when I do throw up, right there on my dusty Nikes. Someone calls out to me. Another runner? My vision blurs and I don't register anything beyond their bobbing dark ponytail as I motion for them to keep moving. I turn back and stumble home in a delirious haze of PTSD and regret. I don't remember all the steps it takes to get home. I do remember throwing my shoes in the trash and b-lining it to the bathroom. I do remember turning the shower to the hottest level, like maybe the heat will scald me into forgetting. I do remember standing there under the pelting water, still in my workout gear.

And then, like always, I remember the night Jaci died. The accident and her limp body and the blood that covered the car. The shards of glass and the stench of burning rubber and the shock of pain in my left shoulder. The grief that followed me like a permanent shadow. The anger. The loathing. The memories like ghosts. The sleepless nights. The early mornings. What Dr. Thomas calls "the dark night of the soul."

My dark night was never figurative. It was literal and endless. Three years now. Three years without my wife and forever to go.

Chapter Two

RAVEN

I'll be damned if I have to wrangle twenty kindergarteners without the appropriate amount of caffeine and sugar. Today the line is long enough to make me nervous and the men in front of me are about as three-dimensional as paper dolls. They order lattes with extra shots, no flavor, no soul. I lean closer, trying to catch their names. I want to hear Steve and Mike or Richard and Robert. Any of those would complete the picture I'm creating of them inside my head, but the girl who makes the coffee is grinding away in the background, and I miss their names entirely.

"Raven, looking especially sweet today." Nicky winks, sizing up my outfit of the day.

I'm wearing a sunshine-yellow sundress and matching

flats, with a hot-pink headband and a rainbow-beaded chunky necklace.

"It's my kindergarten-teacher wardrobe." I sigh, shooting Nicky a pointed look. "Please don't laugh."

He holds up his hands. "I would never. You're very cute."

He's not wrong. We elementary school teachers have the cutest fits of any industry, but that doesn't mean I don't prefer yoga pants and a sweater the size of a small country.

Last week, when I came in here with my tri club, Nicky did a little shimmy and called me spicy, and though I knew the compliment was coming, it still put me in a great mood. Everyone wants to be told they look hot by a sassy male barista. I did look a little hot that day though. Six months ago, I took my mother's advice to subscribe to one of those fitness subscription boxes, and now my workout wardrobe is second only to Gwyneth Paltrow's.

Today? Today I don't look hot. I look positively sunshine sweet, just as Nicky proclaimed.

"What's your order on this fine Monday morning?"

I skim the chalkboard above Nicky's head. No boring lattes for me. I'm a specials with additives type of woman. I can nearly feel the eyeroll from the boring men waiting at the end of the bar for their drinks when I say, "I'll try the raspberry snowball, with sweet cream foam."

It isn't until I finish paying and step to the side to wait for my own drink that I realize that the closest boring man is actually Turner Lawson, father to five-year-old Charlie

Lawson, and he's been avoiding me, which isn't common. Most parents of kindergarteners haven't learned to be afraid of parent-teacher interactions yet. Turner and his wife, on the other hand, are dodging my calls and emails like they think their kid is the next Unabomber and I'm about to call them on it.

I'm about to call him on not calling me back.

"Turner Lawson?" I ask, though I know with complete certainty that this is the dude I met at the kindergarten open house. It's difficult to miss the fact that he and Charlie share the same face, his with a few more lines, but even more difficult to miss that they have the same voice. I had never met a kindergartner with the voice of a man before, yet there was Charlie at the open house, introducing himself with a deep baritone that matched his father's. A month into the school year, and it still makes me giggle.

I see the moment he recognizes me, because dread fills his features.

"Miss Raven, hello," he says.

"Miss Raven?" the man next to him mutters with a raised eyebrow.

One look, and it's obvious this is Turner Lawson's brother. The men are cut from the same gorgeous cloth, though Turner has curls in his dark hair and is slightly shorter and thinner than his GQ-worthy brother.

"Uh, right," Turner mutters. He nods to me and then to his brother. "Miss Raven is Charlie's kindergarten teacher. They, uh, go by first names in class. Miss

Raven, this is my brother." He inches back, obviously stalling.

"Nice to meet you." I smile brightly, then peel my eyes off the eye candy to zero in on Turner. It should be criminal to make a touch of gray look that good. "Have you been getting my emails and phone calls? I've been hoping to set up an appointment to talk about Charlie's progress."

I don't say more because we're not in private.

His eyes widen and I know he must have, but the liar shakes his head. "You should talk to my wife, Samantha. She's better at this stuff."

Better at being involved in his child's education? Sounds like a real keeper. Charlie has been acting out in class and there's only so much redirection I can do at school. I've learned that if I can get the parents involved quickly, the behavior typically resolves itself.

"Your wife isn't answering either."

He has the audacity to shrug, and my heart drops.

"Kindergarten is such an important milestone in child development," I say instead of what I really want to say. "Charlie is a darling boy, but I have some concerns that I'd love to discuss with you and Samantha as soon as possible."

I heave up my overflowing Rainbow Fish tote bag, rummaging for my phone, but the dang thing is hiding from me. "I think you guys added the wrong phone number to the school directory because so far I've only spoken with your nanny." I give him a pointed look. "But she's not Charlie's legal guardian, so I can't discuss anything with her." I pull out my pink polka dot umbrella and hook it on my arm, but that doesn't want to stay. "Here, can you hold this?" I hand it off to Turner's startled brother and keep rummaging.

A stack of orange construction paper slips onto the floor, and I have to keep myself from cursing. I stoop to pick it up and the men follow suit.

I finally locate my phone and hold it out triumphantly. "What's your phone number? I'm going to update the school directory today."

Turner mutters off a string of numbers and I enter them in, then catch the gaze of his quiet brother. The man isn't looking at my face though. No, he's looking at my bare legs and the unfortunate way my dress has gathered around my middle instead of brushing the floor. I shoot up, cheeks burning and wondering how much they saw. I want to kick myself for being unprofessional. Could they have thought I did that on purpose? That I was getting Turner's number for reasons other than my student's well-being?

That's the problem with being a single woman of a certain age. You have to worry that everyone else is worried about you. At thirty, I'm supposed to be married, or at least in a long-term, non-traditional partnership. No one is threatened by the married female staffers at work, but the things you hear in the break room about the singles will make you shake your head. I've never once hit on the parent of one of my students, though I *have* been accused of it.

"Raven!" the barista calls out.

I don't want to exit the conversation without a confirmation that Turner or Samantha will address the situation with Charlie, but I also don't want to stand there long enough for the blush in my cheeks to catch fire and turn my words into a jumble of mismatched syllables.

I quickly excuse myself for a moment and grab my warm, sugary, Monday morning therapy.

The coffee is supposed to be *my* exit strategy, but by the time I pick it up and turn back toward the front of the shop, the Lawson brothers are already making a beeline for the door.

Chapter Three

BRIGGS

"I saw that," Turner says with a sidelong glance at me.

"Saw what?"

We climb into his truck and head out to the first of several job sites we're checking on today. There's one in particular that I'm worried about--a commercial office building that failed a recent inspection.

"Saw you checking out Charlie's teacher." He fastens his seatbelt with a snap and pulls out of the parking lot.

It's not what he thinks. I wasn't checking her out because she was attractive--I was simply studying what ridiculous looks like up close. Miss Raven is like a caricature of a kindergarten teacher. A zany sitcom character come to life. And that dress . . . how is it my fault she flashed her white grandma panties to the entire coffeehouse?

"Really?" I turn it around on Turner. "Because what I saw was you dodging Charlie's teacher. What's going on?"

I know my kid brother, and what I just witnessed wasn't Turner. Six years ago, he knocked up his college girlfriend and has taken care of her and their son Charlie ever since, so to see him cagey with a teacher is concerning.

Turner's knuckles tighten on the steering wheel. "Don't worry about it," he says. "I'll handle it."

"Will you, because--"

"I said I'll handle it."

That is the thing about Turner. If he says something he'll do it. If he challenges himself you better believe he will go full force. I used to think that was a Lawson trait.

I lean back in my seat and close my eyes, this morning's running failure washing over me. Everything Lawson is carefully curated to come off as impressive, successful, and untouchable. Puking on the side of the road hardly fits the bill.

The run today was a mistake. I should've known better than to try something like that. I can get my cardio in other ways, like kickboxing or rowing, things that Jaci would never have considered.

I'm a strategist, which comes in handy when I'm fighting off my demons. My favorite strategies are designed to forget that I'm a widower, and some work better than others. My latest goal is to get through twenty-four hours without thinking about something that reminds me of

Jaci. I'm on a three-year failure streak, though sometimes I surprise myself and I only think about her once or twice a day. Dr. Thomas is not a fan of my strategies. His goal is for me to feel what needs to be felt so that I can learn to process it, to heal. He makes it sound like healing is a real possibility when, in reality, I'm pretty sure I'm paying $180.00 an hour for a hope and a prayer.

The best forgetting strategy is to work. When I'm at Lawson Construction Enterprises, I'm not the grieving loser––I'm the boss, end of story. No awkward questions about my home life, no sympathetic nods or surprise casserole deliveries.

That's why I work around the clock. So what if it makes everyone else work harder? Let them grapple with their priorities however they want, but I'll never apologize for working my ass off. Maybe if everyone else worked as hard as I did, we wouldn't be failing inspections.

Turner pulls the truck to a stop and pivots his body in my direction. His face is a question, and I'm praying it's work related because I do not have the energy to act anymore *fine* today.

"Why aren't you groaning in pain like the rest of humanity does on a Monday morning? Where's your perma-scowl?"

I almost laugh. If only he knew how my morning actually started, he would know what groaning in pain *really* looks like.

"Well, brother, while some people loath Mondays, I find them comforting."

He snorts. "Only you would find Mondays comforting. There is a word for people like you."

"Efficient?"

"Workaholic."

"You're welcome," I deadpan.

The truth is, Mondays hold the promise of five days' worth of distraction. Today, however, it seems the universe is hell bent on keeping me in my feelings. I shake my head, thinking how pleased Dr. Thomas would be that I can't run and bury my head in an excel sheet.

"You didn't tell me Mom and Dad were meeting us here."

"I didn't know," Turner says, but his voice lifts in that way that tells me he's full of shit.

I stride across the gravel lot to meet my parents, the sounds of construction on the four-story structure echoing around us.

"There is an important conversation to be had between the foreman of this job and Turner and me. Can we reschedule the family reunion?" I say.

"Smooth," Turner whispers.

A crease forms between Mom's eyebrows and her lips press into a tight line. She has worn the same expression of disappointment since we were children. It never ceases to deploy guilt.

"This will only take a minute." My father motions for us to enter the building and finds us an unoccupied room away from the rhythmic sound of men at work.

We are standing in what will be a glossy public bathroom. If my father notices the humor in that, he pretends not to. There is no insulation or wiring yet, just concrete floors and framing. I love to visit sites when they are still raw like this. In a few weeks, the place will be sheetrocked, painted, and covered from wall to wall with predictable high-end industrial carpet and tile. For now, it's only a floor plan and possibility.

Like most of our builds, everything here has already been leased off. Since we started owning our buildings instead of just constructing them, our profits have increased tenfold. That was my first goal as CEO. My next goal is to take our company public. I don't just want to be the biggest commercial construction company in Austin, I want to be the biggest in Texas, and I won't stop until I get there.

"You've been putting a lot of energy into work these last few years," Dad says, and Mom nods sagely, as if this isn't the most obvious statement anyone has ever said to me.

"Workaholic," coughs Turner.

Dad levels him with a stare that sucks the humor from his body like a tapeworm.

"As an owner, I'm very proud, but as a father, I am worried." His tone is somber and my mother links her arm through his. Together, they are the picture of grave concern.

This conversation is not new, more frequent lately, but hardly new. It's my role as oldest son to listen with a plain expression and then offer reassurance, but lately, I've been growing more and more resentful. How many times can I say, "I'm fine," before they listen?

"I enjoy the work," I say, trying to stay calm, trying not to snap. They can hardly complain, can they? I've turned them from rich to filthy rich.

"It's all you enjoy," says Mom, untethering herself from Dad's side so that she can place her hands on each side of my face like I'm four years old again and a good dose of eye contact will set me straight. I count to five inside my head before stepping back from her grasp.

"It suits me."

"A little too well." Dad gives me a knowing look, like I should be agreeing with him here. "We've already discussed this with the board, and we'd like to see you take a leave of absence."

My heart rate picks up and my body goes cold. I can't not work. The moments I'm not working are the moments Jaci runs free in my head, and she's already taking up too much space.

Dad must read it in my expression because his voice softens.

"Nothing long term, just a bit of time to collect yourself. Fine-tune some of your old hobbies." He smiles brightly. "You could pull out your trumpet again."

Turner snorts, and I expect Dad to put him in his place again, but he's too pleased with himself for coming up with the trumpet idea. Does he really think I'm going to pull my dusty high school instrument out of the attic, rip into some sheet music, and forget that my life came to a screeching halt three years ago?

My shoulders slump. "Jaci and I met in marching band. The trumpet depresses me."

"Your trumpet playing depresses all of us," quips Turner. This time it's our mother's glare that puts him in his place.

I'd smack him, but I'm grateful for the interruption. I don't need to be thinking about high school band today. "I wasn't any good, Mom." I only stuck it out because of the girl I had a massive crush on, the girl I married, and then ruined.

"You didn't practice enough," says my mother.

My eyebrows shoot to the top of my forehead. Seriously? We're still on this topic? These two are dead serious about the trumpet.

I look to Turner for help, another smart-aleck remark, something to redirect their helpful ire. The bastard just shrugs. Suddenly he's got nothing. If I were really mean, I would throw him under the bus while I had the chance. I could just mention we ran into Charlie's teacher, and it seems he's not doing well. Nothing distracts Mom faster than Charlie.

I glare at my parents. "You talked about this with the board already, but did you vote on anything?"

Mom's mouth thins. "Not yet. We wanted to discuss it with you first."

"No," I growl, "I'm not taking a leave of absence." I motion to the building around us. "Do you have any idea how much we have on the line right now? I can't step away."

"You could," says Dad. "I could fill in or..." He shifts his focus to my brother. "Turner could step up for a while--"

"Turner is our numbers guy," I snap. "He's busy enough as it is." Turner's face has gone sheet white, and I'm not sure if it's because he agrees with them and is afraid of how I'll react, or if he knows that he cannot simply "step up" without losing his marbles.

"Listen," I say, choosing my words strategically, "I hear you. I know I need to work on my self-development a little more, and I have been."

"Oh really?" Mom's face lifts and Dad's pinches. "Like what?"

"Like--" My mind latches on to the first thing that pops into my mind. "Like I started running again."

"Well, that's a start," Dad says, and the tension in his shoulders drops the tiniest of margins.

The words tumble out of my mouth before I can gather them together. "And I've decided to sign up for a triathlon."

"A triathlon?" Turner asks, his eyes widen with disbelief. "The swim, bike, run thing?"

"Yup."

My pulse spikes, and I have to tuck my hands into the pockets of my slacks to prevent them from giving off that tell tale tremble that screams "Briggs is lying!" What the hell was I thinking? Triathlon? I wouldn't even know where that came from, except for the fact that I watched one on late-night television the other day when I couldn't sleep. At the end of the race, the men were strewn out on the ground, pouring water over their heads, and the women were still standing and giving each other high fives and bright smiles. I remember laughing at that, and I rarely laugh anymore.

"How many miles is it going to be?" Turner is looking at me like I just took a bite of a live ferret. He is not playing this cool.

I pat him on the shoulder and squeeze hard to let him know to shut up. "I haven't worked out all the details just yet." I swallow hard.

A shit-eating grin crosses his face. "I have a friend that's really into it, actually. They're long. Almost one hundred and fifty miles depending on the race."

That––I did not know. The blood drains from my face.

"It will take months of training." He snickers and my eyes narrow. "Months of early mornings, long workouts on weekends, lots of expensive gear, and even special dieting. That is a lot of, what did you call it again?" Turner places his hands on his hips while he pretends to catch a lost thought. "Aw yes, self-development."

I could shoot him. Hide the body in the concrete of one of the new builds. This triathlon thing is supposed to be a distraction, and something I'd immediately planned to forget about, but Turner is already turning it into a challenge.

"You don't think I can do it?" I'm suddenly offended. It's not as if I've lost all my muscle and am sporting a beer gut. Who does he think I am?

"Oh, honey, you can do anything you set your mind to," Mom says, the ever-supportive matriarch. "I'm very proud of you. This is a wonderful step for your healing."

So that's what all this is really about. They don't think I've moved on from Jaci fast enough. In their ideal world, I'd be remarried by now with a child on the way. They're calling me out for hiding in my work, but if this triathlon nonsense will keep them from voting me off the island––albeit temporarily––then so be it.

"It's settled then," my father says. "You'll continue on as CEO, but you'll spend your free time training for this triathlon." He levels me with a hard look. "No more company work around the clock, Briggs. We want to see you make some changes and you'll need to if you're going to get fit enough to complete a race like this."

Part of me doubts the board knows much about triathlons. It is very unlikely that a collection of lawyers, businessmen, and development stakeholders are more concerned with my personal life than they are with the state of the business. I could object, of course. I could, and probably should, look my dad in the eye and state the obvious. His concern is noted, but the fact that I am *his* child doesn't mean I am still *a* child. But it is hard not to notice how both of my parents have aged since the accident. Jaci isn't the only one I owe apologies to.

"Fine," I say, letting the fight drain from my body. If this is what they need. I'll do it.

"It's for your own good." Dad pats me on the shoulder.

"Because we love you," Mom adds.

Sure. Call it love or call it manipulation, but the outcome is still the same. Looks like this morning's disastrous run just turned into the first of many.

Chapter Four

RAVEN

Miss Raven's kindergarten class is *the* kindergarten class everyone wants to be in. I know this because I can see the looks of envy on all the other kindergarteners' faces when my class line passes another in the hall. I don't have the best-behaved class. In fact, sometimes I suspect the powers that be purposely put the difficult kids in my class, but we have the most fun. My class enters the first grade with pizzazz.

Which is why it is weird to me that Turner Lawson is dodging me like I'm a Jehovah's Witness at his doorstep. I've called him twice in the last three days and both times it went straight to voicemail. Meanwhile, Charlie is literally cocooning himself in the corner of my room during recess. Yesterday I found him under a pile of blankets in the reading area, and this morning he was crouched behind where the students hang their jackets for a full five minutes before I found him.

I'm used to kids being shy, but an about-face so early in the school year isn't normal. Charlie Lawson has gone from a bubbly jokester to mousy and afraid in a matter of weeks. He won't participate in class, won't talk to anyone, and won't even play on the playground. We're only six weeks into the school year, but I can't just stand back and watch him continue to slip, so I employ my can't-fail secret weapon.

When I drag the big, blue plastic tub from the craft closet and place it in the center of the room, little eyes go wide all around me. Typically, a parade is reserved for special occasions like classroom birthdays or silly holidays like teacher appreciation day, but Charlie needs a pick-me-up, and nothing beats a parade.

"Today, classroom 2B has a *very* important duty. Maybe you have noticed, maybe you haven't, but Glen Eden Academy is suffering from an acute case of boredom."

The class giggles, and I catch a glimpse of a smile twitching at the corner of Charlie's lips.

"This can only be cured by music. Charlie, please come forward." I motion to the spot beside me on the carpet and he cautiously rises from his desk and joins me at the front of the room. I place the red drum major's cap over Charlie's unruly dark curls and hand him a heavily bedazzled staff.

"Today I need you to lead the parade from our room to the cafeteria. Can you do that?"

Charlie worries his bottom lip between his teeth, and for a heartbreaking moment, I think he will say no, but then he looks up at me with those big, brown eyes and nods a quiet yes.

Relieved, I pass the instruments out one by one. Some kids get shaky eggs, some kazoos, one lucky child scores a tambourine, and the rest are left with triangles. I count backward from ten, pull open the classroom door, and let Charlie lead the way out into the hallway. He pumps his red-and-gold staff up and down with pride, seemingly oblivious to the jarring sounds of kindergarten musicians behind him.

"I'm so glad you could meet with me today." I smile at Turner and Samantha Lawson.

"Is this about the volunteer hours?" Samantha asks. "Because we were under the impression that Glen Eden Academy supported working parents. I'm one of Austin's leading trial lawyers, and Turner is the CFO of Lawson Construction Industries, so you can understand that we don't have much free time."

I can only blink at the name dropping.

"Volunteering is optional, Sam," Turner says to his frosty wife, then he levels his rich CFO gaze on me. "Besides, we don't pay thousands of dollars a year in tuition for nothing."

The urge to jump over the desk and wring their necks out is second only to my desire to keep my job. It's not lost on me that my student's tuition is high, and here I am getting paid crap. My salary is more than public school, thank goodness, but it's still barely enough to live comfortably in this expensive city. This is exactly why I've built my tri club business. Well, that's why I started it anyway. I've met so many awesome people through training that I'd continue training people whether or not I had a higher paycheck. Nobody gets into teaching for the money, that's for damn sure, even if the parents can sometimes make you rethink your sanity from time to time.

"This isn't about volunteering. I assure you, we have the classroom well-covered." I lean forward in my seat and give them my serious face. "This is about Charlie's behavior. He's withdrawn emotionally and uninterested in learning. Given the rigorous curriculum at this school, it's important that he keep up, but I also want him to enjoy being here."

"Isn't that your job?" Samantha raises a haughty eyebrow, immediately defensive. "What does this have to do with us?"

"I am here to educate and provide a safe space for Charlie, and we do have special resources for him should he need them, but I always find it best to start with the parents when something like this comes up." I mean, *hello*, they are Charlie's flesh and blood, for crying out loud. "Charlie entered school with one of our highest scoring assessments, and he was enthusiastic about being here, but recently it's as if all that's changed." This is the part I'm dreading with these two, but I have to ask. "Has something changed at home?"

Their faces redden and they won't make eye contact with me, let alone each other. *Bingo.*

Turner clears his throat. "We're fine."

Samantha scoffs at her husband. "Are you serious right now?" She turns to me. "Actually, we're in the middle of a trial separation. We decided to keep Charlie in the house, but Turner and I are trading off staying there. It's called bird-nesting. It's very common these days."

Well, that explains it.

"Thank you for sharing that sensitive information with me." I clear my throat. "As hard as it is, this kind of thing happens with my students all the time, so now that I know what's going on, we can make a plan."

I go into details about our counseling center and what they can do at home, making sure they understand how important it is that Charlie's emotional well-being is balanced with his education. We cannot neglect his emotional growth or Charlie will suffer. Luckily, they seem to be accepting of all I have to say, and the conversation flows easily from there.

When we get up to leave, Turner stops, pointing to one of the framed pictures on my desk. "Do you race?"

I glance down at the image of my tri club after a full triathlon from last year. We were covered in sweat, exhausted to the bone, but bursting with endorphins and pride.

I smile fondly at the image. "Yeah, I'm actually a tri-coach as well as a teacher."

"You have a gift for teaching then." Samantha has softened considerably since the truth of her situation was brought to light without judgment. I'll admit that I no longer want to choke her.

My cheeks redden. "Uh, I guess so. Do either of you race?"

"Oh, heavens no." Samantha laughs, tossing her sheath of blond hair behind her. "I'm a Pilates fanatic."

Turner shakes his head, but there's a plotting glint in his eyes that wasn't there before. What is with this guy? He started out defensive, then forlorn, then the typical "fixer" men often adopt, but this is different. This is *suspicious*. Before I can question him, his phone rings, and he's out the door, talking loudly about fixed budgets and competitive bids, his wife's designer high heels clicking behind him.

Chapter Five

BRIGGS

We used to thrift-store shop for costumes. The Easter day run without bunny ears was sacrilege, the fourth of July without red, white, and blue sneakers, was disrespectful, but Jaci never ventured past a holiday 5k. Though I often ran with her in the mornings, my sole responsibility for the races had been to hold a silly sign at the halfway mark.

A triathlon is different. I can't just sprint for thirty minutes, feel like I'm going to die at the end, and satisfy my parents. A deep Google dive into the sport revealed that I've cornered myself into a tight spot. I should have paid more attention when Turner started railing off the costs and commitment. Instead, I got defensive and stupid.

Of the three legs of the race, I'm most equipped to

run. Given my most recent run, puke, panic attack, that is alarming.

It's not just the physical challenge that's intimidating. I've spent some time scrolling through triathlon forums and there is a whole school of equipment needs out there that goes far beyond buying themed socks and remembering to eat carbohydrates the night before a race. What do I know about wetsuits and lightweight bikes? My last bike was purchased at Target, and it sits covered in dust in a storage unit across town.

I have to tell my parents the truth––I can't do this. Not physically, not mentally. The time it will take to prepare for even the shortest distance event will eat up my schedule. And if I fail? How is that going to improve my mental health? Work is what keeps me going. Time away from work to prepare for something I don't have a prayer of being good at is illogical.

Not to mention, I hate swimming. You couldn't pay me to go to a water park for fun, let alone to swim outdoors in frigid water for sport. It's not going to happen.

Ways to quit bounce around my head like ping-pong balls on steroids. Maybe I can fake an injury. I'm getting gray at the temples, so a bad back is believable. The problem with that excuse is it will launch my mother into full mom-mode. I don't need her pushing an anti-inflammatory diet, or God forbid, trying to take me to see a doctor.

Injury is out.

My phone vibrates across the desk of my home office, and I swoop to catch it just before it tips over the edge and heads screen first toward the black slate flooring. Three cereal bowls and one coffee mug have met their demise in this way. My phone will not be victim number four.

Turner's photo lights up the home screen.

"Ambush not yet forgiven," I answer.

Turner chuckles. "What if I'm calling with helpful information? You forgive me then?"

"Depends on your definition of helpful."

"I've got some tips for your new hobby."

I push my desk chair into reclining mode and tilt my head to the ceiling, watching the fan spin in an endless loop.

"You can table those. I'm currently drafting a list of excuses to quit."

There is a long pause on the other end. Disappointment seeps across the phone line, quiet but familiar.

"You know if you quit, they'll make you take that leave of absence."

"They can't make me take anything," I reply, my jaw clenched and ready for battle. "Dad's a figurehead at this point. You don't really believe that bull about discussing this with the board, do you?"

Turner sighs. "It seems unlikely, but figurehead or not —and for what it's worth I would avoid *ever* saying that out loud in the presence of our father—he has sway over the board, and if he does decide to take this to them, you're going to get railroaded in a vote. What would you rather do? Sit in a board meeting and listen to our dad lay out your personal struggles in front of the men and women you *need* to respect you, or just placate our parents by trying something new?"

Trying something new? Trying something new is enrolling in a cooking class and spending an evening rolling sushi. He has a point though. I have spent far too much time distancing work from my past to have my parents throw it all on the table, with published minutes to commemorate the occasion.

"You going to be joining me?"

"I urge you to reflect back on my senior year in high school."

A smile invades my bad mood.

"That's right." I laugh, springing out of my chair. "You have the curse of the flat foot."

Turner had gotten into his thick skull that he would join the military as a way to rebel against the plans my parents had laid out for him. He never did get past that physical though. The doctor referred him to physical therapy to correct the issue with his feet, with the advice to enlist later, but by then, the novelty had worn off.

I paced across the room trying to imagine Turner running beside me. Maybe his huffing and puffing would be all the motivation I need to shove my way through this thing.

"Doesn't mean you can't do a triathlon."

Turner snorts. "You got yourself into this mess, brother. Don't punish me."

I roll my eyes. That's rich coming from him, considering how quickly he'd jumped on the idea of me training for a triathlon.

"I'll figure it out. Don't worry about me." Even I can hear the robotic tone that slips out every time I have to remind my family that it isn't their job to check up on me. My responses are practically automated at this point.

"I do worry about you," Turner says. "We all do."

I'm about ready to end the conversation there, but something in his voice gives me pause. I know my brother. He's scheming.

"Out with it."

He laughs that devilish little shit laugh of his. "I signed you up for a tri club."

I spin on my heels so fast I nearly lose my balance. "A what-now?"

"Yeah, it's a local club where people train together for triathlons and a professional coach helps them along the way. A bit expensive, if you ask me, but I'm pretty sure everything in that sport is expensive."

I stand and begin pacing around the room, my mind laying out all the pros and cons to the possibility of this club. "Yeah, I'm not doing it."

"You are," he says. "It'll be good for you. Besides, I already paid for the first month. Nonrefundable."

I curse. "It won't be good for me, as you say. It'll be embarrassing. I can barely run a mile."

"That's the point of the club. The coach will help you figure out what workouts you can do now and will get you all caught up with the rest of the group in no time."

"This is a joke, right?" A cruel, cruel joke . . .

"This is a gift." I can practically see his eye roll. "I'll text you the information. Your first workout is tomorrow. Bright and early. It's a shorter run, so you won't need special gear, and the coach is prepared to help you pick out the gear you will need."

"How early?" And also, how short is a short run to a tri club?

He's holding back a laugh. "Five a.m."

It's official. I'm going to prison for murdering my little brother.

We hang up, and I continue pacing, my mind racing through the possibilities of joining the tri club. What if Turner is right and this does turn out to be a good thing? I almost don't want to go simply because I don't want him to have the opportunity to say, "I told you so" in that snarky kid-brother way. But on the other hand, I don't know the first thing about triathlons, and this club could bridge the gap between making this my goal and actually achieving it.

One of the reasons I've been so successful in my current role at Lawson is because I'm not afraid to seek out expert advice. I'm coachable. And I made it a point to find great mentors along the way.

Is this really so different?

With a resigned sigh, I decide I'd better get to bed as soon as possible if I'm going to attempt a five a.m. workout, but my gaze catches on the dusty box sitting in the corner and I pause. It's been waiting there for ages, a ticking time bomb that I pretend doesn't exist. Almost like if I touch it, my whole world will detonate again.

The cardboard moving box holds all that I have left of Jaci's things. I only allowed myself one box of her items when I moved into this place. I packed the things I couldn't part with and taped them inside the cardboard, instructing the movers to put the box in the office. I haven't touched it since. I'm still not ready to go through it, but I carry it into the bedroom anyway, setting it next to the window. Maybe a more visible corner will inspire me to open the damn thing faster, or maybe I'm kidding myself. Maybe I'll be moving that unopened box from now until I die, telling myself I'll get to it later, letting it collect dust instead of memories.

Chapter Six

RAVEN

Briggs Lawson. The name of my newest client is too close to Turner Lawson for comfort. The application and payment came in just as I was finishing up a twice-a-week weight-training session. I'd wanted to read through it right there, but had opted to wait until sliding into the driver's seat of my car to open it again.

I didn't know what I wanted.

Part of me prayed Briggs wasn't Turner's hot brother to whom I'd maybe accidentally flashed my underwear to on Monday. And part of me knew I would be disappointed if it wasn't. How lame am I? That guy didn't show any interest in me.

It's probably a different Lawson. What were the odds, right?

I skim through the application section, my heart squeezing, when sure enough, Lawson Construction is listed under the employment tab. I swipe away from the application and head over to Google for some sleuthing. One quick search is all it takes to confirm the coffeehouse man and my newest client are one and the same. And damn, is he attractive.

I let out a groan and drop my phone to my lap. He's signed up for the three weekly club workouts plus a weekly one-on-one session. We start tomorrow morning. I have no excuse to cancel or put this off. Even if he isn't a good fit for the club yet, I rarely refuse private clients. The pay is too good.

According to Briggs' application, he's an advanced runner, inexperienced in the pool, and intermediate when it comes to cycling. No one ever gets those distinctions right though. In all my years of training, I've yet to have a client's self-assessment match my own assessment of where they stand. But, if my coffee shop memory serves me correctly, Briggs Lawson has the physical potential needed to be competitive . . . and other things. If I were less of a professional, I might focus a little more on the exact makeup of his tri-ready form, but I'm above that, or so I remind myself as I think back on our first encounter. He's got to be a few inches over six feet with broad shoulders that will serve him well in the water.

I'm overthinking this. He's a new client, and a new client means extra income for race season. The race fees alone are in the hundreds, and the equipment gets into the thousands, even tens of thousands. I swallow a gulp of pride, hit accept on his application, then shove my phone in my purse for the drive out to my parents.

Thursday night dinners are a tradition, though I'm not sure who enjoys them. Mom acts like cooking is a punishment, and Dad spends more time out in the garage than he does talking with Mom and me. If I had siblings, we could share this duty or at least commiserate on the experience. Instead, as the only child of academic parents, I have the distinct impression they regret having me. I mean, how many parents take vacations without their only child? Growing up, my parents went on Alaskan cruise ships without me, island hopping in the Caribbean without me, and to at least three national parks. The exotic locations I can somewhat understand, but national parks are family central––just not for our family. Yet, here I am as a thirty-year-old adult, required to eat dinner over there every Thursday evening as if they can't go a week without seeing me.

And still, after all these years, they don't truly know me, or I them.

My mother waves from the kitchen window when I turn off the car and step out into the cool night air. She's got a dish towel thrown over her shoulder, and I know I'm about to enter to the scent of manicotti cooling on top of the oven. We're on a five-meal rotation, and we don't mess with the order. I let myself in and go straight to the kitchen, where a cutting board is already set with cucumber, tomatoes, and green onions. I prep the salad because I burned the garlic bread one time, and it was never forgiven.

My mother pops a cold kiss on my cheek before calling out to the garage for Dad. It takes my dad ten minutes to shut down whatever he is working on out there. My parents are both retired from the university where they taught, and they're bored out of their minds now. Dad pretends to have taken up woodworking, but I suspect he's watching reruns of *Seinfeld* on the tiny garage TV because there never seems to be anything to show for the amount of time he spends out there. He grins and pats me on the shoulder as he walks by to take his seat at the table.

"How's my little bird?" he asks when Mom and I have finished bringing everything over for our meal.

I think about answering truthfully. *Professionally exhausted, a tiny bit lonely, and honestly, at the moment, kinda poor.* Instead, I say what I always say.

"Everything's going well. Nothing too exciting."

Dad nods and digs into his manicotti, and we eat mostly in silence. Then, in a valiant effort to keep the evening from being purely the communal consumption of food in silence, my mother describes in painful detail the latest must-see television show.

"Ray Liotta plays the sheriff and every episode is so surprising. Raven honey, we are talking a cliffhanger every time. It's so unpredictable."

I don't mention that having a cliffhanger in every episode is the very definition of predictable or that I think purgatory might actually be one long network television show starring Ray Liotta. Instead, I lie and tell her I'll check it out.

"And how's school going?" she asks.

"Busy but great." It's my usual answer.

Dad frowns. "Have you put any more thought into a graduate program?"

My parents were thrilled when they thought following in their footsteps meant pursuing higher academia, but when I revealed it was elementary education that had my interest, they'd all but staged an intervention. *But, honey, the pay is so terrible,* she'd say. *Are you sure you want to be around children all day,* he'd question. *Elementary school teachers are overworked and undervalued,* they'd both agreed.

They're more supportive of the triathlon business, though I'm pretty sure they still think my racing is about winning, when in reality it has only ever been about bettering myself. They would know that if they ever attended an event, but they haven't come to a race since my college track-meet days. They had me when they were already older, a one-and-done situation, and now that I'm thirty-three and they're nearly seventy, they act like they can only putter around the house, like rooting me on at the finish line would be akin to running the race themselves.

They don't understand me. But I love them.

I force down a lumpy piece of banana cream pie and make up excuses about needing to prepare for class in the morning so I can bail before Mom suggests we watch the pilot of her new show together. Every time I pull out of their driveway, I'm amazed that eighteen years of my life were spent comfortably under that roof. It seems unfathomable to spend twenty-four hours there now.

It kind of breaks my heart.

I've got a deeper connection with tarot cards than them, and it's not like I pull those out on a regular basis. I've never talked to a therapist about it, but I'm pretty sure my relationship with my parents is exactly why I chose a career being around children, why I like to train with other people instead of going it alone, and why deep down, I'm waiting on my prince charming to sweep me off my feet and give me lots of sex and babies.

LESS THAN TWELVE HOURS LATER, and I can confidently say Briggs Lawson has zero potential of becoming my prince charming. The man is an Ass with a capital A. Case in point: he showed up late and I swear his eyes narrowed like a cartoon villain the second he saw me. That was before he spoke. Not everyone is a morning person, I get that, but he is sporting a terrible attitude, and it's impossible not to respond accordingly.

We're running along an easy park path––most of Texas is flat, training here isn't exactly training for Worlds––but it's only been a mile and he's refusing to run anymore. A little old lady with a Shi Tzu just passed us, and the full grown man beside me wants to slow down?

"I'm done," he says. "I hate running."

Uh, well, you'd better get used to running because there's a lot more where this came from, I think, but I don't say it. Not yet. I can be a tough cookie when I need to be, but we're just getting started so I need to get a feel for his sensitivity-level first. Some coaches are all-out drill-sergeants, but I take a more tough-love approach, emphasis on the love part.

His aging Nikes and basketball shorts aren't exactly top-of-the-line training gear, which is fine, but it might be an indication as to how seriously he's taking this. And honestly, it baffles me. Why pay for private coaching if you don't want to be here?

"I've got you for forty-five minutes. We're gonna cross the one-mile mark in another 200 feet. Done happens then."

He's slowed from jack rabbit to turtle over the last few minutes, and I can tell right away that while Briggs may have sprinted before, he's never trained for anything long distance.

He growls, stopping and leveling me with that hard CEO-stare. "I'm paying for this. I will decide when we are done."

I can tell he doesn't believe that. I tug him forward. It's a risky move, touching him, but there is an icy layer enveloping him whole this morning, and if I don't at least crack the surface, there isn't a chance in hell he gives this a real chance.

"You don't need to pay me anything to quit. You can

do that without a coach. But I can help you push yourself if you'll meet me halfway."

He rolls his eyes but picks up the pace. It only takes us twenty seconds to pass the next tree. The snails we passed along the way will be green with envy. Maybe he's not as stubborn as I first thought. That's good. But it's pretty clear that he's not ready for the group sessions if this is anything to go by. I decide to tell him straight up, just as soon as we cross that 200-foot mark. At exactly one mile, I slow to a walk and watch the relief wash over him.

"You're not ready for the club workouts. We can get you there, but it's going to take a lot of work. Are you prepared for that?"

He grunts.

"Is that a yes or a no?"

He is still breathing heavily, and I have to remind myself to let his body catch up with his brain.

"How do I know you don't just want to make more money off private lessons?"

I count to three in my head, allow my eyes to focus on the winding path ahead, before responding, because my first response of, *You would get eaten alive by my club members* is probably a quick way to piss him off. I don't get the impression people tell him he needs improvement all that often.

"We train a minimum of twelve hours a week." I sneak a peek at him out of the corner of my eye and catch his grimace. We are still walking, which mercifully saves us both from the awkwardness of making too much or not enough eye contact during a tricky conversation. At least it's beautiful in the park this morning and we don't have to pretend like the scenery is interesting. "We're all busy folks, so the club sessions are our longer ones, especially on Saturdays."

"What happens on Saturdays?" He sounds as if he's asking about the plot to a horror movie and I have to keep myself from laughing. My mouth quirks.

"Depends on where we are in our training schedule, but usually a few hours on the bikes or a couple miles in the water."

I know from his application that he doesn't swim, not yet anyway. There is no response, just the sound of his breathing returning to normal. I can't help but wonder what's going through that CEO-mind of his. Is he really prepared for something like this?

"We just struggled through one mile," I say a bit more gently. "Give me a month, and I'll get you moving without stopping, otherwise paying the tri-club fee is going to be a waste of your money. You'll end up being left behind."

He jams his hands into the pockets of his shorts. "How many private sessions a week?"

Dollar signs briefly float across my mind. I could suggest that we meet four times a week. It would strain my schedule, but I would make some serious cash and it would more than prepare him to join the club. He's already defensive though, and I'm getting the impression that everything is a fine line with him. Push too far and he pulls to a stop, don't push hard enough, and again, he stops.

"Three times a week with me, and three times on your own, following the schedule I'll set for you."

His eyes bulge. "Six days a week. Are you kidding me?"

I level him with a hard stare, mustering my Coach Raven persona. "Don't waste my time, Briggs. Do you want to do a triathlon or not?"

Chapter Seven

BRIGGS

N o. The answer to her question is a resounding no. I do not want to do a triathlon. This whole thing is a mistake, which has become embarrassingly clear over the last miserable hour of my life.

But something about the word "no" catches in my throat. I can't seem to utter it. "Tell me more," I say instead.

I've mastered the art of the pitch, and I'm interested to see what she's got. She picks up her speed and my lungs grimace. If she starts jogging again I'm liable to sprint the other direction. Bullshit, I'm liable to hobble the other direction.

"We'll take what you've already paid and prorate it toward private sessions for the next month, maybe longer if you're not ready for the club workouts, but do what I tell you to do and you will be." She flings her ponytail and smiles up at me, the picture of bubbly, endorphin-fueled health. "Once you're ready for the club, you'll join our Monday, Thursday, and Saturday workouts, and workout by yourself the other three days, taking one rest day per week."

I eye the splotchy reds of her cheeks and speak without thinking. "And what if I want to continue our private sessions?"

She blinks in surprise and those red splotches bloom. "You can, but you might not need them. I have a few people who like to meet once a week for a while, especially while they're figuring out their gear, but before long, you'll be cruising." She smiles to herself. "And you're going to love the other club members. Everyone is fantastic."

I nod along with her because that's what this is about. Training. Gear. Prying my meddling parents off my back. Nothing else.

The perma-scowl on my face has been replaced by a furrowed brow and extreme concentration as I weigh my options. This isn't agreeing to a small feat, but it's not actually agreeing to a triathlon either. If I do one month of training and hate it, I can quit. But what if I do one month and it turns into a good thing for me? What if everyone else is right? A flash of Jaci's face fills my mind and I know what she'd say. She'd want me to do it. She'd needle me to death about doing it. If anything, I should do this for her, since she'll never have the opportunity to force me to do it in person.

"Always at five a.m.?"

For the first time since meeting me, Raven is compelled to laugh. It's too big for her body, too loud for the early morning sunrise, and too *something* for me—something I can't quite put my finger on. Something uncomfortable that makes me want to walk away.

"Great. I'll take that as a yes," she says, then starts to jog again. I follow along beside her, my lungs crying the whole way. "I'll send you an invoice tonight and you can schedule your sessions on the calendar widget on my website. Just plan on three workouts with me for this week while you get your feet wet, but beginning next week, I'll send you a full schedule including your solo training."

"Great," I say, with far less enthusiasm.

I guess this is a yes . . .

Raven reminds me of a cheerleader. Way too peppy for my liking. Not to mention, she's a kindergarten teacher, which means she has more positivity in her pinky finger than I do in my entire body. Can I handle this much sparkle at five a.m.? I might kill Turner for this. I truly might.

"I'll also need a full breakdown of your gear so I know what we're working with."

I heave out a sigh and find myself rattling off the truth, that I have no gear yet, and agree to purchase whatever she tells me. Again, I'm reminded of Jaci. This whole ridiculous situation is something she would've loved. She'd be making lists and taking the triathlon world by storm if she were in my shoes right now.

When the path comes to a stop and we leave the shelter of the trees for the crunch of the gravel parking lot, Raven and I part ways. I hobble back to my car, wading in regret. If training makes me think of Jaci over and over, I've got very little chance of success.

"I DESERVE to be forced to think about her."

It's been two weeks since my last appointment with Dr. Thomas, where he'd urged me to start running again. It took five minutes to get him up to speed on my parents holding my job hostage, Turner tricking me into training with his son's annoyingly enthusiastic kindergarten teacher, and the fact that I am woefully out of shape. It has taken much longer to explain why being around Raven makes me feel like I'm trying to grate Velveeta and how everything about triathlons makes me think of Jaci.

"Thinking about your wife can be a joyful experience, or it can be a punishment. Choosing punishment hasn't netted you any results over the last three years." Dr. Thomas furrows his gray eyebrows and looks over the top of his yellow notepad, training his eyes on mine.

If he's waiting for me to have a breakthrough, he'll be waiting indefinitely. It's not the first time Dr. Thomas has said this, or something like it. I'm not an idiot. Nothing I do, say, or feel will change the past or warrant her death, but what he doesn't understand, what I keep trying to explain, is that the guilt of experiencing good moments when she has none left is more painful than self-loathing. I would rather hate myself than go on with my life as if she doesn't belong in it.

"I'm not here for results," I say.

He sits with that for a moment, not saying anything, waiting for me to blurt out some hidden part of myself. I say nothing, not caring if things grow awkward. These sessions aren't comfortable for me. I won't go out of my way to make them comfortable for him.

The two of us are in a stand-off. Him tapping his pen, me my foot. We both watch a fly flit across the room and land on the bookshelf behind him.

"Then why are you here, Briggs?" he asks.

The man is a dinosaur, having been in practice for decades, and well versed in treating grief. I only started seeing him because my mother begged me to, but I kept returning because he was someone I could talk to about Jaci that wasn't from my personal life. Nobody else understands. They act as if her death isn't my fault, as if it was some unfortunate accident, some cruel twist of fate. Any time I point out that I was the one driving and that the police ticketed me, they continue to insist that doesn't mean I killed her. But that's unaccountable bullshit. An accident can still have fault attached to it, and that fault is mine. Sometimes I wish the police or Jaci's parents would've pressed charges, but everyone was so damn sensitive to me being a widower, acting as if I shouldn't be hating myself.

"Because you're the only one I can talk to about Jaci." I swallow my pride and meet his gaze.

"Why do you think that is?"

The answer is obvious, but he's going to make me say it anyway. "I can't do the pity. I hate the uncomfortable frowns. The hysterics. Pats on the back. Unwelcome hugs." I cringe, an involuntary physical reaction to imagining everyone from the admin assistant to the coffee shop attendant trying to wrap their arms around me. "After three years, those are mostly gone, but part of that is because my friends and family know I come to you to talk to about Jaci. It lets them off the hook."

And I'm fine only talking to Dr. Thomas. I prefer it that way. Sometimes he pushes me too much, but he doesn't try to change how I feel. He's not afraid of my darkness.

"Except they've got you signed up for the triathlon training."

I resent the satisfied grin that stretches his mustache from cheek to cheek.

"And little do they know, it's not going to help me get over Jaci. It's only going to make it worse."

"Is that true?"

"Of course. Why do you think I agreed to do it?" I lean back in the padded chair with a heavy sigh.

His mouth thins, and he writes something down in his

notepad. I'm not sure if he believes me or not, and I'm not sure which I'd prefer. "So this is punishment?"

"It doesn't fit the crime, but sure, you could call it that."

Another scratch of the pen, another judgment made. It doesn't bother me too much. I judge myself too.

Chapter Eight

RAVEN

It's our Thursday club workout, and I'm sitting on the side of the rec center pool, stopwatch in hand. Damien is bound and determined to hit a new personal record at our sprint next month, which means I need to push him extra hard in the water. It's his weak link. It's also why he pays me. He slaps the edge of the pool just as I hit the button and tell him the time.

He grimaces up at me from under his swim cap. "That's not going to cut it."

"There are still three weeks to get it right." I jump into coaching-mode, offering tips to improve his form.

He nods and tries again. I watch the numbers tick up on the watch and survey the other members of the team. I've got eleven club clients right now, but Kate is out for a month with a strained rotator cuff and Rob can't come on

Thursdays, so there are currently nine bodies in the water I need to account for. Sometimes that feels like a lot even though my contract states I can let in up to fifteen. Private coaching is easier to help people see quick gains, but I prefer the group gig. It's more fun, and something about the camaraderie pushes everyone to be better, myself included.

I finish up with Damien and move on to the next client, but I can't stop thinking about Briggs. When he agreed to three private sessions a week, I had to physically restrain myself from jumping for joy. Not because I want to see the man three times a week, that part is going to get old real quick, but because that fee is going to pay for two of my most expensive race registrations plus that new pair of running shoes I've been eyeing. And while I am excited about the extra cash, I'm also excited about having a new client.

Everyone on the team has been with me for a while, and while nobody is trying to be a professional athlete, they're all pretty serious about the sport. It's been a while since I've had someone new to mold. He won't have to unlearn bad habits because the man knows nothing—clearly his application was riddled with holes. That's okay. I can't wait to see how the process unfolds, to witness him go from out of shape to competing in his first race.

After a quick shower and a hit from the locker room blow dryer, I peel out of the gym parking lot and cut across town to my place. I have a date, and for once I'm not forcing myself to go through with it because I'm too nice to say no. We matched on my current dating app of choice just over two weeks ago. The fact that he waited a solid seven days to ask to meet in person is a good sign. Plus, he hasn't sent me any annoying good morning texts. It's not like good morning is an offensive phrase, it's just I imagine guys on dating apps who send good morning each day, send the same message in bulk. Like, "good morning to the fifteen different women I'm having vaguely personal conversations with." I never know how to respond. Most of the time, they are sending their good morning mid-workout for me. I don't have time to stop and respond with, *Glad you're rolling out of bed. I'm five miles into my good morning.*

Andre is an exuberant texter. He asks good questions and sends funny memes. Usually, with a guy from an app, I'll wait awhile before I give up my phone number. This guy scored it on the third day. Which is why I raced home to cover the scent of chlorine with perfume and change from my usual wardrobe of activewear and kindergarten color wheel to something grown up. I just haven't decided what that is yet.

I fling open the double doors to my closet and stare at its meager offerings. The best part of my apartment is having a walk-in closet. Too bad I don't have an income large enough to fill it. We are getting dinner at an Asian fusion place within walking distance of my place. When he suggested it, I didn't mention it was within walking distance. I mean, I'm sure he will notice when I don't arrive in my car, or if I get there first, it will happen at the end of the night when there is no car to walk me to, but I'll deal with that when it happens. I still have faith in this guy. I don't want him to think we can cruise through dinner and head back to my place.

Maybe Asian fusion means he is adventurous. I grab a black dress with a cutout in the back that screams *this sophisticated girl can also be sexy*, but pair it with red flats so I don't look too desperate. All the pictures on my profile are selfies, and most from the neck up. It's not like I'm trying to hide anything, and I do have a good one of me during a race. Whoever I date should be somewhat into fitness if they're going to keep up with me. But I don't do sexy body shots. Besides, who is going to take that kind of picture for me? No one. That's the plight of the single woman. No one to take your full body shots.

Hopefully he is into an athletic build. I do not have the delicate figure of a girl who does yoga. I stand back and take in the full effect of my outfit in the full-length mirror fixed to my bedroom door. My upper body is definitely the byproduct of years spent in a pool, strong shoulders and pretty much non-existent cleavage, and this dress does not hide that, but I've got a butt built on a bike and legs for days. I can't picture anyone seeing me head toward their table and deciding to bail early, though you never know these days.

A text from Andre fills my phone.

Looking forward to seeing your face in person when I tell a bad joke.

My lips twist involuntarily into a smile. Sometimes

these online guys don't show up at all. Just go silent the day of the date, never to be heard from again. It's a relief to know he'll be there and I'm not putting makeup on for nothing.

Ten minutes and two tries at wing-tipped eyeliner later, I'm walking down my street. A late-September breeze threatens to undo all the work I put into making my hair look effortlessly wavy, but I'm over it because I can see Andre sitting at an outdoor table just under a heat lamp, and he looks exactly like his picture. He lifts a hand when he sees me and my pulse leaps into overdrive. What I want out of tonight is to not go home feeling lonely.

Please let Andre be interesting, I think as I pull out the chair across from him and sit down.

He grins, displaying lovely Crest commercial worthy teeth. Someone once told me *never* to meet a guy whose profile pictures don't feature at least one smile with teeth. *If they aren't in the picture, they might not exist.* I thought she was joking until I met my first Bumble date missing more than one tooth.

"You look beautiful, exactly as I expected."

A blush warms my cheeks, ten points for the athletic girls.

Andre leans forward, tilting his head toward me like we've known each other for years and sharing little private bits of information is totally normal. "I don't say that because I need you to be a solid ten, though you are, it's just rare to meet someone who really looks the way they present themselves online."

I'm trying not to appear too flattered, but damn, if it doesn't feel good to meet someone who acts and feels familiar almost immediately. "I was thinking the very same about you."

He winks and nudges a menu across the table.

How am I supposed to focus on kimchi burritos now?

Chapter Nine

BRIGGS

"You can't just throw money at the problem and expect it to magically work out." Raven's hands are tight little fists on her hips as she frowns at the row of shiny road bikes. Friday's workout was another miserable run, but this weekend we're shopping. I'm not much of a shopper, especially for something this expensive, but after yesterday's five-mile run, I'm down for literally anything else.

I raise an eyebrow. "Oh, really? Is that what your private coaching is for? I don't recall you telling me to save my money there."

She throws her hands in the air and I chuckle to myself. "Are you trying to piss me off?"

Maybe.

"No," I lie. "I'm trying to get the best gear to make this

whole thing easier on myself. If I'm actually doing this thing, then I'm going to do it right."

She hums to herself for a minute, considering. "Alright then, but you're not buying that bike."

"What if I want to get this one?" I tease. "Red's my favorite color."

"What are you, twelve? As your coach *and* the expert here *and* the person who was a *professional* athlete, I'm telling you this bike is all flash and not worth the fifteen-thousand-dollar price tag."

With each word she emphasizes, her cheeks grow pinker.

As soon as we walked into the rubber-smelling bike shop, I asked the sales associate to show me their most expensive bike. He was more than happy to do so, and I wonder if he works on commission or actually owns the place.

He thins his lips at Raven and clears his throat. "Well, this bike is certainly nothing to scoff at either. It sports state-of-the-art carbon fiber——"

Raven holds up a hand and glares the middle-aged man down. Hard. "I'll take it from here, thank you."

The salesman grumbles something about know-it-all coaches, and Raven continues to glare daggers at his back as he shuffles away. "You'd think he'd be grateful I brought you here and not the competition down the street." She huffs. "On second thought, maybe we should go there instead."

Her assertive behavior is probably intended to be

intimidating right now, but I'm having a hard time not considering it cute, if not downright adorable. I need to focus.

"Tell me what's wrong with it?" My hand glides across the sleek, cherry-red seat. "Aside from the price."

It kind of reminds me of a rocket ship and looks like it's faster than anything else in here. But the truth is, I have no intention of dropping that much money on a bike, at least not right now. I'm a wealthy man because I'm not impulsive. I know I'll be spending a large wad of cash today because you get what you pay for, but I won't be buying a professional-level anything unless it's warranted.

"There's nothing wrong with it," she says, a little puff of frustrated air pushing past her lips. "But it's completely unnecessary." She walks down the aisle and points out bikes that all look the same to me. "Carbon fiber is a great choice but there are other brands that offer the same great quality materials for way less."

I point to a white one. "What about that?"

"I thought you wanted red?" She cocks her head, eyes sparkling in challenge.

"Well, I'm not twelve," I say and then roll my eyes exactly like a twelve year old would. "I think I'll be okay with white."

Why do I love firing her up? I haven't had this much fun in . . . I don't know how long. Years, maybe. We met in the parking lot, and on the way in, she lectured me to let her take the lead and not get sucked into any sales pitches, which was exactly why I'd found the salesman the second we'd walked through the doors. I was being a dick, wanting to get a rise out of her, and I couldn't seem to help myself. But now that he's gone, it's time to get serious. Whatever bike I end up with will have to carry me through the next month, and though I hate to think about it, probably several more months and at least one painful race.

"This is a good choice," Raven says, "but I'm thinking it'll be too small for your frame. Let's take a look at this." She pointed to the bike next to it, also white. I couldn't tell the difference.

"You're the boss."

She chuckles. "Be honest, how hard was that for you to say?"

She must know I'm the CEO and nobody is the boss of me, but even I'm smart enough to step aside for someone who knows what the hell they're doing when I don't. I want to make some joke about my job, but I don't say anything at all. It might be interpreted as flirting. She can't get the wrong idea about us.

Raven waves the clerk back over, and he has me sit on the bike so that he can make adjustments for my height. I think back to all those years in grade school when I would grow a few inches and Dad would have to pull out his tools and raise the seat. I was always so proud when it was time to move it up. This adjustment is a lot more detailed, and I don't understand all that goes into it, just that I can pick it up in a week. It has been so long since I last rode a bike that I'm not sure whether to look forward to it or worry. Obviously riding your bike as a kid and riding your bike competitively look different.

"We can get your bike shorts now if you're up for it." Raven points to a wall of spandex in a variety of bold colors and patterns, and I can feel the blood drain from my face.

"I don't really have to dress like I'm entering the Tour de France. Surely I can function in the same shorts I wear to the gym, right?"

Her lips are pressed in a firm line, and I can tell she's about to censor her response. She probably thinks I'm being vain, but I just can't imagine myself wearing anything that tight in public. Dudes that wear shorts like that make me uncomfortable. More power to them, but I certainly don't want people to know the shape of my genitalia, and the thought of wearing those around Raven already has my stomach on edge.

"We can wait till we pick up your bike if you aren't ready to pull the trigger today."

Never, I'm never going to be able to pull the trigger on those. Especially not the yellow and black striped pair in the corner with *caution* printed around the waistline.

"Are the members of your tri club going to be dressed like that?" I nod my head toward a man who has just entered the shop. He's in head-to-toe spandex with shoes that click when he walks across the linoleum floor.

A grin spreads across Raven's face as she takes in his neon-purple get up. A very douchey pair of sunglasses is propped on his head, and the skin on his face is ruddy from time spent in the sun and wind.

"Oh no, he's not in shorts, he's in a bib."

I choke on my own spit trying not to laugh. "Excuse me?"

"That's what it's called. See how the shorts have an overall piece for the shoulders? That's what makes it a bib."

"So you're saying that these shorts are the better option?" I motion to the wall of spandex.

"Actually, no. The bibs are easier to move in, and we use them or a one-piece for our actual races."

It's my turn to say something, but I'm lost for words. I can't imagine myself wearing an outfit like that, and I don't even want to ask what the hell a one-piece is. For the professionals, it's fine, but I have no delusions about this thing, and I still don't see why I can't just wear basketball shorts.

Her smile quirks. "You'll get used to it."

That's what I'm afraid of. Turner would have a field day if he saw me dressed like that man. Outrageous price or not, I was relieved to be doing private lessons for the time being.

"What next?" I sigh. "Don't tell me you're going to try to get me to wear a speedo because that's where I draw the line."

She snorts. "Don't worry, we'll save the speedos for our next shopping trip."

It's a good thing I can tell she's joking. Wait, is she

joking?

She busts up laughing. "You'll train in a normal swimsuit and wear a wetsuit over your bib for the event, assuming it's cold enough."

I'm not sure what to do with this information. Wetsuits are only for cold water, aren't they? I hate water enough as it is, and cold water isn't exactly a man's best friend, especially a man in tight spandex.

"Speaking of which, have you thought about what race you'd like to enter?"

I grimace. "I don't know--"

"No worries, I'm going to send you a list of races the team will be entering with suggestions for which ones I think would be a good fit for you. You can look everything over before you decide, but you'll have to decide quickly for some of them as they do sell out."

I swallow hard and study her face. She really believes I can do this. Holding her gaze makes my stomach tighten uncomfortably, so I just nod and look away.

We finish up at the bike shop, walking out into the warm sun that kind of reminds me of Saturdays as a kid. Full of opportunity.

"What's next on your agenda?" I ask.

"You'll see." She leads me down the street to a hippie centric grocery store where everything is organic and they sell juice for exorbitant prices.

We spend some time in the supplements aisle where she directs me to buy pre-workout powders and some squishy gel packets that not only look disgusting, but come in the most disturbing flavors. Cookies and cream? Orange dreamsicle? When I pretend to gag, she rolls her eyes and tosses a few generic fruit flavors into my cart.

"It's an acquired taste, but trust me, you'll appreciate having these on hand when our workouts get longer."

The very idea of working out for longer than our most recent five-mile run pains me.

My stomach growls as we make our way through the produce aisle.

"Good nutrition can make or break your training," says Raven. "Talk to me about your diet."

"I usually try to do a large protein portion and a smaller carb."

She doesn't have to know what those carbs and proteins are exactly, does she? The evening before, I'd eaten peanut butter straight out of the jar, with a sleeve of crackers on the side.

"Oh, that's a great start. We won't have to do much with that except up your carb load to fuel the cardio. Just make sure you work in some anti-inflammatory foods and fat. People think fat is the devil, but that's just bad science and good eighties advertising."

My vision fills with images of chocolate cake. Not so bad.

"Healthy fat," she says. "Like avocados, olives, and nut butters."

"So peanut butter." I grin. "I got one right."

"Well, technically peanuts are a legume." She worries

her lip between her teeth, as if she hates to be the bearer of bad news. "They're also highly inflammatory and acidic."

"I'm not giving up peanut butter," I deadpan.

She lifts her hands in surrender. "You don't have to, but think about swapping it out for almond butter. I promise, you'll be used to it in no time."

Damn inflammation. Who would've thought middle-age meant having to think about things like inflammation? One hundred percent, I am going to go home and google "anti-inflammatory foods that taste good" so I don't have to have the peanut butter debate again. Right before I pull tonight's highly processed TV dinner out of the freezer.

Chapter Ten

RAVEN

Sometimes life is like swimming upstream. The currents are brutal and relentless. It's all you can do to keep your head above water, but what choice do you have? Drowning isn't an option. And so you swim, even when it hurts, because you have to, because there's got to be better days ahead. And though you can't see them, that belief is the only fuel you have left.

And sometimes, life is like floating downstream. Things come together easily and the big stressors melt away. Even the little things don't seem to bother you like they once did. Everything just works. It's simple.

Having been through periods of both upstream and downstream in my life, I know how to appreciate the downstream, to let it take me away, knowing that nothing lasts forever.

That's kind of how the last few weeks have been.

Going with the flow.

The growing pains of being new to kindergarten have passed and the kids are doing great—even Charlie has returned to his normal self. Everyone at tri club seems happy with their training, making small gains little by little that will add up to some great races here soon. Briggs hasn't missed any of our training sessions, though I still haven't been able to get him to wear appropriate bike shorts. Mom and Dad haven't had anything to complain about at our last two dinners. And I've gone on three more dates with Andre. All good ones. The kind of dates that make me think this could become a relationship. That maybe we could be something real. Something that could last.

So why do I feel like the other shoe is about to drop?

I shoot a quick text to Andre, letting him know I will be out of range for the next couple of hours and toss my phone in my purse.

"Are you ready for adventure?"

Briggs shrugs, but I can see the curiosity burning behind his October eyes.

We've been on a few bike rides over the last couple weeks, and he's beginning to get comfortable on his new bike. The way I see it, now is as good of a time as any to catch him off guard. It's not like I need to be best friends with everyone I train, but I do like to know something about them. With Briggs, I'm still operating on, "Turner Lawson's brother who wants to do a triathlon, but has no idea why." It's hard to motivate someone whose mind and background is a complete mystery.

I grab the mountain bikes I rented for today and hook them to the back of my SUV, before motioning for Briggs to hop in the passenger seat. He looks hesitant for a second.

"I'd let you drive, but A, you don't know where we are going, and B, I'm more than a little traumatized by the idea of bikes sliding around the back of your pickup."

Briggs' eyes widen and he tugs open the passenger side door.

"I'm not a fan of driving. Have at it."

Not a fan of driving? I'm not sure what to do with that information. Why drive a giant truck if you don't like driving? See, I'm already learning things. I kind of want to ask him what is up with that, but his eyes are already glued to the phone in his hand, and he's typing away at what has to be a work email with enough fervor to signal now is not small talk time.

The drive from downtown Austin to Lake Grapevine where we are riding takes a solid thirty minutes if you don't get caught in traffic. We're lucky because it's a Sunday afternoon and Texans are too busy hitting up the church potluck to want to be out on the road.

"Are we leaving the city?" Briggs sets down his phone and takes in his surroundings for the first time in fifteen miles.

I could kidnap this man so easily.

"Today I thought we would try something different.

We've been training on paved roads, and in the gym up until this point, but a lot of races offer trail rides."

"Yeah, that's not what I'm here for," he says.

"Well, you might be surprised. A lot of athletes like the trail races, so I thought I'd rent some mountain bikes for us for the day."

"I wondered why you told me to leave my bike at home." He scrunches up his face.

"There's a twenty-three mile loop at North Shore Trail. We don't have to do the whole thing today, but if you like it, it might help you narrow down what races you want to register for."

"Race," says Briggs. "One and done."

I'm trying so hard not to shake my head right now.

"What's the point of putting this much effort into one race? Why even do it?" I pause, and a terrible thought crosses my mind. One race sounds a lot like a box to check on your bucket list. "Are you dying?"

Briggs turns toward the window, but not before I see a bemused grin sneak its way across his handsome face.

"I am not dying," he says to the window.

"Then what gives?" The guess work on this client is killing me. "Charity? Is this some kind of charity gig? Like," I clear my throat and put on my best Mr. Radio voice, *"sponsor Lawson Construction, each dollar donated will be matched by Mr. Lawson himself."*

Briggs shakes his head, but he is still refusing to look at me. "Don't you have clients that just want to do a triathlon?"

"Why yes, I do, but they show *some* enthusiasm. I feel like I'm torturing you. Like this is a punishment you're inflicting upon yourself, or a bet you lost."

Something flickers across Briggs' face, like maybe I'm on to something, but he's not ready to give it up yet.

"If this is a bet, it's a *very* expensive bet."

"Tell me about it."

"So it is a bet," I say. Suddenly I feel like Angela Lansbury in the final moments of every *Murder She Wrote* episode. This man thinks he's a tall, dark mystery, but I fully plan to unravel him, one tiny detail at a time.

Briggs just shakes his head, same secretive smile, same lone wolf attitude.

The parking lot to the trailhead is empty today, which is a great sign that we won't be bobbing and weaving around hikers. I love this trail, but it is one of the ten most loved hikes in the area, which means it can be a real tourist trap sometimes.

Briggs moves quickly to the back of the SUV where he takes both my bike and his off the rack. I've taken the liberty of filling both our water bottles in advance. Newbies always underestimate the need for water plus electrolytes, and as strong as I am, I can't really picture myself tossing all six foot two of Briggs over one shoulder and carrying him back to this parking lot.

As we walk our bikes to the trailhead, it is impossible to miss the lift in his mood. The man has transitioned from surly to peaceful. I can see it in everything from the missing tension in his jaw to the lightness of his step. The pieces begin to click into place. Maybe it is the city lights and buzz of early morning traffic that kept him in a permanently foul mood these last few weeks. If Briggs is a nature lover, it opens up a lot in terms of keeping him motivated.

"You want to ride in front or follow?"

Briggs laughs. "Let's just start with me following. We both know it's going to end that way."

I swing one leg over my bike and grin back at him.

"Try to keep up."

I'm only half joking. The point of today is to get Briggs to loosen up and share a bit about himself, but that doesn't mean I'm wasting the training opportunity. Trails are a different kind of challenge, and I am hoping he will dig in and enjoy the work.

The first few miles are gorgeous. The loop is divided into seven different paths, each progressing in difficulty, but the scenery remains idyllic the whole way through. The dirt path ahead of us cuts through meadows and tall, thin trees, which bend and weave above us to create a canopy of shade from the bright October sun. Parts of the trail are bright enough with green ferns and tall grass that it feels like it's still a Dallas summer, but in other areas the dead browns and oranges of fall crunch beneath our tires.

It's the unpredictableness of trail riding that makes it so much more rewarding than the fast, flat ride you get on asphalt. I need Briggs to see and make the comparison himself, so I crank my head behind me, ready to motion for him to stop, but the image of him riding causes my breath to catch in my chest.

He's coasting behind me, standing tall on the pedals, his t-shirt whipping behind him, and his eyes cast upward into the trees. I feel like I'm witnessing something secret and special. It's too big to interrupt, so I turn my attention back to the trail and keep pedaling, but inside my head I'm playing that image over and over again. I'm pretty sure I just witnessed Briggs floating downstream for the first time in a while.

Chapter Eleven

BRIGGS

Jaci hated nature. Like really hated it. I tried to take her on a surprise camping trip for our third anniversary and she got wind of it early, "accidentally" canceled our campground reservation, and sabotaged the tent. I still have a tent for two in my storage unit with three missing poles. Nothing about the North Ridge Trail reminds me of Jaci.

Maybe Raven is on to something. I'm not about to switch gears for the triathlon, but I could see myself out here on weekends. The bikes Raven rented for us seem pretty nice, and I wonder if they run into the thousands like the road bike did. I might just get one either way. I have plenty of money, and it's not like I spent it on much else anyway.

"Just admit it." Raven laughs over her shoulder, her

ponytail streaming behind her under her helmet. "You're enjoying this."

I grunt and she laughs again. "Hang on, it's not going to be easy much longer."

She's right about that. The terrain goes from flat to hilly, and my good mood begins to sour. At first, the exertion is nice, and I dig into it like it's a new acquisition for our company and nobody can close the deal except for me . . . but then my shoulder starts to ache. The same shoulder I injured three years ago when Jaci died.

I growl and push harder, forcing thoughts of her and that day from my mind. But pushing harder only makes the ache worse, and that only makes the thoughts come back with a vengeance. The memories are a bitch.

Raven isn't slowing down. Every minute, she's farther up the path and I'm farther behind. This blasted shoulder is killing me. I've had it act up on me a few times during our runs over the last few weeks, but it's been nothing like this. I blame it on the trail. On the road bike, the handlebars are aerodynamic, so leaning forward on them doesn't mess with the shoulders too much. The positioning is totally different on a mountain bike. It's upright like a traditional bike, and I have to grip the handles hard in order to control it on the steep and winding path.

"You okay back there?" Raven calls, finally slowing down for me. Her mouth thins, and I can see the concern even from twenty feet away.

"I'm fine," I grunt.

I don't want to tell her about my shoulder. Maybe

that's stupid because she's my coach, but I still don't want her asking about how I hurt it in the first place. I have a ready-made lie I can use about a baseball game gone wrong, but what if she questions me further? What if she wants me to see a doctor?

For as much as I hate the injury, I also refuse to get the surgery to fix it. No surgery could fix Jaci. And I don't care what anyone has to say about that. The injury isn't life threatening, but it's a mark on me, a punishment I deserve.

Between one panting breath and the next, my arm goes numb. Before I can get a handle on what's happening, I'm flying off the bike. My shoulder collides into the rocky dirt path, and I'm immediately grateful for the helmet that prevents my skull from slamming into the ground. Nursing a concussion in a dark room is not how I want to spend the rest of my weekend.

Raven is by my side in a second, her face lined with worry. I do a quick scan of my limbs. Aside from my shoulder and a bloody knee, the only real damage is to my pride. Did I really just fall off my bike?

"Sit completely still." Raven inspects me for injuries, moving my ankles from side to side, asking me to bend my knee, rotate my wrists, all those things the team doctor used to do once upon a time when I was an athlete and not a dreary loser struggling to get back in shape.

"I'm fine," I grind out, fully planning to brush her aside and push myself to my feet, until her hands work their way up my body to check for injuries, and I find myself desperate for touch.

In the years since Jaci's death, pity hugs and sympathy pats have been my only human contact. I forgot what it feels like to be calmed by someone else's hands. Raven seems to get it because when our eyes meet hers go wide, and I can tell she's sitting on a question, unsure how to ask it. Which is why I definitely have to stand up. When I push myself up from the ground I can't help it, I flinch. The pain in my shoulder is something else today, and falling definitely didn't help.

"What hurts?"

"My old-man body."

She raises an eyebrow. "I take coaching seriously. And *you* signed an agreement that says you will notify me of all injuries."

She's talking about what just happened, but I am definitely violating that part of our contract by holding out on my bad shoulder. In my defense, I barely read the thing before tossing a digital signature on the document and sending it back.

"Nothing is hurt, except maybe my self-esteem and all that progress I was making toward not looking like an idiot every time we train."

I circle my good shoulder a few times to show her I am good to go before dusting myself off and hopping back on my bike.

I can't tell if she believes me or not, but she takes things slower on the way back, and I'm grateful, not just because I'm tired, but because the view of the lake beside us is too good not to take it in. I've never been super into being outdoors, but all of these bold colors, paired with the sound of the water lapping at the bottom of the shallow cliffs beside us, makes just existing feel easier.

It occurs to me that while I might not want to get a mountain bike after all, I do want to pick a race with some scenery to it. Our morning runs downtown are killing me. Not just because Raven is constantly increasing our mileage and doing ridiculous things like picking routes with hills, but also because the smells and sounds of the city aren't exactly stress free for me. And the air is different here. It's crisp and clean, refreshing in a way I didn't know I needed until now.

We finish and lift our bikes onto the rack. "Maybe we could do some more training like this," I say.

Raven climbs into the driver's seat and pulls her seatbelt across, securing it tightly before putting the key in the ignition. I swallow the trepidation I always feel at climbing into a smaller vehicle and squish myself into the front seat.

"You want to do more mountain biking?" She's smug, sounding like she just won a game of chicken.

"Not necessarily." I don't have it in me to tell her about my shoulder and the mountain bike not getting along. "But I was thinking less gym time and pavement and more running off the beaten path."

Raven smiles, it's a small smile, but I'm beginning to read her expressions, and I know this one. It's the one she uses when she's pleased with herself. The same smile that crossed her face when we picked up my bike and she talked me into buying an extended warranty, insisting that this time it wasn't a scam.

She has a cute little mouth that looks as good when she's giving you one of her know-it-all smirks as it does when she's grinning from ear to ear.

As we drive back toward my truck, Raven is full of energy, talking about all the different parks close enough to where she works for us to run in, and a few that have bike paths we can use. And then there's the lake swims she has planned for the club, which I'll be joining soon. I like how excited she gets about training. It doesn't do for me what it does for her, but damn if it isn't nice to be around someone that loves what they do.

It's not like that at Lawson, where the work keeps me busy and I'm good at it. The kind of good at it that no one can argue against, but you would never hear my voice full of enthusiasm the way Raven's is right now. I like it, and I shouldn't. Not in the way I'm letting myself. It's not okay. Neither was the way my body responded to her when she was checking me for injuries. And neither is the way I find myself comparing her to Jaci.

"Is your shoulder okay?" she says, cutting off my train of thought.

I'm mindlessly rubbing at it, and I drop my hand like I touched a hot stove. "It's fine."

"Are you sure? Did you hit it when you fell?"

"I said it's fine," I snap. Her face drains of the joyful exuberance it held moments again, replaced by shock, and then anger.

"You're lying." Her hands tighten on the wheel and so does that *too close to the truth* feeling that's currently got a death grip on my chest.

"I don't pay you to call me a liar."

She flinches and for a second I feel guilty about being a full-on asshole, but she needs to stop prying into my personal life. I don't care that she's my tri-coach, when it comes to my shoulder, that's tied to Jaci, which makes it off limits.

"And I don't train liars." There's a fire in her voice and as she pulls to a stop next to my truck, I turn to see it blazing in her eyes as well.

This isn't the fun banter I'm used to with Raven. I don't like being challenged like this. It feels like a fight with someone you care about, and that's not what I'm here for.

The moment she clicks off the ignition, I grab my wallet and keys off the dash and push open the door.

"Then I guess it's a good thing I'm not a liar." I'm out of the vehicle and halfway to my truck by the time I finish my sentence. She doesn't follow and I don't care. At least, that's what I tell myself as I tear out of the parking lot.

I don't care.

Liar.

Chapter Twelve

RAVEN

B riggs most definitely has a shoulder injury, and he's most definitely a big fat liar. Okay, he's not fat, but he's big and a liar, so same difference. I have half a mind to cut him from my roster, but I won't, God help me.

There's something about him that makes me want to work harder, and I'm reminded of my most challenging race during my professional triathlete days. I'd gone into it cocky, thinking I had a chance at the podium, but it was a new route and ended up kicking my butt so thoroughly that I was lucky to finish. The elevation was too much, the heat blistering and dry, the hills steeper than anything in Texas, and I hadn't given myself enough travel days to kick the fatigue. I'd left Utah steaming mad, but the next year I'd gone back, humble and prepared, and I'd taken second place. It was my crowning achievement and still a big reason why I had so many clients even seven years later.

I drive home in a fury, comparing Briggs to that race. He wasn't going to beat me. I wouldn't let him quit, and I wasn't going to quit on him either, but he damn well was going to tell me the truth about his shoulder. We were going to get on top of it now before it became a bigger problem.

Once home, I shower and wash Briggs from my mind, dancing around the bathroom to country music while getting ready for my date with Andre. He's taking me out to dinner and then we're going dancing at a club, even though I'm not normally the clubbing type. My schedule isn't friendly with anything that keeps me awake past ten o'clock, but it's Saturday and I want to live a little. Andre seems like the type who likes this kind of thing. He's suave in that stockbroker, money-is-my-domain kind of way. Part of me worries we're too different to make this work, but we've been on six dates without any red flags, and I'm finding myself thinking about him more and more.

Dinner is nice, and before long, we're dancing in the dark club. His hands are on my waist and mine are wrapped around his neck, my fingers playing with his hair. The music hums a low bass that vibrates through my body. We're pressed to each other, and I'm admiring the way his perfectly styled blond hair has curled at the ends with my touch when he catches my mouth in a sultry kiss. It's not our first kiss and it's not a nice kiss. It's a sinful kiss, the kind that makes me consider progressing our relationship tonight. He pulls back to whisper something in my ear, but I can't hear a word over the music. Then my heart skids to a stop, and the alcohol in my system goes straight to my head, because I can't believe what I'm seeing over Andre's shoulder.

It's Briggs Lawson in the flesh. He's dressed in a crisp black cotton t-shirt and jeans, his broad form standing with his back to the bar, a glass of amber whiskey in his hand, and those liquid, golden-green eyes right on me. My stomach tightens and a wave of adrenaline washes through my center.

It's always odd when I see students outside of school, and sometimes the same thing goes for my clients. But this feeling I'm having with Briggs' eyes on me is far from odd––it's disarming. My heart speeds as our eyes lock, his are heated, and I'm certain he must still be thinking about our argument from earlier today. He's still angry, and I'm still angry, and one of us is going to have to back down. That person isn't going to be me.

"I'll be right back," I yell to Andre, peeling myself away from his needy hands. "I need to say hi to a client."

I don't wait to see if he follows. Maneuvering through the crowd, I stomp over to Briggs. His eyes travel down my body, and I'm very aware that I look hot tonight compared to my typical ponytail and athletic wear he's used to seeing me in. I'm sporting long barrel curls and a short, tight red dress. I've even got strappy high heels on, which goes a long way to show how much I like where things are going with Andre. I don't pull out those torture devices for just anyone.

"Briggs. Hello." The fire I felt ten seconds earlier wanes momentarily when I'm up close and personal.

"That your boyfriend?" He nods toward the crowd. I swing around to see Andre coming toward us, his face impassive. The song changes to something more upbeat and the crowd pushes him back.

"Yes," I say, and Briggs brings his glass to his lips for a short hard swallow and suddenly I'm focused on following that liquid in his throat move over his Adam's apple and down beneath the collar of his shirt. He hasn't said a word and yet I keep babbling, keep digging that hole of awkward. "No. I don't know. Probably. We just started dating."

He looks at me like I've grown one extra appendage. "I'm surprised you drink alcohol, Raven."

Great, now he thinks I'm drunk. Maybe I should work with that. Maybe I can pretend I don't remember this conversation. Hell, maybe if I keep making him feel uncomfortable he'll keep drinking and *he* won't remember this conversation.

Truthfully, I rarely drink. It's not just that it's bad for my training, the last thing I need is to show up to work hungover. Between the headache and the kindergarteners, I would die.

"Sometimes," I say with a shrug. "I'm surprised to see you here. This doesn't seem like your scene."

"My little brother is in town, so he and Turner

dragged me out. According to them, I need to get laid." He draws out the last few words lazily, but there's a challenge there too. A dangerous challenge.

I swallow hard at the image of him getting laid and turn to see Turner and a younger man further down the bar. Turner is ordering off the bartender, and the younger Lawson is chatting up a woman who can't be a day over twenty-one. I'm so surprised that I didn't notice Turner at first, that I had zeroed in on Briggs without considering who he would be here with, that I could kick myself. Seeing the parent of one of my students at a club isn't exactly on my short list.

I turn back to Briggs. "How's your shoulder?" It's not the question he wants to hear. He looks away, his drink suddenly far more interesting than me. "We don't lie about our injuries."

"My shoulder is none of your business."

I blink at him, momentarily stunned. "It's literally my business to train you and that includes knowing why you fell off your bike today."

"Old baseball injury. It flares up every once in a while, and it's not a big deal." He meets my eyes again, as if daring me to question him, and I'm certain it's another lie.

"When was the last time you talked to a doctor about it?"

"Lighten up, Raven." He sets his drink on the bar and pushes off, moving in closer to me, his rich spicy scent suddenly everywhere. He's so close and so tall, but I won't let him intimidate me.

He holds my gaze for a second longer before turning away and reaching his hand out. Suddenly Andre is there, shaking it back. My mind goes momentarily blank, but the men figure out introductions themselves, making small talk about careers and who they know in common and the score from some game last night.

"Treat her right." Briggs' gruff voice rocks me from my stupefied state.

Those are the words of an older brother or a jealous ex––not a client. Briggs walks away, and Andre shakes out his hand, clearly the recipient of a death grip.

What on earth just happened? Andre is looking at me like I should know, but my brain is still looping around *treat her right*. Briggs is a challenge, and a pain in the ass, and admittedly, I look forward to both of those things when we train, but a protector? I've never seen any sign of that, not until this moment. My focus should be on Andre, on his hand on the small of my back and his lips dancing over mine. But I can't keep my eyes from scanning the bar, and every time I find Briggs in the crowd, it's like my chest collapses in on itself.

Suddenly going home with Andre isn't what I want.

Chapter Thirteen

BRIGGS

lcohol stopped being fun when I became one of those sad people that can't get out of their own head every time they take a drink. I should have told my brothers no. It's what I wanted to do. My shoulder was killing me from falling on my ass that morning and pain killers, real pain killers, sounded a lot better than a dimly lit club where the music was too loud, and the women all dressed like they were shopping for sugar daddies.

But it's hard to say no to my baby brother. We're lucky if we get him, now that Griffin is mid-residency up in Baltimore. If I said no to tonight, I'd miss what little opportunity there was to check in on him. Only I couldn't focus on anything Griffin or Turner were saying because there, in the middle of the dance floor with her lips pressed to some loser who couldn't keep his hands to himself, was my "coach" and Charlie's kindergarten teacher, not that she looked much like either of those at the moment.

I should have turned away, but the morning had ended with an argument, and I found myself wanting to march over to her and start the whole thing up again just to get that guy's hands off her.

I hated her dress, her shoes, her shiny dark hair falling loose past her shoulders. None of it was her, so when she came over to talk to me, and he followed her like a lost puppy, I snapped a little. I responded to him the way I responded to every guy who had ever been dumb enough to make a move on my sister. At least I hope it came off that way. Because otherwise it looked a lot like I was acting possessive, and I wasn't allowed to be that. Not with her.

"Who was that?" Griffin asks. He's three drinks into the evening and his red cheeks and proclivity for laughing at everything Turner said told me taking him home soon was not negotiable.

"Charlie's teacher," Turner says. "And Briggs' new triathlon coach."

I still haven't found a way to punish Turner for suggesting Raven's tri club without telling me she was leading it, but that didn't mean I wasn't plotting revenge.

"Thanks to Turner."

Griffin's eyes follow Raven across the dance floor. She and her date have settled on a couch in the back of the room. His hand sitting just above her knee makes me want to throw up. That or the whiskey is getting to me.

"That is not what I remember my kindergarten teacher looking like," says Griffin with a low whistle.

First she'd said he was her boyfriend, then she'd taken it back. Is this what it's like to date now? You don't know what you are or have the confidence to call it what it is? I never doubted what Jaci and I were to one another. Not even in the fragile beginning, when getting the courage to ask her out felt like scaling Mount Everest.

"If that was my teacher . . ." Griffin's halfway to a humping gesture, and I'm more than halfway to launching my fist into his pillowy cheeks.

"Watch it," I growl.

Heat rises in my chest, and I actually consider saying something stupid like, *let's take this outside*, when Griffin holds his hands up in mock surrender. All that red I'm seeing is replaced with humiliation. I feel like an idiot. If seeing Raven around other people is going to turn me into this kind of guy, then I need to get my boundaries straight. She is supposed to get me across the finish line and out of my parents' crosshairs, not turn me into a rage-filled assclown.

"Are you going to tell me what's going on there?" Turner jerks his head toward Raven, his blue eyes sparkling.

"Nothing."

"Nothing, like the time you stole my girlfriend or actually nothing?"

I roll my eyes. "It was the third grade, Turner, and she was our babysitter, not your girlfriend."

"She was my first love, and you know what I'm getting at."

Of course I know what he's getting at. It's the same thing gnawing a hole in my stomach. Funny how attraction becomes undeniable once alcohol hits your bloodstream.

"I think she can do a little better than that," I say. "That's all."

Turner cocks his head to the side, inspecting Raven's date. I try to see him how Turner would. He doesn't look the worst. His blue collared shirt is pressed, and his shoes match his trousers. Guys never seem to pay attention to details like that. Case in point, Griffin beside me is wearing black slacks with a pair of Converse sneakers. Those two things don't belong in the same world, let alone outfit.

There's nothing grossly offensive about the guy's appearance, but that doesn't mean he has his shit together. I have a sense about people, an instinct, and it's never wrong. This guy? He's not good enough for Raven. Period.

"He looks a little douchey, sure."

"A little? This is the last type of place you take a girl like Raven to."

Turner's eyebrows lift and he takes a swig of the beer in his hand. "Where are you supposed to take," he pauses, "a girl like Raven?"

. . .

I BARELY ARRIVE to the pool on time. When the alarm went off at an ungodly hour this morning, I had half a mind to cancel. But if I'm going to get Raven to lay off my shoulder, I need to show her that I'm trustworthy. I've been icing it and resting since the mountain biking incident. The inflammation has gone down, and it barely hurts anymore, so I'm sure it'll be fine. If not, I'll suck it up. I refuse to let anyone else know about the pain I regularly endure because I have zero intentions of healing it. I don't want physical therapy, I'll never go under the knife, and I sure as shit don't need anyone's sympathy, especially Raven's.

There are a few other early morning swimmers, and Raven's saved us a couple of lanes on the far end. As I walk over to her, she waves and begins to peel off the sweatpants she's wearing over her suit. I swallow, my eyes glued to her movements, even though I know better. It's not as if she's in a bikini, but her black one piece is cut high on her thighs, hugging her body in a way that is doing unmentionable things to me. The woman has an amazing ass. I didn't notice it until Saturday night when I saw her in that ridiculous club dress. It would be impossible not to notice it now.

What is wrong with me? Maybe my brothers are right and I need a good lay. That didn't happen last weekend, not that I ever had intentions of trying. I don't date and I don't hook up. Ever. Sex with a stranger isn't going to change the fact that the only woman I was supposed to touch is six feet under.

"Are you ready for this?" Raven's eyes sparkle like she's actually excited for this swim. "Your shoulder is okay?"

"How did I know you'd go there?" I ask gruffly. "Yes, ma'am, the shoulder is just fine."

It's supposed to be our last week before I join the tri club crew, and that's a good thing. I've grown too comfortable being one-on-one with this woman. It's distracting. I'm here to make my parents happy. If competing in a triathlon is a means to make that happen, then that is where my focus is. I still don't know much about the race circuit, but Raven says we'll pick one soon. I'm hoping for early spring so I can get this done and get on with my life.

We slide into the cool water and I hold back a curse. I hate swimming, always have. It's the leg of the event that I'm least looking forward to, and probably the one I'm going to need the most help getting ready for. Raven explains that I can use whatever stroke I want in the water, but the best and fastest is the commonly used freestyle stroke. She slips under the rope separating our lanes and asks me to show her what I've got.

I raise an eyebrow. "I do know how to swim."

She blinks, water droplets catching in her dark lashes, her brown eyes filled with mirth. "Then prove it."

I sigh and get to work, pushing off the wall and swimming to the other end of the lane and back. Raven swims alongside me and I wonder what she's thinking. I definitely suck. I'm slow and awkward, but I don't drown, which feels like an accomplishment. We come to a stop, and I ignore the little tinge of nerve pain in my shoulder.

"We're going to work on your form, but not too bad, all things considered."

"All things considered?"

She shrugs. "Considering you're practically a level one minnow learning how to put your face in the water and blow bubbles."

Flashes of swim lessons as a kid come to mind––the overly-chlorinated pool water so far up my nose that my eyes burned, and the scratchy concrete surfacing that rubbed my already pruney toes. I hated it then and I hate it now.

"Don't remind me," I deadpan, and she bursts out laughing.

The sound of her laugh is so happy, so loud and unabashedly free, that one of the old man swimmers a few lanes down stops to see what's going on. Our eyes meet, and he gives me a little nod and a wink. I don't know what that's supposed to mean, other than he is old, and old men seem to think they have everyone figured out.

I take her advice and try again, but the motion of freestyle with my arms brushing against my ears and moving overhead is doing terrible things to my shoulder. This isn't going to work, but I don't have the heart to tell her. I don't want to get into another argument, and I'm too stubborn to admit the truth, especially when I've insisted I'm fine. So I grit my teeth and continue, despite the hot tingling that turns to shooting nerve pain that then goes numb. The gig is up. I'm so angry I could sink to the bottom and scream until I inhale chlorine.

I stop swimming.

Chapter Fourteen

RAVEN

Ding, ding, ding. Raven is right. Briggs is a liar. That shoulder is not okay, and it has not been okay for a lot longer than our bike ride. He's lucky I'm submerged in water and can't break out into a victory dance. He's also lucky I don't yell out, "I told you so," because it's killing me not to.

He's working his way to the shallow end of the pool, trying to use his shoulder the least amount possible. He holds a motionless expression, but he flinches with each step and the pain is etched across his face. I don't understand this stubbornness. He has an injury, so what? It's not like I'm going to take out an ad in the Sunday paper revealing his great weakness.

When he hits the wall, he climbs under the lane divider and pulls himself up the ladder and out of the pool. I watch him grab a towel and sling it around his hips. I'm used to seeing men in swim trunks, but Briggs is different. It feels like I am not supposed to see him like this, like I'm spying on the boys' locker room and might get in trouble any moment.

I should look away, especially since he is angry, but men objectify women every day. These fifteen seconds are my rebuttal. Abs and hip bones that accentuate the "v," and long, powerfully built arms all stand in front of me, while their owner rubs a second towel across his head. He's a walking commercial right now. The brand is "hot asshole" and I feel baited to purchase. Until, that is, he storms off into the men's locker room, and I realize I'm about to lose my client if I don't haul my butt out of the pool and meet him on the other side.

It takes Briggs three minutes to get dressed, pack his gym bag, and try to sneak past me in the gym lobby. I'm too savvy for that though, I'm a coiled and waiting cobra, and as soon as he heads for the sliding glass doors, I spring.

"Not so fast," I call, enjoying the look of sheer annoyance that crosses his face when I intercept his attempt at a hasty exit. "You're still mine for twenty minutes."

I was too afraid of missing him to change out of my suit, so while he has made himself polished and presentable again in brand name sweatpants and a crew-neck t-shirt, my wet hair is dripping onto the carpet, and there are goosebumps crawling up and down my bare arms. I'm hardly as intimidating as I would like to be, but I'm going for it all the same.

"Twenty more minutes in the pool isn't going to happen." Briggs' hazel eyes are blazing with anger, and I still don't understand why.

"Yeah, because you have an undisclosed injury," I say.

He folds his arms across his chest and attempts to intimidate me with one of those cold, hard glares he's perfected. "It's not a good day for me."

"When will it be a good day for that shoulder?"

Briggs rolls his eyes. "I'll let you know."

He's not going to let me know because heaven forbid he admits there is anything he needs to work on that can't be fixed by reminding me how much he pays for my services.

When a woman across the gym waves to get my attention, Briggs makes a second effort to sneak out the door, leaving me no option but to follow him out into the parking lot, the damp towel around my waist the only thing shielding me from the cold morning air. I really should have thrown shoes on.

"Hey!" I call after him. "This conversation isn't over."

He spins on his heels and plants his hands on his hips, his chest rising and falling with each frustrated breath he sucks in.

"What do you want me to do right now? Obviously, I can't do the workout."

"I want you to let me do my job and train you."

"What do you think I've been doing the last few weeks?"

An honest response pops into my head and while I

would normally put a happy little filter on it to keep the client motivated, Briggs hasn't responded to the sunshine approach, so instead I tell it like it is.

"Giving me half your effort, half your focus, a hell of a lot less than the truth, and more than enough attitude."

His jaw clenches into a hard line. "It sounds like you've already decided who I am, so no need for anymore leading questions."

He storms toward his truck, and honestly, I feel like I'm fighting with a high school boyfriend with a flair for the dramatic. I am not chasing him any further across this parking lot, my feet are turning to icicles on the cold pavement and our audience of bystanders seems to multiply with each back and forth.

If we have an audience, we might as well give them a show. So like the jilted high school lover I feel like I am, I shout at him, "I'm working with what you're giving me." Then I hold my ground dramatically as he drives away in a cloud of toxic masculinity.

I honestly don't get what his deal is.

People get hurt. It happens to all of us, but especially to people who put themselves at risk like athletes do. You suck it up and go to the doctor. Sometimes you sit it out for a little physical therapy. Sometimes it's worse than that and maybe you have to get surgery. There might be temporary pain medication to get through the worst of it. But pretending an injury doesn't exist while inwardly suffering? Why would Briggs willingly sign up for that?

All of this and more is traveling through my brain as I

hurry through the motions of drying off and pulling on today's Halloween-themed outfit. Briggs's bad mood is still contaminating my space bubble when I finally exit the gym.

"I thought I saw you!" The same woman who tried to get my attention before beams at me. She's an SUV mom, but it's too early for the gym daycare, which means she's either got a day job or she's an early exerciser. I vaguely recognize her from the carpool lane at school, but I'd know if she was one of my student's parents.

"Oh, hello," I say, pasting a big fat smile on my face. What are the odds she witnessed my super adolescent interaction with Briggs earlier? "Can I help you?"

"You're Miss Raven, right? Raven Oliver?" She extends her hand. In my black baby doll dress and purple-and-orange striped tights there is no hiding my kindergarten teacher status. "I'm Claudia Williams. My three children attend your school. I was just appointed as the new PTO president."

My eyebrows raise and I shake her hand. This isn't someone I want to piss off, so I put on a smile and inwardly kiss the pumpkin spice latte I had planned good-bye. "It's nice to meet you. What can I do for you, Mrs. Williams?"

By the way her giant diamond wedding ring is currently sparkling in the morning sun, it's obvious this woman is married, and it's also obvious she has money from the shiny new Range Rover she's just loaded her designer bag into. Whatever she wants from me, I really hope it's not going to cost me. These women always want something more––more of my time, more of my resources, more of my energy. And I do it because I love the kids, but sometimes the parents are more exhausting than my five- and six-year-olds.

"Well, you see, my daughter Presley is also in kindergarten, and I was hoping to make her experience at school more fun."

I think I know where this is going. I've had several parents try to get their kids moved to my class since school started, but everything is set since we have strict rules on ratios. I feel bad the other teachers aren't as popular but there's really not much I can do about it.

"What did you have in mind?" I ask instead of saying what I really want to say, which is *sorry, but I can't help you and I really need to go now.*

"You see, we're planning parties for the classroom." Standard. Parents love that kind of thing, especially the Pinterest Moms. "And I have some really big ideas that have unfortunately been vetoed."

I frown, wondering how big of parties she's hoping for. We have restrictions on what we can do, a lot of them having to do with the treats involved since there are so many food allergies, not to mention parents who think processed sugar is a gateway drug.

"I'm sorry to hear that, but I'm not sure how I can help."

She sighs heavily, clapping her hands together in frustration. "Apparently it's not fair to bring professional entertainment into the classroom if the other classes don't also get the same treatment."

There are three classes for each grade and the administration tries to keep things fair.

"Yeah, that's the rule. Things like that need to include the whole grade or even the school."

But that's what the PTO is for. They plan a yearly movie night, carnival, and a Valentine's dance, not to mention loads of little fundraisers. I don't understand what this woman is so upset about.

"Right, but do you know how booked professional Santa Claus's get? I was able to secure the best one in town for a thirty-minute window and that's it." She widens her eyes and waves her hands around. "Not enough time for three classrooms."

All this over Santa Claus? Kindergarten does a *Polar Express* party every year where the kids wear pajamas to school, watch the movie, and drink hot chocolate. Apparently the movie isn't good enough, and Claudia Williams wants a professional Santa to show up too. I think a Santa is a great idea, but not if it's only for one class. The amount of unnecessary parent drama I've encountered is endless, but this takes the cake.

"And you need me to agree to your plan?" I say.

"I've already got the other teachers on board. You're my last one."

I don't know what to say. On one hand, it's not fair to my kids. They're going to feel terrible when they hear about this on the playground. But on the other hand, I don't want to start a feud with this woman, and I don't want to deprive any classroom of a Christmas miracle.

"How about this," I say, "give me some time to find a Santa for our classroom and the other one. If everyone can have Santa, then that works for me."

Her cheeks flush pink and her lips thin. "I've already paid the deposit."

"How hard can it be to find someone to dress up in a suit? I'm sure we can manage it somehow."

She laughs as if I'm clueless. Maybe I am.

"Then I'll take that as a yes," she says, unlocking her designer car and sliding into the driver's seat. "I knew you would see the value. I'll let the rest of the PTO know it's handled."

I open my mouth to remind her that I asked for time. I didn't formally promise Santa, but she's already rolling up her window. Her Range Rover peeling out of the parking lot, a tight little smile on her face as she goes, happy to have made her problem my problem.

Chapter Fifteen

BRIGGS

It's Wednesday morning and my body rises minutes before the alarm goes off. I hit the snooze button and squeeze my eyes shut, willing myself to fall back asleep. I should be hopping in the shower, pulling cycling clothes from the clean laundry basket by my bed, and preparing to meet up with Raven. The thing is, there's not much point in that anymore. Swimming is one-third of a triathlon, and I can't drag myself back and forth across a pool for fifteen minutes. There is no prayer I'll make it in open water. Even if I were to survive the swim, I won't be able to peel the wetsuit off my body or lift my bike off a rack once I've torn my shoulder to shreds.

If my parents ask, I'll tell them I decided to do a marathon instead. People train all year for those. It's not like they will be disappointed that I am *only* running twenty-six miles.

I should tell her I can't make it. A quick text would get me off the hook, but I know what will happen if I send that. She'll shoot back with something snarky about my making excuses for my shoulder, and I'll get defensive. She'll get the angry version of me––the version I hate but can't seem to get away from lately. Instead, I climb into the shower and stand under the streaming hot water until it feels like my skin will melt away from my bones.

When I finally get out to start my day, there are three missed texts from Raven and a voicemail that I delete without bothering to listen. I'm being a bastard, but ignoring her is easier than letting her down.

I have an appointment with Dr. Thomas this afternoon, and Raven and my shoulder are going to be a part of the conversation. What I really want to do is ghost the good doctor as well, but I can't do that. If Jaci didn't choose to spend eternity in a wooden box, then I don't get to choose to bag out on the only person that holds me accountable.

By the time I arrive at Dr. Thomas's office, I've built up the conversation in my head to the point where my palms are sweaty, and my pulse is moving faster than that first morning run with Raven. There are pills for this type of feeling. Little round disks to take away the worry, but I've never let myself go that route, and I'm not starting today.

The receptionist calls my name and I enter Dr.

Thomas's office. His wood-paneled walls and the dated framework around the diplomas never cease to remind me of my childhood. My mother used to take me along to her lady doctor appointments, back when I was old enough to protest, but too young to stay home. That place had been covered in seventies wood paneling too. I hated it because, in the waiting room, there was a statue of a mother and child locked in an embrace, with the Bible quote, "I know the plans I have for you . . . to give you a hope and a future" scripted on the bottom.

For some reason this statue made me feel convicted. Every time I spent too long looking at it, I got an unstoppable urge to confess my childhood crimes. The time I stole baseball cards from the grocery store, the action figure of Turner's that I'd sworn I hadn't seen, but was stored under my bed until I could figure out how to fix the broken arm. Sitting in the waiting room with that damn statue was my truth serum, and the interior of Dr. Thomas's office had the exact same effect.

I don't even make it five minutes before I'm spilling my guts out to the man. We've been together enough years that this isn't unusual, but from the sparkle in his eyes, it's obvious he sees this as some kind of breakthrough. "And so that's why I'm changing to a marathon instead of a triathlon."

The silence stretches between us. I have nothing left to say and don't feel a need to fill it. Ball's in his court now.

"Have you been using your mantra, Briggs?"

I blink at him. "My what?" This question is out of left

field. I was expecting a lecture, or at least some leading questions.

"Your mantra. We came up with it together when you first started therapy."

I don't remember shit about a mantra. That first year in therapy is a blur, though, so it's not like I'm surprised that "we" gave me an assignment I've forgotten all about. He gave me lots of assignments I forgot about or plain old refused to do.

"Sorry, I can't say I remember that."

He nods sagely and shuffles through the notebook he uses to keep track of his thoughts on me. Not for the first time, I wonder what's in that thing. Probably nothing good. He thumbs to the correct page and smiles. "Ah, here. A mantra is a phrase I want you to repeat to yourself throughout your day. It might be uncomfortable at first, but give it a try. You might be surprised. Over time, we can change your mantra if something better would fit."

"Okay, so what's my mantra?" I raise an eyebrow, almost thinking that I should change it if it's something I didn't care to remember or follow up on.

"I am open to forgiveness and joy."

I snort. No wonder I didn't use that mantra. Being open to forgiveness and joy has been the last thing on my mind from the moment Jaci died. Dr. Thomas knows that. He's known that for years. It's no coincidence that he brought this up right after I explained why I quit the triathlon.

"You don't like it?"

"No, I don't." It would be a lie to walk around saying that to myself.

"How about we make a deal?" He pauses thoughtfully. "Use it for two weeks until our next session. If you don't like it, then we can change it to something else."

"Like what?"

"We'll discuss that if necessary, but for now, I think you're ready to try this out."

I grit my teeth, wanting to dig my heels in, but in the back of my mind I imagine Dr. Thomas telling me to get lost. If he ever called me out on the truth, that I'm only here to wallow in my misery and I'm not actually doing any healing, maybe that would spur him on to fire me as a client. I don't want to start over with someone new.

"Okay, fine. I'll do it."

He smiles. "According to my notes, you are taking to this mantra better this time than the last time."

"Go figure."

"Even small progress is progress. The key is not to give up."

"Is that what you think I'm doing? Giving up on the triathlon? Because I'm not, it's called a pivot. People do it all the time."

"Do you believe it's a pivot, or do you believe you're giving up?" he says. "Because it doesn't matter what I think. It matters what you think of yourself."

In my gut, I know exactly what I'm doing. I'm giving up. Hardcore. But I'm not about to admit that. "I think I'm open to forgiveness and joy," I deadpan.

He cracks a smile. "Good. Just like that. I know you don't believe it now, but say it enough times and you will begin to believe."

It takes everything in me not to be a total dick and tell him what I really think, that I'm paying way too much for mantras about joy and forgiveness. But I don't and our session ends soon after, with me promising him I'll do my homework. First thing I'm supposed to do is write it on a sticky note and put it on my bathroom mirror. I feel like a complete idiot doing it, but I do it anyway. Only because I promised. Not because I want to. Not because I believe it.

And then I head to bed, my eyes landing on the cardboard box in the corner.

Without letting myself think too much, I stride right up to the box, heft it to the bed, and rip off the tape.

And there they are, among the photo albums and old ticket stubs and two of her favorite ratty t-shirts. Jaci's stack of journals. They're the real reason I kept this box taped up for so long. I meant to open these journals ages ago, but I haven't been able to. It's easier to pretend that because I moved them to my bedroom that I actually had intentions of reading them. I didn't. I haven't. I still don't.

They're another one of Dr. Thomas's assignments. The journals belonged to Jaci. She wrote in a journal every night from the age of eight all the way up until twenty-nine. Start with the first one and work your way up, Dr. Thomas had said. But I didn't. And every time he brings them up, I tell him that I haven't read them yet. He continually urges me to start, but leaves it alone beyond that. I guess your dead wife's journals and a stupid mantra don't hold the same weight in the therapy community.

What the hell? I've started my homework--have a bright-yellow sticky note to prove it--might as well go all in. I take the first journal off the pile and crack it open. Her handwriting is curly and sloppy, the telltale sign of a child's writing. My throat burns and my eyes water, but I force myself to read.

DEAR DIARY,

Today I started at a new school. Third grade is going to be the best ever! I wonder who my new friends will be. Will I finally make a best friend? I've always wanted a best friend.

Chapter Sixteen

RAVEN

Briggs is no longer my client. There are rules, and one of the rules is that it doesn't matter how much money you have to offer, if you blow me off without explanation, you are fired. I've fired him. In my head, anyway. I can't fire him in person because he won't answer his phone. Not that I care. I absolutely don't care that after several weeks of training, some of the most challenging sessions in my career, the man dropped me like a hot potato.

Okay, that's obviously a lie. I always care when I lose a client, especially like this. I'm just saying I don't care more than I've cared about anyone else. Briggs isn't special. There's more to life than being hot and rich, like maybe being a decent person and picking up your goddamn phone, or canceling appointments ahead of time instead of straight up ghosting people.

"He's basically an overgrown child. I bet he pouted every time he didn't get picked first in gym class," I say to Leonard, my favorite client. Maybe coaches aren't supposed to have favorites, but if you met Leo, you'd understand.

I'm pedaling like a maniac, the spin bike wobbling beneath my attempt to burn off the last few ounces of rage I've been bottling up all week. It's windier than the tornado scene in *The Wizard of Oz* right now so we had to take our session indoors. Leonard doesn't say anything about my haphazard riding or the fact that today's training is supposed to be about *him*.

What he does say is, "No refunds for douchebags." Sweat pours off his chin and glues his shirt to his chest like a second skin. He's been in the tri club for going on three years now and my friend for almost as long. His dedication to the sport is admirable, considering the fact that he has never once placed in a race, not even a local 5k.

"That's not an official policy, but I'll keep it in mind." I imagine adding it to my contract with a satisfied grin.

We hit the forty-five minute mark, and Leonard pulls his hands away from the handlebars and stretches them above his head, allowing his heart to return to a resting rate.

"You're better off without him."

"I am, but do you know how hard it is for a coach to deal with a quitter? It makes *me* feel like I failed."

"Well, shut those feelings up. You don't fail. Look, how many people in the club have gone from holding your hand to hoisting a medal in the air?"

"Every finisher gets a medal, you idiot." I laugh. Leonard always makes me smile. His husband is a lucky guy.

"You know what I mean."

And I do. There are the finisher medals but then there are the three coveted plaques for the overall podium placers, and while it's rare for us to place at the events with pros intermixing, my club is kick-ass in the elite-amateur league. I've lost count of how many age-group awards we've scooped up in the five years that I've been doing this. I've even had a couple of my clients go on to get pro-cards, which not only mean paid sponsorships, but coveted race positions and invitations to elite events and prestigious teams.

He's right, I *don't* fail. In the entirety of my coaching career, no one has given up the way Briggs has. It was Briggs who gave up, not me, so why do I feel like this is my failure and not his?

KIDS CRY. Kindergarteners especially cry. I'm used to it. There's a reason why I hoard Kleenex boxes like they're toilet paper in a worldwide TP shortage. But something about seeing Charlie Lawson cry hits me in a way it usually doesn't.

We're sitting in the office after school with the other

kids who didn't get picked up. There are always a couple, and the staff are well versed in calling parents and charging late pick-up fees to their accounts. None of the other four kids are crying, probably because they're all older, or maybe because they're used to this which is its own league of awful, but adorable, curly-haired Charlie in the corner with the crocodile tears is eating me alive.

"Don't worry, Raven," the front desk admin says. "I got this. You can go back to your classroom."

I swallow hard, eyeing Charlie. I want to scoop him into a big hug.

"What happens if you can't get a hold of them?" I whisper, careful to keep my voice low.

"We're here until five," Lisa whispers back. "If he's not picked up by then, I have to call child welfare services."

It's already four fifteen, and I've been waiting with the kid for an hour. It's not my job, but I couldn't leave him there. He's got a soft spot in my heart. Child welfare services are supposed to look out for children, and calling them is something we do from time to time, even in our fancy private school setting. Sometimes that phone call is for the best, but I don't think the Lawsons are the type to warrant such a call. This has to be a mistake––but even so, it's not okay that they're not here, and I want to wring their necks for it.

"And you've called all his emergency numbers? His parents? What about grandparents? Aunts and uncles?"

My mind flits to Briggs. I haven't seen him in over two weeks and doubt I ever will again. What a waste that was.

"I've got numbers for his mom, dad, the nanny, and an uncle." She frowns. "None are answering."

"What's the uncle's name?" I step around the desk to peer at the computer. "Is it Briggs Lawson?"

"Yeah, but his number is a dud."

I squint at the computer, then whip out my phone to compare what I have with what's on the screen. Two of the numbers have been inverted. "Look here, you have the wrong number."

I give her the correct one and explain that he used to be a triathlon client, which is why I have it. She thinks nothing of it and begins to dial, but I don't think nothing of it. Why do I still have his number? I should've deleted it by now. Blocked it. Scrubbed it, and him, from memory.

I can hear the deep rumble of his voice on the other end of the phone as Lisa explains the situation, but I can't make out what he's saying back. I'm glad she was the one to call—I have nothing to say to him and the very idea makes my stomach clench.

I return to Charlie and kneel in front of him, squeezing his clammy little hands. "Your Uncle Briggs is on the way. No need to worry."

He brushes the tears away and looks up at me with those adorable hazel eyes, eyes that remind me of said uncle. "Can I go play on the playground until he gets here?"

I wince. There's no duty out there right now, so it's not something we let the kids do after hours, but I can't say no to him, not when he's so vulnerable. "Alright, buddy. Let's go."

Lisa gives me a questioning look when I take Charlie by the hand and head out of the office, but she doesn't stop me. Until this afternoon, I was prepared to simmer over the Briggs situation. There is no sense going over what you should have, could have, would have said to someone when you aren't going to see them again. But now that Briggs is about to be face to face with me, I've got some thoughts on how the conversation is going to go.

When he arrives fifteen minutes later, I'm pushing Charlie on the swing. Apparently, my daydreams have worked themselves into my arm strength because I quickly notice that Charlie is swinging pretty damn high and looking mildly terrified at that. I grip the chains and slow the swing as Briggs steps out of his oversized, overcompensating truck.

He's in his work attire. A dress shirt, pushed up at the sleeves and trousers that have been ironed within an inch of their lives. I glare at him across the playground and imagine how nice it would be if we still handled things the way they did in western movies. Get mad. Challenge to a duel. See, shoot, repeat. I mean, I don't actually want to shoot the man, but some kind of revenge seems necessary.

Chapter Seventeen

BRIGGS

She looks like she wants to shoot me. An impressive feat considering she's standing there in tights covered in cartoon crayons and a t-shirt that says, 'Complimentary colors always have nice things to say.' I knew there was a chance I would see her when the school secretary called, but I was hoping it would be a brief passing in the hallway, or at least in the presence of another adult. Instead, the only other soul in sight was Charlie, and he was pumping away on the swing set, oblivious to the fact that I, and not his parents, had come to his rescue.

I dig my hands into my pockets and begin walking from the parking lot to the playground. Our last conversation ended with her shouting at my truck as I sped out of the gym parking lot, and I won't be all that shocked if this one ends the same way.

"Good afternoon," I say, when she stops directly in front of me, arms folded over her chest, eyes burning with contempt. I didn't think that level of death-glare was possible in kindergarten teachers. I stand corrected.

"School got out an hour ago."

I look over at Charlie, still swinging, still appearing content, but I know better than to assume it has been an easy hour. The kid has probably spent most of that time dripping with tears and anxiety. It isn't like Turner to be late. His wife, sure. Samantha has always been a bit of a flake for anyone who isn't connected to her law firm, but my brother?

"I'll talk to Turner. I'm sure something important came up."

Raven rolls her eyes. "More important than picking up your kid?" She leans closer, her body language still giving off murder vibes. "You know, if you hadn't gotten here when you did, they would have called child services? You would have been picking Charlie up from DHS and not the playground."

My eyebrows lift without my permission as my stomach sinks. "I'll take care of it."

Raven nods once, and I think our conversation is done here. Do I want our conversation to be done here? My gut reaction is a resounding no that unsteadies me.

"You know, I'm surprised you made it, what with all the trouble with your phone lately," she says.

"Trouble with my phone?" Now I'm really confused.

"Well, surely something is wrong with your phone.

Why else wouldn't you have picked up the phone all those times I called and texted you?"

A blush is creeping up and over the collar of my blue button down. The truth, that I decided to give up at the first sign of struggle, is not something I can verbalize, not to this woman who projects an unflappable air with every ounce of her being.

"Some things came up. I meant to respond."

She shakes her head. "Just stop. You quit, people quit, it's part of life, but do yourself a favor. Next time you drop the ball, have the courtesy to own it. Nobody likes a jackass."

A lump forms in my throat, and I have to fight off the urge to undo my top button and suck in deep breaths, like I've been holding my breath under water for the last thirty seconds.

She's after an apology and I owe her one. Instead, Charlie comes bounding across the parking lot and leaps into my arms. I've never been so grateful for the skinny little limbs that wrap around my neck as he snuggles into my chest.

"Uncle Briggs," his voice is hoarse and it's obvious he's been crying, "where are my mom and dad?"

I'm wondering the same thing. "Let's go find them, okay, buddy?" I hug him one last time and then strap him into the backseat of my truck. I close the door and turn back to Raven with a frown. "I don't have a booster seat. Do you think that's okay?"

She blinks a few times. "He's probably fine. Most of

the kindergarteners are still in booster seats, but not all of them."

She would know, she's here at pickup every day. I, on the other hand, know very little about children, let alone what the weight and height restrictions are for something like this. Future children disappeared from my life plans the moment I let lack of sleep turn them into a roadside memorial. Maybe I am lucky because I lost them before I knew what being a father really was. Imagining Turner losing Charlie puts a knot in my throat.

Raven and I stand staring at each other for a beat too long, the unsaid apology weighing heavily between us. Yup, I *am* being a jackass. I clear my throat, prepared to say what I should've said two weeks ago, when Raven backs up a step.

"Drive safe." Then she turns and strides back into the school.

I stare after her until she's gone, my mind spinning. I gave up, she's right, but she herself said that giving up was a fact of life. I've accepted it, and at the end of the day, I don't give up on the things or the people that really matter to me. The triathlon simply wasn't that important of a priority, and Raven got her payment. I already told my family that I switched to a marathon, and they didn't seem any less enthusiastic. The matter has been resolved. It's done.

So why then do I feel so unsettled?

· · ·

TEN MINUTES LATER, we're at Turner's place and nobody is home. Where the hell are they? Charlie and I wait on the doorstep for a good ten minutes before giving up. I wouldn't hesitate to break in, alarm system be damned, but Charlie's on the verge of tears again and aren't uncles supposed to make life fun?

"What's your favorite flavor of ice cream?" I ask.

He blinks up at me, lost in thought for a moment, before declaring, "Butter pecan."

I stifle a laugh. "Aren't you supposed to like rainbow ice or bubblegum sprinkles or something like that?"

He wrinkles his nose and shakes his head. "Too sweet."

"Butter pecan it is." I take him back to the car and look up the closest ice cream shop.

When I got the call from the school, I almost didn't answer it, assuming it was spam. Thank God I listened to my gut. Whatever is going on with Turner and Samantha, they have some serious explaining to do, and I can't help but be worried. He wasn't in his office and his admin didn't know where he was either. Playing hooky from work isn't like my brother.

What if he's dead?

The intrusive thought razors through my mind, but I don't entertain it. I shove it away and focus on getting Charlie ice cream instead.

Hours later, we're back at my place when a knock finally sounds on the door. Charlie's full of butter pecan and cheese pizza, happily perched on the couch with *SpongeBob Square Pants* cackling away on the television.

"Where were you?" I hiss the second I open the door.

Turner winces and steps back. "Can we talk about this later?"

"No."

He ignores me and pushes his way inside, beelining it for his son. Charlie wants to know the same thing I do, and Turner gives some excuse about work and an apology, which Charlie seems to take at face value.

"Finish your episode, Charlie," I say, and fix my brother with a hard stare. "Your dad and I need to talk."

Turner sighs, as if I'm the annoying one in this situation. If anything, that makes me even more frustrated with him. I lead him into my home office and shut the door.

"I'm sorry, where's the gratitude for saving your ass today?" Maybe I'm overreacting, and I love spending time with Charlie, but not like this.

"Thanks for your help." Turner won't meet my eye.

"What happened?" I step closer. "And don't you dare lie to me."

He drops onto the edge of the desk and rubs his hand through his disheveled hair. "It was a miscommunication. The nanny is on vacation, and I thought Sam was picking up Charlie, but it turns out I was supposed to do it. I'm so sorry. I owe you."

He owes Charlie.

I narrow my gaze and force myself to calm down a little. "I know things happen and I can't pretend to understand what it's like to be a parent--"

"No, you can't." Turner's face pales.

"*But,* that doesn't explain why you left work early or why it took you hours to answer your phone. And I know you weren't at the office because when I left to get Charlie, you weren't there, and your admin didn't have a clue."

He looks up at me, his jaw set. "Did it ever occur to you that where I was is none of your business?"

Anger races through me all over again. "It's my business when I'm picking up your slack."

"You're such a hardass. Not everyone is perfect like you, Briggs."

"Don't turn this around on me."

"Fine." He throws up his hands. "I was out with a woman. Okay? I was on a date, and I accidentally left my phone in the car."

My stomach hardens. Of all the things he could've told me, I wasn't expecting it to be this. "You're cheating on Sam?"

"Technically, she's cheating on me too. And anyway, we're separated." He lets out a long breath and his news hits me like a ton of bricks. "We've been struggling for years. We finally separated a couple months ago and recently agreed to start seeing other people."

Seeing other people during the workday? Skipping out on his responsibilities for hours? Possibly hooking up with this new woman too? These are all questions I want to ask, but I don't. It's unlikely he'll answer them all, so I go for the most important one instead. "Does this mean you're getting a divorce?"

He nods once and looks away. My heart sinks. This is

huge news, and I wonder if I'm the last to know because, apparently, it's been in the works for a while.

"Charlie didn't say anything." Which is kind of surprising, considering I've had three uninterrupted hours with the little man.

"Charlie had a hard time at first, but he's getting used to the new normal. His teacher set us up with some resources to help him. She's really good, you know."

Part of me wants to let him steer the conversation over to Raven, but I'm not taking the bait. "Why didn't you tell me?"

We're close, always have been. I was the first one he told when he got Samantha pregnant. I'm the first one he goes to when we're having an issue at work. I didn't realize he had things this big going in his life that he wasn't telling me.

"Because you had this perfect storybook love with Jaci. I know you'd give anything to have her back. You two would've never gotten divorced." His voice softens and he stands up, brushing out his dress pants. "I didn't want to admit defeat."

I can't pretend to understand what he's going through, but I can understand that sometimes life gives you shit, and you can't make lemonade out of shit. I hug my brother then, something we never do, but I think maybe we should start. "You're not a failure. You're just a human."

It's easy to mean those words to someone else, even though I've never been able to believe them in my own life.

Chapter Eighteen

RAVEN

Santa remains elusive. Every working Santa in Austin already has plans for the date of the kindergarten *Polar Express* celebration and, according to my online research, a legitimate-looking Santa costume is something like three hundred dollars.

"Who in their right mind pays three hundred dollars to dress like Santa?"

Andre looks over the top of his morning paper and grins. "Is this your way of asking me to play Santa?"

I nearly spit my coffee across the breakfast table. "You? Santa? We can strap a pillow to your stomach, but no one's going to believe your face is a day over forty."

He folds the paper in half, and that grin becomes a big, toothy smile. The kind that sparkles in cartoons. The kind that makes you think of old Hollywood actors. Andre circles behind me and pops a kiss on my cheek before grabbing his gear to head off to work. I'm still not sure what he does in finance, and now that we've been seeing each other more frequently, I feel silly asking.

He probably knows far more about my job than he would like to, but that's the thing about me. I'm a talker. I try to be a listener, too, but Andre rarely talks about himself and it's uncomfortable trying to pull details out of someone when they clearly aren't interested in sharing.

He's not totally off base about Santa though. It doesn't have to be a professional. I could get someone I know to fill in. Andre, however, is not an option. I never introduce anyone into my work life unless I have full confidence that they are going to stick around. I like Andre. I'm pretty sure it's mutual, but mutual and serious aren't the same thing. Besides, I need a tall man with a wrinkle or two. A touch of gray wouldn't hurt, but I suppose a bald cap could hide their hair with the right Santa wig.

I could ask one of the old professors from my parents' college friends. Some have got full-grown beards of their own. The thing is, I don't love spending time with that crowd. Even though my parents are retired now, they're still fully immersed in their old work cohorts. Every year for Thanksgiving, the college hosts a tenure and family Friendsgiving, and though I've been plenty of times, I've yet to enjoy one. It's one long evening where someone, or three someones depending on the year, imbibes too much overpriced liquor and starts explaining to me the value of getting my doctorate. That or some old man's hand magically makes its way to my knee under the table. Neither circumstance carries too much appeal.

There is still time. That's what I tell myself as I hop on to my bike and pedal toward the school. Briggs' truck is in the drop-off line when I arrive, and I can't help but train my eyes in that direction. I step off my bike and pull the lock from my bag, trying not to make it obvious that I'm spying. While I haven't heard one word from Turner or his wife after both neglected to show up for Charlie last week, I have noticed that Charlie's uncle has suddenly become more involved. As much as I want to know the details, I am not willing to give Briggs an opportunity to redeem himself. Not when he refuses to apologize for blowing off training.

Charlie waves goodbye to his uncle before running into the main building. Despite my covert attempt to mask myself behind the bike rack, Briggs raises a hand and waves at me before pulling out of the line.

Claudia Williams, a.k.a. Ms. PTO Pres herself, sidles up to me, her eyes bouncing from me to Briggs' truck and back to me again. "I haven't seen that dad before. What's the scoop?"

I eye her left hand. You know, the one with a big flashy wedding ring on it when I met her. She catches me staring and waggles her fingers. "Oh, I'm definitely single," she says, fluffing out her hair. "I only wear that thing when I go to the gym because I hate getting hit on while I'm working out. You know how that goes."

I do to an extent, but I don't say so. So she's single, and

she's a woman who does not share the same boundaries as I do when it comes to dating the parents of students. So what if she wants to actively target the single dad population here at Glen Eden Academy? It's none of my business.

"He's not a dad. Just an uncle helping out."

She clutches her chest like I've said he donated a kidney to a child in need.

"Does this uncle have a significant other?"

I open my mouth to say no, but then it dawns on me that I really don't know. As many early morning sessions as Briggs and I had, he never once delved into his personal life. He didn't wear a ring, but he wasn't hitting on women that night in the club either. Truth be told, most of what I knew about Briggs Lawson I had learned on the internet.

"I'm not sure."

Claudia raises an eyebrow. "He seemed pretty familiar with you."

Clearly she doesn't believe me.

"His nephew's in my class. That's the full range of my knowledge on Briggs Lawson."

Her eyes light up at the use of his name, and I am already mentally kicking myself for letting it slip. That woman is going to scour social media for any and all information she can get on Briggs.

"As in Lawson Construction?"

Oh, so she's already got intel on all the wealthy families in town. Of course she does. I almost want to warn him, but I'm not that nice. "That's the one. Now if you'll excuse me, I've got to get to class."

I begin to walk inside, and the woman follows me. She's not supposed to enter the building without stopping for a guest pass, but that doesn't deter her.

"And tell me, Miss Raven," she clucks her tongue, "have you found a suitable Santa Claus, yet?"

I let out a frustrated sigh, not letting myself lie to her, which I really want to do right now. Anything to get her out of my hair. "Not yet."

"Thanksgiving is only two weeks away and Christmas is only six." Her voice transforms from soft and happy, to sharp and angry. It's almost frightening––someone ought to get this woman an acting agent. "Don't tell me you're going to let this slide because I am not going to allow that."

I turn on her then, doing my best not to glare. Students stream past us, but she's oblivious to everyone but me.

"What do you mean, you're not going to allow that?" I ask carefully. I'm pretty sure she's threatening me, and I'm not sure how much weight that threat holds. If it was a regular run-of-the-mill parent, I wouldn't worry so much, but this is the PTO president, which means she's not afraid to pool her resources. I like the administration here, but if she starts a crusade against me, I'm not sure I'll win.

"I mean, Santa Claus *will* be visiting my daughter's class. That is non-negotiable." She steps closer. "What is negotiable is whether or not Santa Claus visits *your* class-room on *Polar Express* Day."

Someone clears their throat. "Miss. Raven."

I whip around and blink up in surprise at none other than Briggs Lawson himself. "I thought you left?"

The man is blindingly handsome today in a gray suit and shiny black tie. His dark hair is styled perfectly, those sexy streaks of gray around his ears matching his outfit as if he planned it. The rich scent of his woodsy cologne envelops me like a glove and it takes a massive amount of self-control not to visibly swoon. This isn't the ornery five a.m. Briggs I spent three weeks training. This is someone else entirely--CEO Briggs.

He holds up Charlie's backpack. "He accidentally left it in my truck."

"Oh," I breathe, but I don't know what else to say.

My cheeks are burning, and I wonder how much he heard of the Santa Claus scandal. I know Claudia should be the one embarrassed, but I can't help but feel two inches tall. I reach for the backpack and our hands brush. I swallow hard, hating my body for how it reacts to the feel of his calloused fingers. It only lasts a second, but his touch sends adrenaline spiraling through me. It's like the exact moment when a race starts, when everything goes from zero to one hundred in a single breath.

"Aren't you going to introduce me to your friend?" Claudia says. She's back to her soft and sweet persona, reaching out her hand to shake Briggs'. She doesn't wait for me to introduce her despite the question she directed at me. I don't know if I'd be able to anyway. My throat has suddenly grown tight. "I'm Claudia Williams. I'm the PTO president, so if you ever need anything or if this one gives you a hard time," she nods to me with a little laugh, "let me know."

Briggs drops her hand and steps back. His eyes are hard, even though he's got a fake smile plastered to his face. I wonder if she can tell the difference. "I'll keep that in mind, Mrs. Williams."

"Oh, please, it's Miss. I'm *very* single." Giggling, she bats her perfect eyelash extensions. "On second thought, let me give you my card. Just in case." She rummages in her designer purse and pulls it out in two seconds flat, hardly enough time for him to refuse. Not that he does.

She hands it over and then the bell rings. "Time to get to work," she says, waving a coy goodbye to Briggs and slipping into the crowd.

I can't help but wonder what she does for work to be able to afford her lifestyle. Does she work? Is she some kind of heiress? Or did she divorce a wealthy guy, getting a fat settlement out of the deal, and now she's looking for rich husband number two?

"Have a good day, Raven," Briggs says to me, his voice barely a whisper, and then he's leaving too.

On his way out the door, he casually drops Claudia Williams' card into the trash. My legs don't want to move even though I will them to. Instead I watch him go, taking in the shape of his broad shoulders and the way he so easily moves upstream through the mass of children.

Why am I so unnerved?

Because I don't have this fluttering feeling with Andre.

Because I am obviously inappropriately attracted to Briggs.

When did this happen? Maybe it started seconds ago when he tossed Claudia's card into the trash. Or maybe it started the moment I laid eyes on him in the coffee shop. Either way, there's not a damn thing I can do about it. He's untouchable, grumpy as hell, with walls even the most seasoned rock climber would struggle to scale, and he quit on me.

That's right. He quit. Remember?

"Get over it, Raven," I whisper to myself, whipping around and hurrying to my classroom. For the first time this school year, I arrive late.

Chapter Nineteen

BRIGGS

Reading Jaci's journals doesn't exactly go how I imagined it would. For one thing, I'm not swallowed by grief the way I'd feared. Surprisingly, I don't wallow in the paralyzing guilt that has dominated the last three years of my life. Instead, it's like getting to know her again. The parts she kept secret and the parts I recognize from our life together merge seamlessly into this new person. This whole person, this vibrant woman, who is more than the girl I had a crush on, more than my partner.

But sometimes I find myself laughing out loud and then turning to where she should be, so I can tell her about what I've just read. Those are the moments that shake me back to reality.

I flew through her middle school years, then read all

four years of high school on repeat for the better part of a week. I knew what was coming of course, but it was different reading it from her perspective. When I met her, it was a no-reservations, this-is-your-future kind of meeting. When she met me, it was a blip. I got one sentence. *The guy with the trumpet won't stop staring at me.* The first time I read it, I wanted to grab a pen and scribble in response. *I couldn't stop staring. There's a difference!*

Reading about our growth from bandmates, to friends, to high school sweethearts, all through her eyes, has been both painful and beautiful at the same time. I find myself thinking what I always thought around her, *how did I get so lucky?* Only now, I can read in detail about exactly what made her change from mildly annoyed with me to head over heels.

According to Jaci, it was my personality, not my family's money or the way I looked. Although my looks didn't hurt, she made sure to write that right next to the tiny hearts and little muscle arm doodles. I wonder what she would think of my personality now. Most days, I felt like a hollow shell of a human. Moving, eating, working, repeat, repeat, repeat. It was a good thing I was forever hers because no one was going to fall in love with present day me.

Unless you counted that tart at Charlie's school. Her business card was obviously a cheap excuse to give me her number, an excuse made even more obvious considering she had no actual business. The thing read 'Claudia Williams, branding strategist and entrepreneur.'

Entrepreneur of what? I'd only heard roughly thirty seconds of her conversation with Raven, and the whole thing felt like a low budget PSA for bullying.

I should have said something, but watching it happen felt like that night in the club. Raven didn't need protecting, and if a time came that she did, I wasn't the guy responsible for doing it. Her eyes were still full of resentment anyway.

For the third time this week, I return Jaci's senior year journal to my nightstand and prompt myself to get out of bed and into the shower. I stop at the mirror to examine my face. Are those wrinkles at the corners of my eyes the sexy kind? Am I one step closer to Harrison Ford or did I just pole vault past aging gracefully to Old-Man River? My stubble is more salt than pepper these days. If I didn't start drinking more water, I could actually be Raven's Santa impersonator. The thought makes me laugh. Me, Briggs Lawson, playing Santa Claus for children's parties, pumping himself up by chanting his mantra, *I am open to joy and forgiveness.*

I didn't keep the Post-it Note on the bathroom mirror longer than a few days. I have internalized the message, and the message is not realistic. I am not open to joy or forgiveness. This afternoon when I see Dr. Thomas, I have a few mantra suggestions of my own. My favorites are, *Remain closed to bullshit,* then there's *Master Excel, Not People,* and last but not least, *Therapy is temporary, Self-loathing is forever.*

I won't feel quite as guilty when I plant myself in Dr.

Thomas's cozy green chair. While I may have failed my mantra assignment, I'm carrying the fact that I've begun reading Jaci's journals like an ace up my sleeve. As soon as he strikes with his disapproving look and frantic pen scribbling, I'm going to bust that information out. Who's not a total failure this month? This guy!

I should keep getting ready, but those damn journals are calling to me, so I wrap a towel around my waist and plop down on the bed. Jaci and I got married at twenty-six, and I lost her at twenty-nine, but that doesn't account for the other eleven years we went through together. We went to the same college. I studied business and she studied music. She loved music. All kinds. She wanted to be a composer. Not an easy feat, but she worked on it on the side and got a job in marketing at my parents' company. We did everything together. Only had one car at one point, because we were just starting out and wanted to prove we could do it on our own. Or she did anyway. At the time, I was still so used to my silver spoon that sharing one car felt like the ultimate symbol of poverty. I begged her to let us borrow money, but she stayed firm, and I'm glad now. If it wasn't for that time, I wouldn't understand half of what I do now about work ethic.

I wonder what she wrote about those times. They were so good. Even the bad times were good when I look back on them.

I grab the first journal off the stack and crack it open. It's from the first year of our marriage. The wedding. Our honeymoon in Florida. Breaking ground on the house I built for her. I thumb through it as I read as quickly as I can, forcing myself to get through every word. I'll come back to savor them later, but right now I just want to know.

Know what she thought.

What she felt.

Did I make her as happy as she made me?

I land on something that rocks my world off its axis the moment I realize what it is, something she never shared with me. My heart drops to the floor, and I have to sit down while I read the words over and over again.

FIVE GOALS IN FIVE YEARS

Number One: Make friends with people in our new neighborhood. Dinner parties?

Number Two: Score the music for a television show or movie, even if it's just for fun. I can use it on my demo.

Number Three: Travel and start a blog. Can I combine travel and original music?

Number Four: Compete in and finish a triathlon. Frame the medal. Briggs?

Number Five: Start trying for a baby, or two, or three.

THAT QUESTION MARK after my name haunts me over the next few days. I try to put it at the back of my mind, but I can't. Travel and start a blog? Score a movie, her demo? It's basically a list of five ways to have a life, and I didn't know about any of them. Maybe she told me? What if I just wasn't listening? I'm listening now. I can't seem to stop listening. I've reread the list a dozen times. Each time I skip over babies. Thinking about that is jumping into a pit I can't get out of. But the triathlon. It grates at me.

Does that question mark mean she wanted me to do it with her? If she's looking down on me now, is she disappointed in me? Did I let her down, make her think I was going for it, then quit at the first sign of a struggle? Dr. Thomas says I have to stop thinking of every moment of my life as a moment taken from Jaci's, but with this, it's impossible not to see the parallels. She wanted this and I'm letting fear and a completely salvageable injury stop me from even trying.

Raven's tri club schedule is still saved on my computer. Before I can talk myself out of it, I pull it up and check the address of the next training session, adding it to my calendar and setting an alarm.

Chapter Twenty

RAVEN

"Oh hell no."

Leonard follows my gaze to the corner of Sixth and Baker where Briggs Lawson stands, not in a suit for work, but in running shorts, a technical t-shirt, and a brand-new pair of Nikes. Sunglasses shade his eyes, but I don't need to see them to know he is headed directly toward our group.

"You didn't tell me you were letting him back in."

Leonard is the only one who knows about my private sessions with Briggs. I confessed the whole story when it all went down, to which Leonard had immediately googled him and pointed out that Briggs could be a cover model. Not very helpful.

I turn and scowl at Leonard. "That would be because I did not and am not. He's out of his damn mind."

"He looks very serious." The word serious sounds like it could double for the word sexy.

"I don't have time for this," I grumble.

Time is the excuse I'm using for the flock of butterflies that are currently destroying my stomach. I know it's stupid to take a client relationship personally, but him not texting me back felt like being ghosted by someone you aren't ready to give up yet. And it pissed me off. Where does he get off rejecting me? I'm the one that let *him* in the club!

"Do you want me to pace the group while you handle this? Because dude does not look like he's going to go gracefully into the sunset at your request."

He has a point, which only further pisses me off. Not only is Briggs ambushing my tri club, his doing so means a disruption to the day's planned workout. The workout *everyone* already paid for. A roiling heat fills my belly. He can't just keep showing up. First at the school and now here.

The group is busy stretching their calves on the curb outside of our meeting spot. If anyone other than Leonard has noticed the newcomer, they've decided to ignore him. I wish I had that luxury. Pointing to a grassy patch at the entrance to today's park run, I take Leonard up on his offer.

"Can you circle everyone up and lead them through the usual stretches?"

Leonard could do these workouts blindfolded,

dancing over lava, but I still hate that he has to fill in for me.

"No problem, that will just be a twenty percent reduction on next month's club fees."

I shake my head and give Leonard a stern shove toward the group. The man already pays less than everyone else because I don't have it in my heart to ask him to pay my now-raised prices. Not that I mind, I'd train him for less. Case in point, he's wearing a devilish grin as he jogs off to do exactly as I asked of him. It's not lost on me how lucky I am to have such loyal clients. The kind that do not ghost you for the better part of a month and then show up like nothing has changed.

As the group begins their warm-up, Briggs strides directly to where I stand waiting. My arms are crossed over my chest in the universal pissed-off posture for, *this better be good*.

"Good morning," he says, pausing for a response I have no intention of giving.

When it sinks in that I'm not going to make this easy on him he removes his sunglasses, tucks them into the collar of his shirt and matches his stance to mine. From a distance we must look like caricatures. Two angry people about to face off.

"This run is for tri club members only."

"I paid in full," he says.

"You paid for October. It's November."

"I can pay for November. I'll pay for December too. And January. However many months until race day."

He doesn't know when race day is because we never picked out his competition schedule. We were days away from that conversation when he quit. That's on him and it's not my problem.

"Participation is about more than money," I say. "I sent you several texts alerting you to the fact that not communicating with me about your absences would lead to your removal from the training process. Texts that you never responded to."

There's a tick in Briggs' jaw, like he's clenching his teeth so hard they might shatter. Standard Raven would let him off the hook here, but I can't seem to let go of the way I felt those first few days, standing outside waiting for him to show up, texting repeatedly, then finally leaving pathetic voicemails.

"I was going through a difficult time." He's being earnest and I feel myself soften, but only a little. He still hasn't apologized. It's still all about him. And I'm still not giving in.

"There will be difficult times in the training process. You can't just stop all progress every time you have to address an injury. On any given day someone in this club is out nursing an injury. We work around it, we change plans, adjust workouts, we get help, but we don't quit."

Something changes in his expression. A crack in his armor, and though his arms are still crossed over his chest defensively, the tension leaves his shoulders.

"I'm not normally a quitter." I can't tell if he believes those words or not. "I want to try again."

Until I hear the words come out of his mouth, I don't realize how badly I wanted him to say them. I don't know why this is important to Briggs, but I find myself wanting him to want it.

"You have to show commitment."

Briggs nods. "I'm here now."

I shake my head. "More than that. You broke my trust."

He pauses before responding, and I catch myself wishing that he would put his sunglasses back on so I'm not so easily sucked in by his hazel eyes, all crinkly around the edges and able to plead his case without words.

"Tell me how to earn it back and I'll do it."

This part I really haven't thought about. How do I know that he won't pull the same shit a second time? It was a mistake to assume the best so easily before. I barely knew him, and I went into training him at full speed, no reservations, and no protection policy to prevent myself from getting hurt. This is the hard side of my job, the side I hate. Sometimes people let you down. Sometimes you mistake them for your friends, when they only ever saw you as a means to an end. When they change their mind about that end, they change their mind about you too.

It always sucks, but it hurt worse with Briggs than it did with others. I'm not sure I can go through that again.

"I mean it," he says, dipping his head so that I am forced to meet him eye to eye. "I'm going to do a triathlon with or without you."

He wants it. That much is clear. But why? "What changed?"

Something raw flashes in his eyes, but I can't quite name it. "I had a change of heart."

So it's personal. But it always is, isn't it? Nobody pushes themselves to these extremes if it's not personal.

"You answer your phone when I call," I say.

Briggs grimaces.

"Or text."

The relief on his face is palpable.

"If you are going to miss a workout, you give me notice."

Briggs nods.

"And you see a doctor about your shoulder."

Across from me, he intakes a sharp breath.

"And you do physical therapy."

"I don't have time—"

"You make time," I say. "As often as Leonard thinks is necessary."

Briggs' eyebrows knit together, and I can almost read his thoughts. *Who the hell is Leonard, and why is he weighing in?*

"Leonard is a club member, the longest standing actually, *and* he is a licensed physical therapist. You won't be the only person seeing him. Several of my clients work with Leonard. I've worked with him for a variety of injuries over the years. He's good. I promise."

"I'm not sure I like the idea of being assigned a physical therapist. Shouldn't my own doctor do that?"

"Your own doctor hasn't gotten you to address this problem in the past. Why should I believe he will be able to now?"

"Any other requests?" he asks, his lips pursed in a tight line.

I feel my eyes widening, does that mean he agrees to all of my terms?

"That's it."

Briggs doesn't look happy. Not happy enough anyway, considering he's been given a second chance he doesn't deserve, but I don't care how he feels at the moment, because I am elated. I am going to whip this man into shape. He has to see that triathlons are as much about fighting the demons in your head as they are the miles of road and strokes in the pool.

It's true that I don't know who Briggs really is, or why he holds himself back the way he does, but one thing is certain, this man has demons, and whether he likes it or not, this process is going to unearth them.

Chapter Twenty-One

BRIGGS

"What happened in there?" Our father corners me and Turner after a particularly brutal board meeting. "I thought we had that hospital bid in the bag."

"I thought so too." I exhale through gritted teeth. Large commercial and government projects are our bread and butter, and the newest city hospital is one of the projects we'd been preparing a bid on for months. This morning I was informed that we lost that bid minutes before walking into our quarterly board meeting. It was like walking into a lion's den with a fresh wound.

Nobody's happy. Everyone's pissed. Me the most because I do not lose. Failing isn't an option in my book. My work is my life, and losing this big of a bid isn't acceptable. I could blame my team, Turner on his vague financials, Lisa on her lack of design innovation, Brent and his tumultuous relationship with the city zoning commission, but at the end of the day, it's my ass on the line here. I'm the leader. I'm the one who should've seen this coming and prevented it.

"It's my fault." Turner closes the door to my office, so it's just the three of us in here. "I've been distracted."

Our mother is the soft one in our parents' relationship. Our father is the opposite. He's the hardass that shaped us into the successful type-A family we pride ourselves on today. Yes, we've had a shit-ton of privilege to grow up in the family we did and be offered high-ranking positions within the company after college, but that didn't come without a lot of hard work and ass-kicking on our father's part. If Turner thinks Dad is going to be sympathetic, he is barking up the wrong tree. Excuses are what you pull out when Mom is around.

"It's the divorce," Turner says, "things aren't as cut and dry as I thought they'd be." He sighs heavily. "And lawyers. God, I hate lawyers."

"You went to law school," I say. "And you're divorcing a lawyer."

He also went to business school for undergrad and has a master's in economics. He did all this while raising Charlie. My brother is smart as a whip and an even harder worker, but things haven't been the same with him in months. Not that I have room to talk. I'm off my game too.

"Yeah, and I hated law school." He raises his eyebrows. "There's a reason I don't practice law."

"Do I need to come out of retirement?" Dad asks, and Turner and I both still. It's the last thing either of us wants. His influence is too strong around here. He says "jump" and people ask, "how high," even if we're telling those same people to sit down. He steps closer, those boardroom eyes locking on me. "This is not an empty threat. I'll right the ship if I must."

"I'll handle it." I grit my teeth so hard it feels like they'll snap into a hundred fragments.

He points at me, then Turner, then back to me. "You'll make it up to the board by the February quarterly meeting, or I'm coming back."

He storms from my office and I curse. I want to take my anger out on Turner, and normally I would, but I find myself holding back.

"Well, let me have it," he says, falling into the seat across my desk and raking his hands across his face. He looks older than I've ever seen him. More tired. Less himself.

I sit down too. I'm not sure what to say, afraid if I open my mouth, I'll say the wrong thing.

But this is Turner.

I should be able to say whatever needs to be said.

"Have you gone soft?" he asks, his voice laced with vitriol, as if he wants to goad me. "I've never seen you like this. Normally you'd be ripping me a new asshole for losing a bid as big as that. And now, what? You lost for words?"

So he wants to take his shit out on me. Got it.

He heard the reasons why we lost that bid when I took the phone call this morning. He walked into my office right as I had the city on speaker phone. Our bid lacked direction, and the financials were murky, at best. Their words. Not mine.

Silence stretches between us.

"It's not lost on me how lucky I am to have this job," he says. "Most of my classmates are still early in their careers, clawing their way up corporate ladders or biding their time and billing their hours until they make partner. And here I am, CFO of a billion-dollar company, all because of my name."

"So do better," I say softly, slowly, carefully--but I still know it's a blow.

He nods and meets my eye again. "I'll do better if you do better."

I lean back in my chair. "And tell me, brother, how would you suggest I do better?"

Turner's not one to challenge me, and this is a definite challenge. "My work shit is suffering because my personal life is a mess. That's predictable at least. What's up with you? My numbers were garbage, and you didn't notice?"

Again, he's blaming me. But he's also kind of right. Why *didn't* I notice? I've spent as many hours in the office these last few weeks as any other. I knew what this bid meant for the company. Why didn't I intervene? Truthfully, I don't have a good reason. Failing at work is unfamiliar territory.

I know it's a shitty thing to say before the words leave my mouth, but it's like I've got too much experience being a grumpy asshole to stop myself now. "I can't babysit you all the time, Turner. At some point, I have to be able to trust that your work is accurate."

Turner leans forward and rests his elbows on his knees, dropping his head in his hands.

"I'll take that as an *I don't want to talk about it*," he mumbles.

Part of me wants to explain Jaci's journals, and the way her five-year plan is messing with my brain. He's been open with me about his divorce, so shutting him out feels like I'm not being fair, but for some reason I bite my tongue. It's one thing to have these conversations with my therapist, it's another to bring family into it.

I'm supposed to be the big brother. The strong one. The one who runs the company, the next patriarch of the Lawson family, the winner.

Not the loser.

"I need you to redo the numbers on all open accounts." I lean forward, knowing he's going to hate this. "I'm talking a full audit on everything."

Turner winces but nods. It's a huge undertaking, but if things weren't right on one project, then chances are they're not right on others. Lawson can't afford to take those chances.

"And focus, I need you to focus. I know this divorce is

shredding you, but trust me, throwing yourself into work can help keep you from spinning on other things."

It's the closest I'm willing to go to admitting I'm anything less than a machine, and Turner accepts it for the olive branch that it is, pulling his shoulders back and smacking his palms on his thighs. He agrees to get his shit together before exiting my office. I owe him a moment of brotherly condolences, but not today. Not when Turner needs me to be the boss.

Today has been a pile of shit. The only highlight is that Raven is willing to take my sorry ass back into the tri club. Her conditions, however, have the ever-growing knot in my stomach growing larger by the moment.

WHEN LEONARD SENDS me the address to his physical therapy office, I'm a little shocked. He's located at the YMCA, a location we have never once trained at. It's bizarre to me that he would pay for a gym membership elsewhere when surely, it's a perk of the job. But then again, Raven is worth it.

I've only seen Leonard once. He took over for Raven while I begged her for a second chance. He was wearing neon-pink that day, and he looks different in a subdued polo and khakis.

In a sea of protein-shake-guzzling overcompensates, Leonard has the lean, athletic physique of someone who actually practices daily health and wellness. He probably eats a lot of kale. I awkwardly reach out my hand to shake his, and he leads me through the gym, past the guys benching twice my weight, past the ladies on ellipticals, to a door marked rehabilitation.

The moment it opens, I want to turn around and run. There are old men everywhere. This is senior citizens' domain and I am mortified.

"Have you done physical therapy before?" Leonard is holding a little clipboard, and I am reminded of working with Dr. Thomas just long enough to keep me from bolting.

"Nope."

His eyes narrow. "Your doctor didn't prescribe you therapy after your shoulder injury?"

He asked if I had done physical therapy, not if I had been prescribed it. Of course it had been recommended. After the accident the doctors had insisted on it, saying it was that or surgery, to which I did neither. I shrug off the question. Raven said I had to attend physical therapy, she didn't say I had to lean into it, nor that I had to give this Leonard guy my entire life story. I was here for the bare minimum required to get back into training, just enough to get my shoulder into a functional place again, and debating my previous choices didn't fit in that category.

It takes Leonard all of five minutes to note what my doctor pointed out three years ago.

"You have a rotator cuff injury."

"Had," I say. "It was years ago, and it's hardly an issue."

I don't mention that the day-to-day pain associated

with that injury is how I remind myself that an inconvenient injury is a hell of a lot more pleasant than a permanent residence at Lane Valley Cemetery.

"Your shoulder disagrees. I'm sure your doctor informed you that leaving this untreated can result in increased symptoms, including *permanent* loss of motion."

He probably would have mentioned that had I ever returned for treatment.

"The swimming portion of a triathlon training involves a great deal of repetitive motion, which is exactly the type of activity that aggravates and worsens an injury like this. If you want to continue training, then you're really going to have to work at rehabilitating that shoulder."

"That's what I'm here for."

Leonard smirks. "You're here because Raven threatened to kick you to the curb otherwise."

"About that. Is she always this bossy or did I earn special treatment?"

He only winks and then begins rubbing my shoulder. At first, I want to smack him. I'm not a guy who allows touch without permission, or at all really, but within a few seconds I've lost my edge. The man has magic hands. I've deprived myself of anything to relieve this pain, especially something as comforting as massage. When was the last time another human touched me who wasn't a direct family member?

I honestly can't remember.

And I honestly don't know how to feel about that.

"Lie down." He directs me to the massage table. "We need to start here. You're ridiculously tense."

I do as he asks, practically melting into the table as he kneads the shoulder. I can feel myself relax, like I've got shards of ice finally thawing out in there. A few minutes later, he pulls out a massage gun and begins to carefully circle the areas of pain. The massage gun is not my idea of fun. My eyes water and I close them, willing the emotions rising within me to go away. The more I want them to leave, though, the more my eyes water. Leonard doesn't see, or if he does, he doesn't say anything.

We go through the appointment, and he shows me some exercises to start working on at home, then gets me set up for twice-weekly appointments with him.

"You won't be cleared to swim until I say so," he instructs. I reluctantly agree as he walks me to the door. "And another thing." His voice softens, and I turn to look down at him. I've got a couple inches on the guy, but his self-assuredness could fill a room. "Healing the body requires releasing trapped emotions. It's all tied up in the nervous system. With how tense you are, I wouldn't be surprised if your body has been caught in fight-or-flight mode for some time now."

Yeah, for three years, I think, but I say nothing.

"It's going to be okay. What matters is you're showing up now. It's going to be hard, but you can do this."

I thank him and quickly leave, but his words follow me back to the office. He doesn't know my story, but it's almost as if he can see right through me, as if he knows everything I've been through, the shame I carry, the grief, the pain, the anger. He wasn't just talking about healing my shoulder today. I won't be surprised if he's assigning mantras by the end of the week.

I am open to forgiveness and joy.

I laugh bitterly and roll my shoulder until it pops, the familiar nerve pain shooting through my arm, reminding me of why I'm doing the triathlon in the first place. I'm not "showing up," as he says, for myself. I'm showing up because I think Raven can help me and I don't want to let her down again. I'm showing up because I want to put myself through the physical experience of a triathlon, not in spite of the difficulty, but because of it. I want to feel something again. Something real. Something intense and meaningful. But most of all, I'm showing up for Jaci.

Chapter Twenty-Two

RAVEN

The incredible aroma of buttery, well-seasoned turkey wafts through my two-bedroom apartment, and I do a little happy dance on my way to my closet to finish getting ready. It's an expensive sweater dress and ankle boots kind of moment, complete with a salon blowout and a full face of makeup. I look good, my turkey looks even better, and I'm giddy with excitement.

Thanksgiving has always been a disappointing holiday for me. Most holidays are for an only child of parents who would rather not be parents. Instead of wallowing in self-pity again this year, I decided to do something about it, hosting my first-ever Friendsgiving. I picked the weekend before the actual holiday so people wouldn't have conflicts, and several of my club members and work friends agreed to come and bring side dishes.

The doorbell rings as I zip up my bootie, and I nearly trip over the heels as I dash over to let Leonard and his husband Dan inside, but it's not them at the door. It's Briggs Lawson.

It's Briggs Lawson holding a cake.

"I hope this is okay," he says, lifting the chocolate cake up in its plastic Tupperware holder. "I don't like pie, so I figured I'd make this instead. It's my mom's recipe. I promise it's good."

One: I didn't know he was coming.

Two: I didn't know a man baking his mom's cake recipe could be so attractive.

Three: I have a boyfriend. Another man's cake has no impact on me.

Yeah, I'll be repeating that to myself as many times as it takes.

"Hi." I catch my breath, nearly screaming at the poor guy. "I'm so glad you made it."

His eyes travel the length of my body and I blush. "Can I come in?" He chuckles and I jump out of the doorway. I'm only rattled because he didn't RSVP and I had no idea he was coming tonight. It has nothing to do with the fact that Andre is on his way, and the last time they met, Briggs seemed on the verge of threatening bodily harm.

Briggs scans the room and when he realizes he is the first one to arrive, it's as if his confidence visibly flops to the floor. Good, we are evenly matched now. Both awkward, nervous, and uncomfortable.

"So, can I help you in the kitchen?" he offers.

Ordinarily I would issue a big fat no. I'm not exactly a dinner party professional, but good hostesses don't put the guests to work. However, no one else is here and according to the slow tick tock of my clock, they aren't going to be here for a good fifteen minutes. I don't have fifteen minutes of small talk in me.

"You can help me make the salad." I direct him to the cutting board where all the ingredients are laid out and ready. Briggs grins at the Roma tomatoes and soft mozzarella cheese.

"I'm not sure I've ever had a Caprese salad at a Thanksgiving celebration before, but I'm happy to see it." He grabs a sharp knife from the block and begins slicing the tomatoes into perfect little steaks. "I was afraid this was going to be all health and no food."

A laugh bubbles out of me. "What does that even mean?"

Briggs looks up from the cutting board, and I'm momentarily silenced by the way his hair flops in front of his eyes. "It means I thought there would be a lot of kale and possibly even a meat substitute."

I have to answer and stop staring. Why are words suddenly so hard to find? "Like tofurky?"

He points the knife at me. "Exactly what I was afraid of until you opened the door. You have no idea how relieved I was when I smelled actual turkey."

The conversation is flowing fine, but if I stand here staring at him chop vegetables much longer, I'm going to feel like a creeper, so I break my own rule of not opening the wine until everyone has arrived and pour us each a glass of cabernet.

"I can't compete on tofu, and besides, the texture is weird."

"Oh, I know." Briggs laughs, and watching his expression change from mild to amused, I can practically see the happy memory wiggling through the cracks in his tough exterior. "When we were in high school, Turner wanted to date this girl in his anatomy class who was really into animal rights. Like really into it. So he kept inviting her over to the house for 'study sessions' and requiring our mother to make vegetarian meals. Our mom is a great cook and all, but she raised three steak-loving boys. She had no idea what to do with tofu. Those were some of the sorriest meals I've ever eaten."

Picturing a young Turner trying to impress a girl with his mother's forced vegetarian cuisine almost has me forgiving him for dropping the ball with Charlie.

Almost, but not entirely.

"Okay, but did he get the girl?"

Briggs sets the tomatoes aside and begins julienning the basil like a man who has seen a lot of the Food Network.

"They both got B's in anatomy, but nobody got any boo . . . " A blush creeps up over his collar.

I'm dying a little. "Booty. Were you about to say booty?"

Until ten minutes ago, I was certain Briggs Lawson had absolutely no sense of humor. Now I'm wondering what else goes on inside his head while he's pretending to be captain calm, collected, and boring. Briggs' blush is deepening by the second.

"I regret beginning this story."

I'm about to tease him unmercifully when the doorbell rings.

Briggs smiles, the smallest, cutest, relieved little smile. I want to ignore whoever is standing on my welcome mat and lean into this opportunity to dig beneath the surface, but the bell rings again, and I know that isn't a real option.

This time, it really is Leonard and Dan at the door. Leonard is an "early to everything or you're late" kind of guy, but his husband is a "give me five more minutes" man. Their arms are full of wine and flowers, but there's no side dish to be seen. I suppose I should be grateful they ignored my directions and didn't try to cook. I've tasted some terrifying things out of Leonard's kitchen. They love food, they just suck at cooking it.

Leonard leans in for a hug and whispers in my ear. "There is a big, masculine-looking truck in visitor parking. Is that Andre's? You did *not* mention he was an alpha type." He looks so proud I almost feel bad correcting him.

"Actually, Andre isn't here yet. That's Briggs' truck."

Dan's eyes go wide as saucers, and I wonder how much Leonard has shared about Briggs.

"We need to open the wine," says Leonard. "We need to open and serve the wine very quickly."

Forty minutes later, everyone has arrived except for Andre. Dan and Leonard are busy regaling everyone with the story of how they first met. They happened to sit next to each other at a Celine Dion concert in Vegas and hit it off so quickly that an Elvis impersonator was marrying them by the end of the weekend. Hands down the craziest wedding story I've heard, but they've been married for five years now and are still going strong. I guess God—and Celine Dion—work in mysterious ways.

Briggs is chatting with my best teacher friend, our school librarian, Remi. She's brought her hunky husband, Derek, and from the way the three of them keep looking over at me, I know they're talking about me. I'd give my right ovary to know what they're saying. That, or a kidney––people don't need both of those.

I pull the turkey from the oven and lower it onto the counter top. The thing is majestic. Golden brown, that shine on the skin that lets you know it's crisp, but not dry. Stuffing pouring out the nether regions like the back end of a cornucopia. I retrieve a carving knife from the butcher block and stab the damn thing. I'm not supposed to carve the turkey. I made the turkey. This was supposed to be Andre. It seems silly to care about something like that, but I had visions of us bonding over my beautiful bird. Visions of his triceps bulging from beneath a sensible T-shirt while he said things like, "I can't believe you made this, babe" and "My mother's turkey was never this glisteny." Instead,

I'm stabbing my masterpiece with unnecessary force and the side dishes people brought are growing cold. I can't wait around for Andre. I've already checked my phone for the umpteenth time––no text messages, no calls, no nothing.

"Everything okay?" Remi approaches. Derek and Briggs are still chatting in the living room, so it's just the two of us standing over the main entrée.

"Yeah, why wouldn't it be?" I slice into the turkey like the heroine in a seventies horror film, and she raises her eyebrows.

"You seem tense, is all."

I sigh and grip the knife a little harder. "Well, my boyfriend decided to be a no-show, so there's that."

She's quiet for a long minute. Not her usual style. "Speaking of boyfriend, why don't you dump Andre's sorry ass?" And there she is.

"I just might."

Her eyebrows jump. "And it seems like Andre's taking a risk leaving you with Briggs unattended. Now that man is into you."

My cheeks warm. "Did he say he was into me? Because I highly doubt it."

Remi hasn't met Andre. That's what today was supposed to be for. I hate that this guy I've been gushing about has immediately earned himself "guy that sucks" status in the eyes of all of my friends.

"Not in so many words, but he did ask a lot of questions about you."

I don't know how to feel, especially with a carving knife in my hand, so I don't say anything at all. Briggs and Derek wander over and eye the poor bird.

"Pretty sure I'm ruining it," I say, exasperated. "I researched how to cook it but not how to cut it."

"Here, let me show you." Briggs comes around behind me, and I expect him to take the knife, but he takes my hand instead. His fingers are calloused, large, and cool over mine—a direct contrast to his body heat warming my back, or maybe that's just me having a totally irrational physical reaction to a totally innocent move. I mean, everyone teaches Patrick Swayze in *Ghost* style, right? I make panicked eyes at Remi, who gives me a told-you-so smile and leads Derek away to chat with the others.

The moment seems to stretch out and my heart pounds. Briggs is explaining something about the grain of the meat, but I can hardly hear him. I'm too focused on his clean, Irish soap scent and the way his breath spreads across the back of my neck like a promise. My mind flits to images of what that promise might be like . . .

Stop it, Raven.

He steps away, and I wonder if he feels what I just felt. I peer up into his eyes, bravely searching for an answer, when my phone rings on the counter next to us. We jump apart, rom-com style. Andre's name lights up the screen, and my stomach twists with guilt.

"Here, take over for me." I hand off the knife and take the call in my bedroom.

"Are you okay?" is the first thing I ask, even though

I'm feeling angry and guilty and have many other things I'd like to say to Andre right now instead of worrying about his well-being.

"I'm sorry, Raven. I had to come in to work tonight. There's an emergency." He sounds rushed. Stressed out. Apologetic.

A financial emergency on a Saturday night?

I don't know what to think, but I decide to give him the benefit of the doubt. I don't understand his work, but I do know that things happen. Heaven knows teachers work on weekends sometimes.

"Alright, I'll save you a plate," I say slowly.

"That would be great. I'm sorry to do this to you with all your friends over. I was looking forward to meeting them."

I analyze his voice, trying to tell if he's actually being sincere or if he's playing the part. Is it really plausible that he had an evening work emergency tonight, of all nights? The night he was meant to meet everyone I hold near and dear? And why couldn't he have called me an hour ago instead of waiting until I had a full house?

"It's okay. We can talk about it later. Good luck with your *work emergency*." I know it is spiteful, but I find myself saying work emergency in a mocking tone.

We hang up and I sit on the bed, dropping my face into my palms. I haven't wanted to admit it, but it's glaringly obvious to me now—this relationship is failing.

And not just because I'm upset with how he handled tonight. If I'm honest with myself, I felt more in two minutes with Briggs than I have in two months with Andre.

That hopeful glimmer that Andre brought to the table in the beginning has diminished over time. Honestly, my heart leaped for all the wrong reasons when his call came through tonight.

I hate that I don't know if Andre is telling the truth, and I hate that after two months of trying to connect on a higher level, I'm ready to bail over a missed dinner party, but I am. I have to end things.

Again.

How many short-term ex-boyfriends is it now? I've honestly lost count.

The part that hurts most is knowing that when it comes to love and relationships, something greater exists, and I'm never able to make it my own. Where is my damn Celine Dion concert?

I want to feel like the man I'm with is the only man I ever want to look at for the rest of my life. I want to be so consumed by him that even the act of cutting a turkey together is downright sexy. If I wasn't so frustrated, I would laugh at that notion. Truth is, Andre and I both deserve better.

Chapter Twenty-Three

BRIGGS

I'm not really sure why I came tonight. This was clearly a blanket invite to the entire tri club, but that didn't mean she really wanted me here. I'm the newbie asshole who had to beg my way back into her good graces after I quit the first time. So of course there wasn't an expectation that I would attend her party, nor did I bother to RSVP. It wasn't like my absence would come up during training.

But I made the mistake of mentioning it to Turner, and my brother lectured me about the importance of forming a connection with the club. After I finally relented to his badgering, he helped me make the cake. Insisted upon it, actually. His way of apologizing without apologizing. It was the sort of thing we did when we were kids. "Sorry I broke your bike," always looked a lot more like, "here take mine" over an actual admission of wrongdoing.

So when I arrived here, I expected the whole thing to feel forced, but the moment Raven opened the door, it was like sunlight sneaking through your office window at just the right time of day. Somehow, she's painfully good at helping me forget what a miserable sack of boring I usually am.

So now, as the evening winds down, I find myself disappointed, like I could keep drinking wine and picking away at that turkey carcass long into the night. Since that would be overstaying my welcome, when Leonard and his husband leave, I duck out as well. My curious side wants to pick Leonard's brain on the way out the door. Not about things I have any right to ask, but about Raven's no-show boyfriend. Where was the snappy dresser from the club who couldn't keep his hands off her?

You would think tonight would be a boyfriend sort of thing. Swooping around the room, refilling wine glasses, carving the turkey, doing all that boyfriend shit that earned you props when a relationship is young. She hadn't even known what they were that night, so clearly, they were still in the honeymoon phase now.

It was him on the phone, for sure. She'd come back with red-rimmed eyes and a nervous energy that was hard to ignore until dinner started and everyone was silenced by delicious dish after dish. I wanted to assure her the turkey was perfect. It wasn't too dry, like everyone always worried a turkey would be, but the words were glue in my throat.

One thing was clear, I was very out of practice when it came to being normal in social situations.

I didn't end up saying anything comforting, but I did save a piece of cake and left it on her kitchen counter. If she cried at her own dinner party, there should at least be midnight cake for later.

A WEEK LATER, both Capri and Griffin flew in for Thanksgiving. The holidays were the one Lawson activity my grieving did not excuse me from. Since the first year, Mom has insisted I be present at everything, even Easter, and we aren't religious, we just like recipes heavy on the egg. I've given up trying to back out. This year, however, is a double whammy. Not only do I have a four-day weekend with no work to keep me distracted, plus an evening filled with family dysfunction, I also have my first fun run.

"Why do I feel like I've been tricked into something terrible?"

Raven stands next to me in silly running pants with turkeys wearing pilgrim hats all over them and a shirt that reads 'Will Run for Pie.' Most of the tri club is here with us, dressed in varying degrees of ridiculousness. We're doing the 10k, which isn't a lot, but I'd have opted for the 5K if I wasn't peer-pressured by the club. Who am I kidding? I wouldn't be here at all if it wasn't for them.

I have to admit, they're growing on me. Only a couple of weeks of training, and I already feel bonded to these people.

Raven must catch the skeptical look in my eye because she nudges me and laughs. "There aren't a lot of race options during the holidays. You've got to start somewhere."

"Must somewhere involve full-grown men in stuffed turkey hats?" I still can't believe my first official race is a damn Turkey Trot. For once in my life, I'm happy to be underdressed.

A wide grin stretches across her face. "Are you mad you didn't get one? I specifically asked you if you wanted a turkey hat when I signed us up. You declined, remember?"

There is a man behind us bobbing his head to the music in his earbuds, his turkey hat swaying along with him. I point him out to Raven and mutter, "It's like the turkey's ass is swallowing his head."

Raven snorts with laughter, brightening her already pink cheeks and nose. It's a chilly seven a.m. and I'm dancing back and forth on the balls of my feet to keep warm.

"If you were wearing the hat, the drumsticks would keep your ears nice and cozy."

"Nope. Not going to happen, Oliver," I say. Her grin grows wider at my use of her last name. "I don't like the look you are giving me right now."

Now she's not just smiling, she's giggling, hardcore giggling, clutching her stomach, bent over at the waist giggling. Her eyes are fixed on something behind me, and I am terrified to turn around. She must sense this because she grabs me by both arms and spins me to face the starting line.

"Oh, for Pete's sake."

There in turkey hats, their arms filled with handmade signs, stand all three of my siblings. Capri is beaming, Griffin is laughing, and Turner is filming the entire thing with his phone. I swear if he's live streaming this moment, I'm going to kill him.

"Why does it say, 'I hope you're better at this than the trumpet'?" Leonard sidles up next to me, nodding toward Capri's neon-pink sign.

I'm about to answer that everything my siblings do should be ignored, when a man steps under the starting line and raises a bullhorn to his lips.

It's a mad scramble as everyone takes off, and the energy blossoms from excited to a full-on frenzy. There's a sense of camaraderie that I haven't experienced since high school band, and even then, I was terrible. I'm not so terrible at running, not after the last two months of cardio-vascular training, but I'm no Usain Bolt either. The tri club splits up into three pacing groups, and Raven leads the fastest one. I stick to the back and make it my goal to keep up with our leader Chris. I'll feel pretty stupid if I can't finish with the club, even if I'm the newest member.

A few minutes later, Raven's group leaves us in the dust. I don't let myself think about it too much. I'm only sad to see her go because I'm not fast enough to keep up, not because I enjoy her company any more than I should. I was spoiled by the one-on-one sessions. Those are over.

Now I'm simply one of twelve club members, only deserving of a small percent of her time and attention.

There are three of us in this slower-pace group, and Chris and Richelle chat as old friends. They try to include me, but I'm too focused on getting through the race to offer much in the way of thoughtful conversation.

"You okay?" Chris asks. His pacing is remarkable, the man has obviously done this before. "How are you feeling?"

"Feeling like this is harder than I thought it was going to be." I grit my teeth as we pass mile marker four. It's taking everything in me not to slow my pace and just say to hell with keeping up. My pride won't let me. This shouldn't be so hard, it's certainly not for the rest of the team.

"I remember my first race," Richelle says. "I threw up three times. You haven't thrown up once, so you've already got me beat."

"I haven't thrown up yet, but there are still two more miles." And if I take another swig of my water bottle, I just might.

Chris must read my mind though, because he tells me to remember to drink every mile. "And not too much. Eight ounces is my sweet spot unless it's really hot, then I'll do more."

"I can only do five or six ounces at a time," Richelle says. "But again, I'm a puker."

"Can we stop talking about puke?"

They laugh as my stomach cramps, and I force the

vomit talk from my mind, making myself ask different questions instead. Where are they from? What do they do for work? What got them into triathlons? Are they married? Kids? All the small talk I usually try to avoid with new people but it's better than thinking about how much water I should be drinking or listening to the sound of my own labored breathing.

It feels like an eternity later when we reach our last mile.

"I'm going for it," Richelle announces, pushing ahead of us. The spritely woman has got to have at least twenty years on me. I'm a little jealous and a lot impressed.

"What do you think? Can you go faster?" Chris asks.

At least Chris is my age, so I won't feel as bad when he smokes my ass. I want to tell him to leave me if he wants to go faster. I don't care about keeping up anymore. Just finishing is going to be good enough for me.

"I'm good," is all I say.

He nods knowingly. "Come on, you got this. Let's finish strong."

Thoughts of Jaci filter through my mind for the next several minutes until the finish line comes into view. The rest of the tri club is there waiting for us alongside my family, waving their arms and cheering like banshees. I would be embarrassed if I wasn't so exhausted. Their faces send a renewed sense of optimism bolting through me. My mind clears, memories of Jaci fading as my body takes over. Pumping my Nikes one in front of the other, I push myself into a full-on sprint.

Chris whoops. "Let's go!"

We fly through the finish line and are surrounded by our ragtag crew. I'm disgusting and sweaty, but so is everyone else so they don't care. They pat my back and yell congratulations, and I yell it right back.

I did it.

I finished my first race.

Raven throws her arms around my neck. She fits me better than a race medal ever could. It feels amazing, like winning, butt-ugly turkey hats and all.

Chapter Twenty-Four

RAVEN

There is nothing quite like post-race endorphins. Post-race endorphins will have you thinking things like, *I should reseed my backyard this summer, maybe construct a porch. How hard can it be?* They are basically free drugs. This, and only this, explains why I jumped on Briggs like a spider monkey when he crossed the finish line. This, and only this, explains why he leaned into that hug like it was a lifeline. Other explanations, like I am developing a raging crush on him, are totally implausible. *Emotional unavailability is not hot.* Now there's a little gem I should embroider on a throw pillow.

Ordinarily, the tri club would grab a beer after a race like this, but holiday races necessitate different traditions. Mainly because the bulk of the club have their own family function to attend or facilitate. Briggs most certainly does.

What started as only his siblings at the starting line ended up including both of his parents by the finish. I tried not to be invasive and kept my distance while I waited for the last group of our club to complete the race, but Turner was all too eager to introduce Charlie's teacher to his siblings and parents, so I found myself making small talk with the whole Lawson crew, laughing along with them when Briggs rounded the final corner and they got to wave their silly signs one last time.

He's being a good sport about it. Again, likely because of endorphins, but after a handful of hugs and barbs from his brothers, he sneaks off to the vendor tables. Either he is really interested in what new flavors of gel packs are being distributed, or he needs a breather from all the family affection bubbling up around him.

My own parents are nowhere in sight. This would have bothered me back in college, when whether or not I placed well really mattered, but nowadays it's normal not to see them. Sports are not my parents' jam, and there are few things more miserable than watching them fake enthusiasm for my benefit.

A glance at my pacing watch reminds me that I've got a little under three hours before it's time to join them for one of my least favorite evenings of the year. I wonder if I can get out of it. If I tell them I'm sick, will they ask me if I raced this morning? Do they even have to know?

"Raven," says Mrs. Lawson, breaking me from my train of thought. "What does your family do for Thanksgiving? What's on the agenda?"

The use of the term agenda cracks me up. Of course his parents speak like life is a never-ending board meeting. They've raised a son who may or may not know the difference between business relationships and actual relationships.

"My parents are both retired college professors. They go to a big, retired college professors' dinner every year, while the other grown children and I hang out near the liquor cabinet, wishing the night would end quickly."

"Brutal," says Turner. He seems to interject himself into conversations a lot, but he's so personable that I find I don't mind. "What happens if you don't go?"

I shrug. "I eat leftovers at home and feel mildly guilty." Which is exactly what I'm hoping for this year. It's not a hard question to answer. After all, I've skipped roughly fifty percent of these dinner parties since turning eighteen.

Mrs. Lawson scowls, and it pulls at her pretty matriarch features. The woman reminds me of a model for Better Homes and Gardens. "That simply can't happen. You can't spend the holiday alone."

"It's okay, really."

She shakes her head and pats me on the shoulder. "No, dear. This year, I would like you to feel mildly guilty at our dinner table."

My mouth pops open, but nothing comes out. I don't know what to say. I definitely don't want to go waltzing into Briggs' family home without his permission, but his mother doesn't look like she hears no a lot, and Turner is vigorously nodding beside her in a way that makes me feel like declining the offer would be a grave insult. I'm racking my brain for a believable excuse when Briggs returns, his hands full of sample products and the complimentary water bottle offered to each finisher.

"Charlie's teacher is joining us for dinner." Mrs. Lawson's tone is kind and maternal, but it's also firm and indisputable. This is a woman who gets what she wants. "Charlie will be thrilled. He's with his mother right now, but he's coming to dinner, isn't that right, Turner?"

Turner shoots her a thumbs-up and elbows his brother. I hope to God that Briggs catches on to the fact that I haven't actually been given a choice here. Otherwise I look pretty desperate homing in on his family's Thanksgiving at the very last minute.

I can feel his eyes on me, probably assessing me like some kind of business proposition, but I'm too embarrassed to look at him. Instead, I smile and nod, fixing my gaze over his right shoulder. Either dinner will be fun and I'll leave knowing a lot more about Briggs, or dinner will be as awkward as this moment. I have no idea which outcome is more likely.

After the podium ceremony, which we end up sweeping, I say my goodbyes and head out. I'm distracted with doubts about tonight as I go through my after-race rituals of stretching, lymphatic massage, Epsom salt bath, and finally the best part, an afternoon nap. But as I lie in bed staring up at the ceiling, sleep ain't happening. I'm too busy wondering if Mrs. Lawson invited me to dinner out of obligation, and if Briggs will be annoyed that I'm crashing.

Probably true on both counts.

Maybe I shouldn't go. I could send an excuse and go to my parents' thing instead. Or stay in bed all night, ordering Chinese takeout and watching reruns of *The Office* in my pajamas. But when my phone rings with Mom's name lighting the screen, I know my answer. I quickly tell her I have another dinner planned, and I'll see them next week, to which she protests only enough to make it obvious she doesn't really care.

Resolved, I drag myself into the shower and get ready for tonight, hoping this isn't a terrible idea, and also hoping for something I'm not quite ready to admit.

THE LAWSON HOME could be described as an estate. Their cobbled driveway is long and wide, framed on either side by towering willow trees. The largest private lawn I've ever seen surrounds the largest home I'll ever step foot in. I know people live like this because I drive past these insane neighborhoods on my way to work, but I've never been privileged enough to be invited through the gates of one.

This is normal. This is perfectly normal, I repeat to myself as I lift one of those enormous brass knockers that I thought were used solely as movie props, and conk it against the front door.

Mrs. Lawson swings open the front door "You made it." She beams. "And you look lovely."

She ushers me inside their gorgeous home, which I compliment her on right away and hand over the pumpkin pie I picked up on the way over.

"Sorry, it's store bought," I admit. Store bought seemed fine this morning, but now that I'm standing in her home, every inch of which is carefully decorated in a fall pallet, it feels like I could have made the effort to at least make cookies. I can feel the start of a blush rising in my cheeks, and I wonder if I look appropriately mortified, considering how silly I feel.

"It's perfect."

"So is this house."

She's unfazed by my compliments, leading me through a marble entryway into an elegantly designed kitchen and living room. Art hangs on the walls that could just as well be hanging in a museum, and the scent of an expert Thanksgiving dinner permeates the entire home.

"Can I help with anything?" I ask. I don't actually see any food in the kitchen, which is a bit puzzling.

"The staff have it handled," she says, and I nod awkwardly.

Of course they have staff, and probably multiple kitchens. Why cook your own Thanksgiving dinner when you can have professionals do it for you? My cheeks warm and I wonder if Briggs found my ragtag Friendsgiving in my aging apartment lackluster. No wonder the guy had zero qualms about buying an expensive bike or paying for one-on-one sessions. This family is out of my league.

"We do desserts. We leave the turkey business to the

professionals. It's hard to screw up a pastry, but Lord knows the same cannot be said of the bird."

My mind wanders to the heaping slice of chocolate cake Briggs left waiting on my kitchen counter, and I feel a little less like I'm standing in the White House.

"You made it." Briggs appears dressed in dark jeans and fitted black t-shirt. My nerves are simultaneously relaxed and frazzled. It's good to see someone dressed casually in this kind of environment, but the fact that it's someone I'm attracted to makes me feel off kilter.

I smile. "Thanks for having me."

Mrs. Lawson goes to check on the food, and Briggs and I sit on the couch. Is this a set up? Is Briggs on board with it if it is? If so, I'm really glad I ended things with Andre on Monday. He came over to eat the leftovers I'd saved for him, and after dessert I gently let him down. I expected some kind of fight, but the man didn't even seem hurt or rattled. Which is probably the biggest indicator that I did the right thing. After two months of dating, you're supposed to feel things. Someone should be sad, or at least angry. The two of us ended things with a hug and a promise to stay friends. That doesn't happen when you care.

Normally, I'm a mess after a breakup. Even if I'm the one to end it, I still feel awful about losing the possibility of a forever love with someone I saw potential in. But these last few days have been different. I haven't thought about Andre once since he walked out of my door and out of my life. I've been busy with work and then the race today, and now here I am, sitting next to Briggs Lawson in his family's mansion.

I don't know what to say to him. Where to put my hands. Where to look.

Cheers emit from the television, so I look there. Football. We can talk about the game. Not that I'll have much to offer, but it's better than stoney silence.

"So, do you have a favorite team?" I ask, nodding toward the screen.

He gives me a funny look and shakes his head. Note to self, football is not a conversation starter with Briggs.

"You made it." Griffin bounds into the room, diving onto the couch next to Briggs. It's strange to see such a large man acting like a teenager, and I laugh.

"Scoot over, fat ass," Griffin says, pushing his brother closer to me.

Briggs growls something with the word juvenile in it and readjusts, but now there are three of us on a couch distinctly made for two. I suck in a breath. There's another couch and two empty chairs he could've switched to. Instead, Briggs' warm muscled arm is resting against mine. I have a thing for men's arms. Abs are nice and all, but they've got nothing on the way a well-defined bicep presses against the sleeve of a man's t-shirt. A man's black t-shirt. I am side-eyeing the shit out of Briggs when Griffin interrupts my deeply inappropriate thoughts.

"So, Raven, why did you slow down at the finish line?" Griffin asks.

Briggs shoots me a questioning look. "You slowed down?"

I shrug, hoping they can't see the blush I'm fighting. "I'm not a pro anymore and I don't need to win anything. Besides, I trained those guys. It's a lot more satisfying watching them get excited over a win than it is to get another one for myself."

Griffin laughs. "Imagine that in residency. *No sir, you take today's transplant observation, when one of us wins, we all win.*"

"Maybe I take too much credit, but their accomplishments feel like my accomplishments too."

Briggs doesn't say anything but Griffin nods. "I respect that, in medical school everyone was out for themselves, even the professors. And now that I'm in residency, it's even worse."

"Raven's not like that," Briggs says quietly.

It makes me grin. I can't help it. Griffin shoots me a thumbs up. "No judgment, just thought it was an interesting strategy."

"It's not really a strategy. I won a lot of races when I was younger, and I don't get joy in that part anymore. My joy comes from seeing my clients succeed."

"That's why she's the best," a voice says from behind us, and we turn to see Turner standing with a sleeping Charlie on his shoulder. The little boy blinks down at us through sleepy eyes and curly dark hair.

"He fell asleep in the car."

"Let me." Briggs reaches out and tugs the child into his

lap. Charlie instantly falls back asleep in his uncle's arms and my heart does a little tug. A moment ago he was regular-hot, now he's great-with-kids hot, and I'm not sure I can take it. So I pretend to watch the game while actually watching Briggs and Charlie. I like strong arms, but wrap those arms around one of my favorite kindergarteners, and I can't look away.

Chapter Twenty-Five

BRIGGS

It's unnerving sitting next to Raven in my parents' home, watching my siblings joke around with her as if she's the girl I brought home from band practice. Jaci and I were so young when we met that there weren't any others. I've met a half a dozen different girlfriends for both Turner and Griffin, and Lord knows Capri's always in a relationship with some douchebag or another, but bringing someone in to meet my family is a completely foreign concept.

Not that that's what this is.

Raven has become a family friend. That's why she's here. That's the only reason why she's here. It just doesn't feel that way, thanks to her body heat pressed firmly against mine. Holding a sleeping Charlie is the only thing keeping my heart rate under control. I haven't touched a woman in years, a choice to make it easier to live with myself, but now all I feel is out of practice.

When Capri and her flavor of the week finally arrive, my mother stops guarding the dining room. With the aroma of a full-scale traditional Thanksgiving dinner as bait, we all filter in and take a seat at the table. When we were kids, Mom spent all day making the meal. Now she hires it out, a decision everyone secretly loves. Afterall, the stressed-out version of Mom tends to result in the stressed out version of all of us.

There is talk at the table of this morning's race. A few stories from Capri that remind everyone how painful dorm life is, but mostly we shove our faces until everyone is both miserable and happy all in one.

My body is growing increasingly sore by the minute. I followed Raven's after-race instructions, but I still feel like I've been hit by a bus and stuffed full of turkey. I could curl up and take a nap between dinner and dessert. On any other year I probably would, but not with Raven here. My brothers would have a field day with that. The last thing I need is for them to fill her head with a bunch of embarrassing stories from our childhood.

Charlie isn't having downtime anyway. As soon as the dishes are cleared, he makes his rounds, tugging on the hems of everyone's shirts and insisting we go outside.

"He needs a cousin," says Turner.

It's a joke. One he clearly didn't think through, but the moment he says it the room goes silent. Maybe Raven notices, maybe she doesn't. I haven't learned to read her yet, and at the moment, I really don't want to. Instead, I hop up and head toward the front door.

Despite the fact that Texas rarely gets cold enough for more than a light jacket, Mom is already bundling Charlie up in a fitted cap and puffer coat, signaling to all of us that we aren't getting out of going outside. Raven doesn't seem to mind. Apparently, all those turkey hormones that are supposed to make you lethargic have no impact on her, because she bounds past me and out the door with a smile on her face while the rest of us are still hemming and hawing.

I have to remind myself that this morning's run is a typical workout for her. While she moves with fluidity and grace, I hobble around. My quads and calves are aching something terrible, and my arms are like two anvils hanging at my sides.

When Charlie begs to go on the trampoline, I actually groan.

"It'll get easier, I promise," Raven says, as if positivity is enough to sooth my angry muscles. "Before you know it, thirteen miles won't be a big deal."

"I'll remember you said that next time we run thirteen miles." Which I have an inkling will be sooner rather than later.

"Don't worry, you're off the hook." Turner chuckles. "I'll jump with the kid, while you rest your old-man bones."

The desire to shoot a barb back at him is strong, but the pain in my body is stronger, so I find myself standing to the side watching as he, Raven, and Charlie play wake the dragon, a game in which someone lays quietly in the center of the trampoline and everyone jumps as hard as they can till the person in the middle springs to life and starts wreaking havoc. Turner is the best dragon. One minute his eyes are squeezed tight and his arms lie peacefully over his chest, and the next he sprints around the trampoline, making both Charlie and Raven scream in terror.

When my brother says something in an obviously flirty tone, my hands ball into fists. I'm about to fly up onto that trampoline, sore or not sore, and insert myself into their conversation, but Raven doesn't return his flirty tone in her reply, so I make myself calm down. She's not like that, but Turner still needs to back the hell off. She's his son's teacher, for Christ's sake. Besides, she's got a boyfriend.

A boyfriend who's nowhere to be found, but a boyfriend nevertheless. And *Turner* is going through a divorce. The next few relationships will be about rebounding. He's not ready to date wife material, and Raven is definitely wife material.

Shaking my head of these unnecessarily protective thoughts, I retrieve my phone and snap a picture as Turner roars like a fire-breathing dragon and scoops Charlie into his arms. He hasn't looked this happy in months. For the first time, I wonder what it feels like to lose the person you love and still have to see them. No one expects an explanation for my grieving, but it's not the same with divorce. I keep expecting him to get over it, be better at it. I'm starting to feel like a real jackass for the way I came down on him the other day. If he wasn't trying to flirt with Raven, I might even apologize.

After a few more minutes on the trampoline, Turner clutches his stomach and tells Charlie it's time to call it a day. I expect Charlie to pout, but he is on his best behavior for his teacher, grabbing her hand and pulling her out from under the net.

Raven's cheeks are flush from exertion, and it's impossible not to notice how striking she is with a background of autumn leaves enhancing the little gold flecks in her deep-brown eyes. Autumn suits her. Turner nudges me in the side, and I realize I'm staring.

"I'd better get home," she says in a regretful tone.

I can't decide if it's wishful thinking or if I am actually reading her reaction correctly, but I don't think she really wants to leave.

"No, you can't go," Charlie whines, dropping his teacher's-pet attitude like a sack of potatoes. "We haven't had pie yet. Or cake."

Her smile quirks. "I've had your grandma's cake before. It's very good."

Turner shoots me a satisfied look. Does he think he's being my wingman or is he purposely goading me? One second, he's flirting with Raven, and the next he's acting like she belongs to me. I don't understand it, but I don't understand the possessiveness I feel around her either. I mean, technically Turner saw her first, and he's the one out there on the dating market. If fate put them together, I shouldn't be mad.

"Well, thanks to Briggs' hatred of pie, we have another cake." Turner inches closer to Raven, who is turning bright red. Maybe she doesn't like that he's so clearly hitting on her.

"I'm so sorry." She turns to me. "I completely forgot you hate pie and here I am showing up with one."

I stare at her. "Everyone else likes pie. It's fine."

Her cheeks pink as I hold her gaze, but I can't seem to look away.

"So, chocolate cake or pumpkin pie, Raven? What'll it be?" Turner says and when she looks from me to him, I inwardly curse myself at the pang of jealousy. There's something daring about his question, like he's asking her to choose between men instead of cake.

"Um—cake?"

Her answer makes me smirk.

"Great choice. What do you say I cut you an extra slice?" He winks at her and this time she laughs.

What the hell? Then he leads her inside, Charlie running ahead of them, shouting to Mom that he wants to put the whipped cream on his pumpkin pie all by himself. I trail behind them, jealousy slapping me upside the head like a wet blanket. I'm obviously full of shit if I think I wouldn't be mad about these two hooking up. Just imagining it has me thinking all sorts of horrible things a brother should never think about his own flesh and blood.

What a joke I've become. If I can't control whatever I'm feeling for Raven, I'm going to have to start avoiding her, and I don't want to do that. We picked out my first triathlon--a seventy miler the first weekend of April. I've got four more months of training with her, and I can't be feeling anything other than professionalism if I'm going to get through it without making an ass out of myself and quitting again.

Self-preservation is cruel, but necessary.

I make myself shut down, something Dr. Thomas would consider regression. When we all gather back in the kitchen for dessert, I keep as far away from Raven as possible. I don't talk to anyone, letting my family take over. It's not like I invited her here anyway. If someone asks me a question, I answer in one-word replies. It's hard but I don't look at her either. Not when she laughs or answers unnecessarily prying questions or compliments Mom on the cake. Not even when she tells them I made her the same cake for Friendsgiving and the whole room falls silent for the second time.

"That's surprising," Dad says, and Mom holds her chest like her baby just took his first steps.

"Oh, for hell's sakes," I grumble. "It's not a big deal."

"I didn't know you boys could bake." Capri snorts.

Her boyfriend interjects with something completely unhelpful about feminism and the two of them jump into the kind of spirited debate that can only happen when someone is still a college kid living on their parents' dime and hasn't had to work in the real world. Turner catches my eye, and I almost expect him to tell Raven the cake was his idea, that he even helped me bake it, but he simply slips a bite of pie into his mouth and watches me with a mischievous grin.

He knows.

He knows I feel something I shouldn't feel for this woman. Do they all know? I'm suddenly disgusted by the heavy chocolate in my mouth. I force it down and throw the rest in the trash.

"I have to get some work done. Thanks for the dinner, Mom. It was wonderful as always." I nod toward Raven. "I'll see you Monday for club training."

Before anyone can protest, before I can register the way Raven's mouth pops open or Mom's disappointed frown, I'm out of there.

I drive home in an angry daze, pissed at myself for feeling the things I know I shouldn't. The excuses pile up in my head.

One: I'm overly tired from the race.

Two: I'm weary from years of grieving.

Three: I've allowed Raven to become my friend. I'm not friends with beautiful women for good reason.

And four: None of this has to change me.

I don't have to go back on my commitment to my parents or Dr. Thomas or Jaci's five-year plan, just because I felt something I shouldn't. Feelings don't have to mean anything. They're fleeting. Insignificant. They go away.

That's what I tell myself anyway, even though little amber flecks fill my vision the moment I close my eyes and attempt to sleep.

Chapter Twenty-Six

RAVEN

Briggs' hasty goodbye leaves everyone standing with plates full of dessert and slack jaw expressions. Well, not everyone. Capri's boyfriend makes a snide remark about seeing why she refers to him as the town grump. A remark that earns him a sharp elbow to the ribs from Capri and a hard glare from Mrs. Lawson.

With Briggs gone, it feels like I should leave. Only if I do then it's like I've assumed I'm his guest and that's not really the truth. Technically, it was Mrs. Lawson who invited me, and her who I would insult by traipsing after Briggs like that kid on the playground that can't take a hint when the other kids run away.

I crave this man's approval and I hate that. It's completely undeserved on his part. Almost every interaction I've had with him either starts or ends with feeling like

I'm not enough. Not interesting enough, not professional enough, and definitely not a snappy enough dresser. I still cringe thinking about that first encounter at the coffee shop.

Mrs. Lawson might be a psychic because before I can spit out a valid excuse to leave, she's looped her arm with mine and is leading me out of the kitchen and into the family office. I can't help myself, a snicker slips out when she closes the door behind us, and I see that the walls are covered in photos of the Lawsons. Their home is beautiful, no one could dispute that, but all evening I've been searching for signs of Turner and Briggs' childhood. Instead, the mantelpiece was topped with a shot of Lawson Constructions first ever property development. There were no family photos on the end tables, just crystal awards, fancy little trinkets to remind guests that this is no ordinary household, but one built on a successful business. If I needed an internship this would all be interesting, but what I want is ammunition. Something to tease Briggs with when we reached the crankier parts of his training regime. Distraction, I have found, is an awesome tool for getting someone through a tough physical challenge.

There is definitely ammunition in this room. Starting with an incredible shot of Turner in a full body leotard. "Are those jazz hands?"

Mrs. Lawson grins and lifts the photo from its spot on the built-in bookshelves covering two-thirds of the wall space in this room. "He was passionate about dance. Right up until he hit middle school and his friends started teasing him."

His skinny little arms and legs are hard to look away from, but it's his long curly hair that I can't get over. I say, "Why do boys get the perfect eyelashes and dark shapely curls? Do you know who I most resembled in middle school? Wednesday Adams, and not in a hot Christina Ricci sort of way. Just pale, with stick straight hair and a tendency to wear horizontal stripes."

Mrs. Lawson smiles and sets the photograph back down. "Is that why you are so colorful now? Out to prove all those seventh-grade rivals wrong?"

I shake my head. "No, no, I got over all of that as soon as I started excelling in sports. If you're fast enough, no one cares how you dress. Nowadays, I just like the bright colors and goofy accessories because it makes the kids smile. You can't be a boring kindergarten teacher. That's totally against the rules."

"Whose rules?" she asks playfully.

"Maybe just mine," I admit, "but it works to break the ice. Kids like Charlie have enough going on in their lives. They need school to be fun. It's a lot easier to make school fun if they aren't intimidated by you."

The playful smile leaves her lips replaced by an expression of concern. "Kids like Charlie. Well, I guess nobody gets out of a divorce unscathed."

I know I've misspoken, but I'm not sure how to get myself out of it so I quickly scan the shelves for a photo to make small talk about. The one that catches my eye however is anything, but a conversation starter. I can't hide my shock at Briggs in a tuxedo, his chin resting on the bare shoulder of a beautiful blonde––a beautiful blonde in a strapless wedding gown. My hands grab the frame before I can stop them, and I'm inspecting the photo like it's all the missing pieces of a puzzle I've spent months trying to assemble.

"I didn't have the heart to put that one away." She clears her throat. "It's probably best if you don't mention you saw that."

There are a thousand questions running through my mind. Who is she? Where is she and how come there are no other photos of her? Did Mrs. Lawson bring me in here to show me this photo?

"Charlie's not the only one who could use a break from what they are dealing with at home," Mrs. Lawson says.

"Did Briggs go through a divorce too?"

Now that I think about it, it makes sense. He's heartbroken because this woman must be the one that got away. Maybe he made a mistake and ruined the relationship, or maybe she cheated and that's why he seems so bitter and prickly. But none of those things really explain why there'd still be a picture of this woman in his parents' home.

"Briggs is a widower," Mrs. Lawson says, and I can tell from the way her tone changes and her hands reach for the photo that this is a conversation she's had more times than she would like.

She carefully removes the frame from my hands and

sets it back on the shelf. I can't stop staring at the photograph. Whoever this woman was, she was gorgeous, but that's not what's so captivating about the photo. It's the startling way Briggs is smiling down at his bride, like he can't believe his luck.

He loved her. Clearly. A man like that will always love a woman like her.

"What happened to her?" My cheeks warm as I realize I'm overstepping. "Never mind, it's none of my business."

"It's okay to ask." Mrs. Lawson rests her hand on my shoulder and squeezes. "They were in a car accident three years ago. Briggs was driving. He blames himself."

Everything clicks into place. His reluctance to address his shoulder injury. His uncomfortable reaction to riding in my smaller vehicle the day we went mountain biking, insisting on taking his gargantuan truck. How he abruptly left tonight when I brought up the cake he made for my party. His steadfast dedication to his work above anything and anyone else. The man pushes people away––pushes me away.

I don't know what to say. It's a terrible revelation, like a tidal wave that has me swimming in circles of debris, not knowing which way is up. Embarrassment washes over me. I've been worried about finding "the one," feeling sorry for myself that my parents aren't attentive to me, daydreaming about having a family of my own one day. Meanwhile Briggs has been trying to move on without the love of his life, blaming himself for her death.

"Can you tell me about her?" I know it's not appropriate to keep pushing, but I can't stop myself either. I have to know more, and I know there isn't a prayer of Briggs opening up to tell me himself.

"Jaci was his high school sweetheart. They met in band, if you can believe it. He played the trumpet and he was terrible."

I let out a strangled laugh at the image of a burly Briggs Lawson on the sidelines with a horn instead of out there on the football field like I automatically assumed. He's got the build for athletics, and I know he's played some baseball. He's picked up on our training faster than most, so it seemed obvious that he would've been a jock in high school. Then I remember his siblings' sign at the race today and it all makes sense.

"Did he ever play baseball?" I ask, thinking about his excuse for a terrible rotator cuff.

Her frown lines deepen. "Just little league, and he quit after two seasons. Sports weren't his thing. He's so analytical and exacting. He excelled in academics and was the president of the robotics team. He only did band because he heard a musical instrument would make him smarter, and then he met Jaci and stayed on for her."

I only realize my mouth is hanging open when I snap it closed. "I never would've guessed."

"I know." She smiles proudly. "Our other kids all played sports though. And Griffin, oh my, now he was our star athlete. He even played college football in undergrad."

She goes off about all her kids' accomplishments, the adoring mother that she is, but all I can think is that Briggs outright lied to me about his injury. There's no way it came from baseball, so it must have happened during his car accident. Does anyone else know about it? My stomach hardens and I must look upset because Mrs. Lawson drops her storytelling mid-sentence.

"Are you okay, dear?" she asks gently.

I nod. "I know it's none of my business, but I wish he would've told me about Jaci."

"Maybe he should have, but I'm his mother, and he won't talk to me about it. When and who he chooses to open up to is out of our control. I'm telling you now because you're good for him. I can see that. You deserve to know the truth, but he deserves his privacy too."

Right. That.

My mind is floating away while my heart is shutting down, my body torn into halves. There's no denying it now––I was opening myself up to Briggs. I've felt something for him for weeks now, maybe even since I met him. I told myself that breaking up with Andre was about me and not Briggs, but doing so only gave those feelings for Briggs license to grow. What a fool I am.

"I know it's selfish of me, but can I ask something of you?" Mrs. Lawson says, and I meet her eyes. They're so much like his that it's hard to look at them for long. "Don't give up on him?"

I smile softly. "I'm not planning to." Not that anyone plans that sort of thing. "But it's late and the turkey hormones are starting to get to me. I think I need to go home now. Thank you for dinner."

She nods. "Of course. Let me walk you out." We don't talk as she leads me from the office and out to my car, and it's only as I'm pulling on to my street that I wonder exactly what Mrs. Lawson is asking of me.

Don't give up on Briggs as a potential partner, or don't give up on him as my triathlete client?

Maybe she meant both.

Or maybe she doesn't see any possible way he could ever love me, because she knows Jaci was his endgame, and I was yet again shoving hope where it didn't belong.

Either way, I won't give up on Briggs as my client, but I'm not going to put myself through the hell of wanting someone who won't allow himself to want me back. I've spent too many years settling for the table scraps of love-- with boyfriends, with friends, even my own parents seem to need a pep talk when it comes to showing the world I'm theirs. If there was one good thing to come out of today, it's the realization that I can't keep doing that. I want a whole feast.

The whole damn feast with an adoring husband and children who I love enough to frame a zillion photos of, and the eventual grandchildren who will binge on whipped cream for dessert, and I'll let them because that's what grandmas do. I want it all, and I'm going to keep searching for the person who wants that with me, even if I have to break my own heart a time or two along the way.

Chapter Twenty-Seven

BRIGGS

Early Monday morning, by the time my alarm clock blares, I've already been awake for hours, unable to move from the bed. I can't be late for training, but my body is stiff.

That, and I want to keep hiding from Raven.

After leaving my parents' house, I'd spent the rest of the holiday weekend finishing Jaci's journals and slipping Post-it Notes into the entries I wanted to reread. Half of me plans to come back to study every single letter, and the other half never wants to touch these journals again. The Post-its are my compromise.

But there's one note in particular that has been glaring at me from across the room since the moment I stuck it to the page last night. As the morning sun creeps through my windows, there it is, tortuous neon yellow. I didn't want to process Jaci's words when I stuck that note in yesterday, but I know I have to.

So I peel myself from the bed and crack open the journal, internalizing the entry from only a few months before she died. Her words sink in so deep the second time, it's like I hear it in her voice.

SOMETIMES I WONDER what it would have been like if my family never moved to Austin. If Briggs Lawson wasn't my whole life, who would Jaci Renolds be? I think if I knew my fate and had to choose whether to live it out as is or take a different path, I would still choose to turn around that day in band class and catch him staring at me. I've never even dated anyone else. We have the kind of everlasting love story that other people envy, but there was a moment the other day when I saw what it might be like to not be half of a couple.

I was at the library of all places when an attractive man struck up a conversation beside me. I had nowhere else to be, so I stopped and listened to him, really listened to him. He liked the books I picked, and I could tell he wanted to ask me to meet again. Then he spotted my ring, and he didn't ask me anything more after that. I wondered what would have happened if I wasn't married. I think it's natural to wonder about these things sometimes.

I'm not trying to run off with another man, and I'm so happy with our life together, but sometimes it's hard to imagine a version of myself that isn't tied to being a Lawson. And that's a little scary.

He's been my priority since day one. I didn't think too hard about my career goals because I wanted his to be the priority. I thought his focus, tenacity, and drive were enough to sustain us both.

But lately I've been feeling like something is missing. Who do I want to be? What will challenge me?

Truth is, I need more than a happy marriage. I need a passionate career too. I don't want to work for Lawson Construction anymore, and I haven't since I was twenty-five. Now that I'm approaching thirty, I feel like I'm running out of time. I can't just sit around journaling goal lists, picking out future baby names, and waiting for inspiration to strike. I have to quit and start trying new things until something sticks. I hope Briggs will understand. He loves having me around the office, but I feel like working there is a participation trophy for marrying him. I hate that I'm scared to tell him the truth, but I am. I've never been scared to tell him anything before.

I'M the world's biggest asshole. My own wife and best friend for over a decade was afraid to tell me how she was feeling. I had her so wrapped up in my passions, in my absolute drive to grow the business, that she didn't know how to find her own passions, her own growth.

I drop the journal onto the bed and go to the closet, going through the motions of preparing for today's workout. We're scheduled for a short run followed by yoga in the park. It's the last thing I want to do right now, but am I really such a selfish prick that I'm going to dishonor Jaci even in death?

I took down the mantra Post-it Note, but that bucket list? It still hangs on my bathroom mirror, the triathlon circled in red ink.

I can't quit on her now.

THE RUN itself isn't as brutal as I'm expecting. Everyone is exhausted and bloated, not a great combination. Thank God Raven knows how to be gentle when she needs to be. I stay in the back of the group, my mind spinning with thoughts of the journal entry.

I still can't believe it--Jaci didn't want to work for Lawson. She hadn't wanted to work for Lawson since she was twenty-five. She was almost thirty when she died. So that was years of wasted time for her. Not months. *Years.*

I want to be angry with her for keeping such a big thing to herself, but I can only blame myself. Of course she was scared to tell me. I was CEO by the time she wrote that entry. Our whole lives were wrapped up in my career, my company, me, me, me.

We finish our run and move to the mat. I've never done yoga before so I'm certain I'll be pathetic, but I don't even care right now. Because besides the self-loathing, I'm numb to everything else. I don't look anyone in the eye as I roll out one of the extra mats Raven brought, again sticking to the back of the group.

I follow along with the poses, and most aren't that hard, but a few are way more challenging than they look. The movements force me out of my head for a bit, which is nice. But then we hold one of the more challenging ones and everything I've been feeling washes over me again.

After college, my father hired Jaci at the same time he hired me. She went to work in marketing while I was groomed for CEO. That was always his plan for me, and when he retired, I took over at only twenty-six years old. It was full steam ahead and Jaci went along with everything, never once complaining. In fact, she always seemed happy about it.

She wasn't happy.

How could I have missed that?

For years, I missed that.

Guilt sweeps through me, so sudden and so deep that I drop the pose and move into the child's pose Raven told us we could use at any time. With my face pressed into my chest, tears slide from my eyes and my breathing grows labored. Crying during yoga is not how I planned to end this workout. I'm reminded of the one and only time I attended our local church youth group. Somehow, by the end of the thing, everyone was overcome by emotion. To this day, I blame the Jesus music and swaying. I never went back. Too bad I don't have that liberty with yoga. I've already been informed it will be a regular part of training.

I'm wondering how long I can get away with holding

child's pose and trying to cry quietly, when I hear Raven wrap it up and remind everyone that our next training session will take place in the pool. I wait till the majority of the group leave before moving off my mat and start rolling it up.

Do I look ridiculous, focusing on putting the damn thing away, like I'm taking my SATs? Probably, but if I stand up right now, it's going to be obvious I've been crying, and I'm not sure I can bear that awkwardness on top of everything else.

I can see Raven's running shoes in my peripheral. She's going to want to talk about this, and I don't want to lie to her. For a brief moment, I actually consider running away, just rising to my feet and sprinting in the other direction. Of course, she is a former college athlete, and I'm not even three months into training, so this is probably a pretty poor idea, but what's the alternative?

I stand and hand her the yoga mat, careful to avoid eye contact.

"Yoga will get easier," she says. As if holding her goofy poses is what brought me to my knees, and not the constant internal struggle I keep failing to put behind me.

I nod, but stay silent, just in case my voice cracks and I go from being embarrassed to mortified.

"I'll see you Thursday?"

"At the pool," I mumble, and she gives me one of those megawatt smiles.

It's so bright and genuine and goddamned free that I can't look at her for long. It draws something out in me, something I don't want to name, something so frustrating that on the drive home I have to call Dr. Thomas and leave him a message requesting an emergency session. I've never done that before.

And then I do something else I've never done--I call my administrative assistant Carla and tell her I'm sick and to reschedule my day. Her response is professional, though I'm sure she's curious. Maybe even worried.

After my shower, I crawl back into bed, and do another thing I haven't done in years. I turn off my phone. The heightened emotions from the last few days soften as my mind slips under the headiness of sleep. Within minutes, I'm out like a light.

Thump, thump, thump.

My eyelids peel apart and I blink rapidly, taking in my familiar bedroom. Something about it isn't right. The light is too bright from the windows. The air is too warm. I sit up as clarity seeps in--I took a nap. I canceled work to take a nap, something I said I would never ever do.

I check my phone, but it's still turned off. The very thought of turning it back on makes me want to weep, so I toss it on the nightstand. I fully intend to go back to sleep but that incessant thumping sound continues.

Someone's at the front door and they're clearly not going away.

I pad over to the peephole to find Turner on the other side.

"I know you're in there. I can hear you breathing," he calls out.

I open the door reluctantly and glare down at my little brother. "I'm sick. Leave me alone."

His eyebrow arcs and he sniffs. "You're something, but you ain't sick." Then he pushes past me and into the condo.

"I am ill," I growl.

He turns on me. "You didn't show up to work and you never do that."

No shit. I shrug. "I'm also a human."

He laughs at that.

"It's not a joke."

This is what I have planned for the day: sleep, feel like shit, wonder how else I may have hurt Jaci, and ignore the sudden onslaught of problematic feelings for Raven. I'm not completely irresponsible—I'll see Dr. Thomas too.

"I'm here because I obviously care about you and if you're not going to listen to Mom and Dad, then maybe you'll listen to me."

"I already have a therapist," I snap.

"As if that's done you a lot of good." He throws his hands in the air. "Eventually you're going to have to actually apply what you're learning in therapy, Briggs."

I hate him for saying that, as if he's ever gone to therapy a day in his life. "What do you want, Turner? I needed a personal day and you're interrupting."

"You need more than a personal day and you know it. You need to move on and allow yourself to be happy again. It's what Jaci would have wanted."

This conversation is exasperating. "Look around you,

Turner. We're standing in a condo that is nothing like the place Jaci and I made our life. I have never had the luxury of not moving on. My whole life is moving on. It's *hers* that isn't."

I hate the words coming out of my mouth, almost as much as I hate Turner for making me say them out loud. Turner shakes his head. He's grappling for the right thing to say, when all I want him to do is shut up.

"Selling your house, working seventy hours a week, and even running these races is not what I mean by moving on."

"Then what would you like me to do?" My whole body is white hot. I'm beyond pissed that he can't see all I've been through, that I'm doing my best.

His eyes narrow. "You know."

"Spell it out."

"Raven," he says, and my stomach drops. "I mean Raven. I know you have feelings for her and it's obvious she feels the same way."

Guilt racks through me and I feel about two inches tall. Turner never should've sensed something between me and Raven. The fact that he did has my brain spinning in circles. I can't very well deny what I'm feeling if everyone around me can see it.

"You need to stay out of my personal life."

"Nope." He walks into the kitchen and helps himself to a can of coke, like this entire conversation isn't a border-line argument. "I've stayed out for three years, and I'm done pretending like all of this is okay. You finally have a chance at happiness, but you're going to screw it up and choose to be miserable instead. Do you want to know why?"

"I really don't."

Turner pops the tab on his soda and takes a long fizzy drink before leveling me with the kind of cold stare that only family can get away with. "Because you like being miserable."

"Get out." I point to the door, but Turner holds his ground.

"It's true. You get a payoff for being a miserable son of a bitch."

A payoff? I get a payoff for being miserable that the love of my life is dead and I'm stuck roaming Austin like she never existed and my whole world didn't crumble like that piece-of-shit car she insisted on buying?

Silence falls between us, and I'm so angry I could punch him right in the mouth. Knock the smirk from his face, along with a few teeth for good measure. We haven't had a physical fight since we were kids, but right now, it's hard to care about being a mature adult. Right now I want to hit first and think later.

"Get the hell out of my house," I snarl.

His lips thin and he stomps toward the exit. "Talk about this next time you go to therapy." He slams the door so hard the entire condo vibrates.

I pace back and forth for a bit and then go check my phone to see if Dr. Thomas replied to my message. Sure enough, he did, fitting me in at the end of his day. I decide to bring Turner's argument up to the good doctor to prove that I'm in the right. A mental health professional will be able to explain exactly how wrong Turner is about this.

Except when I see Dr. Thomas later that afternoon, he considers Turner's argument thoughtfully and way too close for comfort. "Well, let's entertain the question so we can see if it has any merit. So what could you be gaining from living how you've been living?" he asks.

Just whose side is he on anyway? I don't answer that asinine question. I never wanted to answer in the first place because it's bullshit.

"Or . . . " He leans forward across his oak desk. "Ask yourself, what is it *costing* you to keep living like this?"

I clear my throat, because this one is a little easier. "It's not about me. I can't just move on like they want me to. I'm the one responsible, so it's my job now to make sure I'm never in a position to hurt another person."

"Or could it be that by keeping your heart ransomed to the past, you believe *you* will never be hurt again?"

I hate it when he does this. Slaps the truth in front of me like it's been sitting there all along and I've been purposely closing my eyes so I don't have to see it.

His honesty cuts to my core––so exacting, so punishing. What is it costing me to keep living like this? Everything.

Chapter Twenty-Eight

RAVEN

I'm not supposed to know that Briggs is a widower, not supposed to notice things like red-rimmed eyes and uncontrollable emotions. But this new information about him is not ignorable. I already decided I wasn't going to go after another unavailable guy, but I can't keep thinking about the tortured way he looked at me after that yoga class last week, and how he's continued to look at me ever since. There was enough tension between us before I knew that he's an *I'll never love again* type. Now I'm over here watching Nicolas Sparks movies like there's going to be a test on how to woo a widower.

Remi's patience is epic. I ramble on and on about Briggs, and she continues shelving books in the school library, like nothing I'm saying is distracting her from her work, when in reality it's probably fairly difficult to adhere to the Dewey Decimal System while your coworker is having a tiny mental breakdown beside you. She waits until I pause to take a breath before interjecting.

"So, his wife died. And *now* he's a real possibility for you? I could swear at your dinner party you were not interested. If this is the benchmark for gaining Raven's interest, it is no wonder you're still single. Must you really require personal tragedy?"

I wince at her candidness. "That's not the appealing part."

"You don't think so?" She quirks one eyebrow, and it is obvious she doesn't believe me.

"Seriously, it's just . . . "

Remi shelves a book on the life cycle of a bee before returning to face me. She's looking for an explanation, and I'm having a hard time coming up with one. What exactly is it that I feel?

"It's like, before, he was a challenge. A stereotypical, emotionally stunted, alpha male. We all like going for that type of guy. It has its own appeal. Granted it's the kind of appeal that makes you feel like a traitor to your gender . . . "

My single-lady problems are clearly amusing to Remi because I can tell she is biting back a smile while trying extra hard to be an active listener.

"But now it's like he has a genuine reason to be that way. He's emotionally stunted because he has experienced great pain. He's an alpha because he failed to protect his last partner."

"He's got quite the backstory," Remi says.

"Exactly."

"So what are you going to do about it? When I suggested you dump Andre and date Briggs, I was kind of joking."

Guilt punches me square in the stomach. "I didn't dump Andre for Briggs. Andre wasn't really all that interested in me. Actually Briggs isn't interested either, that part you're wrong about."

That eyebrow pops up again, and I can feel my cheeks changing colors.

"Andre wasn't right for me. Andre's backstory was that he wasn't invested in our relationship and wasn't going to get invested any time soon."

"And this attraction to Briggs had nothing to do with your realizing that?"

A deep sigh escapes my lips. "He had everything to do with my seeing that."

The bell rings, and as much as I want to stay and probe Remi for seasoned married-lady advice, I don't have that option. Ms. PTO will be dropping by my class before the buses arrive, and I need time to come up with yet another excuse for why I haven't located Santa yet. There are only two more weeks until *Polar Express* Day, and I'm out of ideas.

"I have to go," I grumble. "And you haven't solved any of my life problems yet."

A soft laugh tumbles from Remi as she stands to bid me goodbye. "I'm afraid you get the therapy you pay for, my dear. My specialty is listening, with a side of snarky but necessary commentary."

Walking out of the library, it occurs to me that my conversation with Remi is the first time I've admitted out loud that Briggs is more than a member of my tri club. As his coach, it's my responsibility to get him over the finish line. Part of that process is identifying *why* he wants to compete in the first place. I have my suspicions, but that's not the same as an answer. I've never had feelings for a client before, and I'm afraid that my motivations as his coach and my motivations to dig beneath the surface and uncover the unreserved version of him are going to cross at some point. How am I supposed to know which boundaries need crossing, and which ones I just want to cross?

THE NEXT TWO weeks fly by in a blur of activity. December has a way of doing that. It's one of those months where life seems to speed up and slow down all at once. It's also one of those months where I feel the most conflicted about my career choices. I embrace being a part of my students' holiday magic, but my heart grows heavier every year that I still don't have children of my own. Heck, it has been years since I had a serious relationship I could even see leading to children.

Something about being thirty and single hits me harder than it has before. Harder than it ever did in my twenties. If I'm still single in a few years, I'll have to hit up a sperm bank and do the whole parenting thing on my own. It'll flip my world upside down, and I'll probably have to quit coaching until my kids are in school with me, but I can't imagine myself childless forever. I understand why some people don't want kids, or why people like my parents probably shouldn't have kids, but I've wanted them since I was a lonely little girl with a baby doll.

And what if it isn't easy? What if I'm not one of the lucky ones, and I can't get pregnant right away? These years could be my only shot . . . I blame all of these thoughts on Hallmark Christmas movies. Must there be a happy ending every night to remind me that I'm marching toward an endless quantity of single-serving microwave dinners?

Burying those feelings for now, I take in my classroom and smile as big as the Grinch when his heart grew three sizes. I decorated the room with twinkle lights right after Thanksgiving but waited to add the extras for *Polar Express* Day until this morning. In a couple minutes, my students will wander in wearing their pajamas and carrying teddy bears to find their very own train car with a golden ticket waiting inside. The train cars are actually cardboard boxes I got from Costco that I've covered in holiday wrapping paper, but they are big enough for the kids to sit in and Lord knows kids love cardboard boxes.

I'm dressed up in the train conductor costume I invested in a few years ago and will punch their tickets before the movie. During the movie, they'll get hot chocolate, candy canes, and a little Christmas bell necklace to wear for the rest of the day. It's the kindergarten version of

Rocky Horror Picture Show, and though it is not polite to brag, I'm convinced that this little event is exactly the sort of thing that creates happy little memory bubbles for the kids to hold on to as they grow older and lose their enthusiasm for the holiday spirit.

Everything will come to an end in the afternoon, when a group of parents arrive with party games to finish us off. It's the perfect kindergarten day, the only dark cloud is that I never found a Santa Claus to compete with the professional one surprising the classroom next door.

The first child arrives, and her eyes brighten as she takes it all in.

"Right this way, Miss Audrey." I show her into her train car, and she insists on punching her ticket by herself.

Fifteen minutes later, and everyone is in their boxes when the morning bell rings. They're excitedly whispering to each other, showing off their teddy bears, when I dim the lights and start the movie. Tom Hanks' deep vibrato fills the room.

I chuckle at the awed faces as I slide into my chair at the back. *This.* This is the reason I teach kindergarten. It's considered the most challenging grade by most of my coworkers because emotional regulation is hard for five- and six-year-olds, but I thrive among these wonderful little humans. They embrace life with a special kind of wonder that adults never could, living for learning and fun, and they're honest with their emotions. They're *present,* not bogged down like the rest of us. I'm constantly inspired to be more like them.

Also, only a kindergartener can enjoy this boring ass movie. The only reason I enjoy it at all is that this Tom Hanks animated monstrosity has prevented me from having to read the book over and over again. No amount of getting into character can make that book an interesting read aloud. But now that Dr. Seuss has been put on half of the parents' no-no lists, admin says we need to play it safe with *Polar Express*.

Once the bells have been handed out, it takes everything in me to keep from tipping my conductor hat down over my eyes and snoozing through the end of the movie. Twenty minutes later, a booming "ho, ho, ho" from across the hall startles me out of a daydream and my heart takes a deep dive. The credits will be rolling any minute and there is no way my kids aren't going to hear the commotion next door. I should have stood up to the super mom and stuck with the school's policy. Policy exists for a reason, and it is now painfully obvious that this one was meant to protect my kids from feeling left out.

I'm mentally preparing for the mountain of tears about to come my way when an unexpected jingling noise starts somewhere in the distance and grows closer with each second that passes. The kids hear it, too, and I can feel the excitement building up in each of them. After all, we've spent the last hour and a half connecting the ringing of bells with Santa's sleigh. When the jingling reaches just outside our door, I find myself holding my breath.

Knuckles rap against our oak door. Did Claudia Williams grow a conscience and pay her Santa to hit up the other rooms? I doubt it because I can still hear kids giggling across the hall and there is no way Santa got through twenty-five kids in the few minutes since I first heard his jolly "ho, ho, ho." I don't know exactly what I am hoping for when I turn the knob and pull open the door, but the Santa before me is not what I expect. I gasp, my hand flying to my mouth and my eyes widening. His suit is authentic, the best the internet can buy. I should know because I looked at each and every costume available. The handle of bells he clutches in his fist is a nice touch. One I bet the mall Santa across the way didn't think of. But it's his eyes. Bright hazel and brooding, with little crinkles at the corner that take my breath away.

Briggs takes in my startled expression, winks from beneath his long, white beard, and walks past me to greet the children. He grabs his overstuffed belly and lets out a big Santa-style chuckle. It's the most cliché and surprising Christmas miracle of my life, and I'm left completely speechless.

Chapter Twenty-Nine

BRIGGS

Charlie sits on my lap and peers up at me with a discerning expression.

"What's your name, little boy?" I ask in my best Santa voice.

"Charles Donovan Lawson."

I chuckle to myself. Leave it to Charlie to answer so honestly. Nobody calls him Charles and probably never will. Not even his mother. Charlie's lips twist as he studies my face, and I'm sure he's about to out me as his uncle, but instead he asks if I'm the real Santa.

"Of course I'm the real Santa," I say in mock offense.

He shakes his head. "My mom told me that the real Santa is at the North Pole with the elves getting ready for Christmas and the other Santas are just his helpers."

Well, that makes more sense. I don't know how

parents handle these kinds of questions. I look around for Raven's help here, but she's busy wrangling the rest of the sugared-up kids. I can't very well tell Charlie that his mom is a liar, so I go for a redirect instead. "I have it on good authority that you're on the nice list this year, Charles. Is that true?"

He nods. "I'm always nice."

"Of course you are. And what does a very nice boy like you want for Christmas?"

I'm expecting his answer to match with the other kids in his class who want gaming consoles or Legos. If he mentions something about his parents' divorce, I don't know how I'll respond, maybe with something about how his parents love him no matter what.

But in true Charlie fashion, he surprises me entirely. "I want a big box of Lucky Charms cereal." I hold back a laugh as he elaborates. "My parents won't let me eat it because they say it's not a healthy breakfast, but I had it at my friend Olivia's house and it was so good, and I want some for my house."

"A big box of Lucky Charms, huh? Alright. Anything else?"

His chocolatey eyes widen into little round saucers. "I can pick two things?"

"Sure, why not?" If I have to, I'll buy the damn cereal box and demand Turner put it under the tree with whatever they're getting him from Santa this year. I can't wait to tease his parents about this one. Your kid is so sugar deprived that he wants Lucky Charms from Santa Claus--how do you plead?

Charlie rattles off the name of some toy I've never heard of, and I nod along like I know exactly what he's talking about, whatever it is, I'm sure Sam and Turner have it handled.

A few minutes later, and I finish up with the kids but I'm having so much fun that I'm not ready to go. Raven's job is entirely different from mine, and I'd love to stay and help out with whatever she has on next, but that's really not my place. She walks me to the door and the kids yell their excited goodbyes. The energy is magnetic, taking me right back to similar memories of my childhood, memories I never think about anymore. Maybe I should. They feel good. More than good--they're damn near therapeutic.

"Thank you," she says, "you have no idea how much this means to them and to me."

I'm sweating profusely in this outfit and probably look like an idiot with the white beard, but I'd do it a thousand times over if it meant I got to see so many smiles, especially the one on the woman standing in front of me. Who knew train conductor outfits could be so attractive? And why do I get the impression that Raven nails sexy Halloween every year? I find myself thinking that she's just as gorgeous today as she is every day, and I have to laugh internally because I haven't always felt that way. That first day we met, for example, sexy was definitely not the word I used to describe her in my head as she dug through that ginormous purse of hers.

"I'm glad I could help. Is there anything else I can do?"

She considers for a second. "How would you feel about visiting another classroom? There are three kinder classes but only one got the professional Santa treatment. I still can't believe you remembered."

"How could I forget? I was fuming the day I heard that lady going off on you about this ridiculous Santa Claus business, as if you don't have enough to worry about while teaching kindergarten."

She looks startled by my answer and her cheeks go pink. Maybe I said too much, but honestly, it's been in my mind ever since it happened. I even ordered the suit the next day, just in case she never found anyone. I called the school this morning to confirm that it was okay that I come, and I may have fibbed to the staff and told them Raven was expecting me. I wanted to surprise her and I'm glad I did.

"Show me the way to the next classroom." As I follow her across the hall, I get back into character, ho-ho-ho-ing so loudly she bursts out laughing.

One more class full of sugared-up kindergarteners and about three pounds of water weight lost from sweating under my suit later, and I feel a bit like a rockstar. Maybe I'm high on Santa's celebrity status—or maybe it's the fact that I've managed to make Raven smile, genuinely smile, not pity smile, or over exuberant coach smile—but I find myself asking her if she wants to celebrate a *Polar Express* victory with a lunch somewhere without a playground.

The moment the words come out of my mouth, I realize it sounds like a date and I want to retract them, but it's too late, and besides, she hasn't said yes yet. This is what it feels like to be an adult pursuing a woman. Terrible, it feels terrible. Each second, I stand there in my Santa beard waiting for her to issue a rejection, or worse take me up on the offer, is a second where my heart is beating so loud and so hard that it could do me in for good. Just when I think I'm about to keel over, that obnoxious woman who shook Raven down about hiring a Santa Claus interrupts our conversation.

"Santa's asking you out, Ms. Raven. Don't leave him hanging."

"No!" I say. Quickly, too quickly, because Raven's cheeks turn scarlet, and Claudia, the *branding strategist and entrepreneur,* peers at my face for the first time, realization dawning on her. I'm no Santa for hire.

"Oh my goodness." A mean-spirited laugh pours out of her. "Of course you aren't. Briggs, I didn't even recognize you under there."

I hate the sound of my name coming from her mouth, and the familiarity with which she uses it. We haven't had a single conversation since that day in the hallway, and I don't want Raven thinking otherwise. But more irritating than all of that is the fact that she called me by my first name, and there are still students milling around the hallway, including my nephew. My nephew, who thinks he just met Santa's helper.

"What I meant was," I say, "I would like to thank Ms.

Raven for the opportunity to be here today. I am not trying to pressure her into a lunch date with *Santa*."

I'm not sure if that is better or worse than what I said to begin with, but it sounds less like I'm appalled to date Raven.

"How about it?" I ask, directing all my attention back to Raven and away from the busybody standing uncomfortably close to my side. Standing there in her conductor suit, being asked to lunch by a man dressed as Santa Claus, only fazes Raven a little.

"Let me grab my things," she says with the cutest smile. Then she pops into her classroom, leaving me standing alone in the hallway with Claudia.

"Is this appropriate? What with Charlie in her class . . . "

I turn to give her my sternest glare, despite the circumstances of my wardrobe.

"Charlie is my nephew, and I hardly think having a good relationship with his teacher is anything to be concerned about. I do, however, think it is inappropriate to pressure a teacher into a difficult circumstance in order to benefit your child. You knew what a challenge it would be to get a Santa last minute, and it didn't stop you from berating Ms. Raven repeatedly for the benefit of your own child's classroom."

She reaches up to twist the expensive looking pendant dangling from her neck around her fingers. "I only intended to improve the day for *all* of the children."

"It seems you stopped short then."

I'm used to being cold at work, but belittling PTO moms who walk like they've got a permanent stick embedded in their ass is a new kind of thrill. It feels disturbingly good, coming to Raven's defense.

I leave Claudia standing there with her mouth hanging open to walk Raven to my truck. I peel off the itchy red suit the second we reach it and throw it in the back seat. I'm wearing my work clothes underneath because I'd planned to go to the office after this, but now I just want to go home and savor the goodness of a day unsullied by work stress.

Raven hitches her hands on her hips. "Dang, I was hoping you'd keep that on. I agreed to go to lunch with Santa, not you."

"Santa has left the station," I deadpan, but I snatch the hat and pull it back on. "Compromise?"

She nods and slides into the passenger seat. "Lookin' good, Briggs. Who knew Santa could be so sexy?"

She's joking, laughing and light, but I wonder if she's also flirting. I have no idea how to flirt back, if I even should flirt back, and I don't want to say the wrong thing, so I ask her where she wants to go eat instead.

Between lunch and recess, we only have forty-five minutes to find food and get her back to campus, so she directs me to the quickest restaurant that isn't a fast-food joint. This really isn't a date, because if it were a date, I wouldn't be doing it over lunch. A real date with a woman like Raven would be over a gourmet dinner and expensive drinks somewhere with a romantic atmosphere, somewhere quiet enough that we could talk for hours without interruption. A real date certainly wouldn't take place at an Italian deli that doubles for a grocery store with lines of patrons practically out the door, not enough tables for half the people in here, and a staff calling out loudly to each other in thick Italian accents, many of which sound fake.

"Half of these workers probably grew up in Texas." I snort as we stand side by side in the busy line.

She nods and a little grin turns her lips. "What do you mean? You don't think Miguel is Italian?"

She points to a Hispanic man at the cash register. When he yells across the poor sap ordering to a kid stocking grocery shelves, Raven and I simultaneously start laughing.

"His accent is equal parts Italian, American, Mexican, and fake. I love it," Raven says.

"I love it too. I need to find more restaurants like this one."

"This place has great food and they're fast. We'll be in and out in no time."

She's right. It only takes ten minutes to get through the long line and another ten to get our sandwiches. Luckily, the sandwiches are authentic with imported meat and cheese and fresh-baked crusty bread. They're wrapped in paper, so we opt to walk around the block instead of waiting for a table to open up. It's unseasonably warm today, and the sky is a cheery blue. Nothing like December should be if this were truly a *Polar Express* kind of day, but I love it regardless. If it weren't for the decorated storefronts and holiday music pouring from them, it would feel like springtime. I wouldn't mind skipping the holidays altogether, truth be told. Holidays aren't fun for grieving assholes.

A few people give Raven's outfit funny looks, but she doesn't seem to notice. If she does, she clearly doesn't care. She has such a strong sense of self that I find her refreshing. I always thought I had a strong sense of self, but she makes me want to reevaluate everything. Why do I wear what I wear? Why do I do what I do? Live where I live? Work where I work? I've taken so many of these things for granted and never truly thought about why I do them or if I even want to. Thinking about this, it's hard not to think about Jaci's journal entry. Is this how she felt? Like maybe her life wasn't bad, just a little too scripted?

"Thanks again for being Santa today," she says between bites of her sandwich. "It was the best surprise ever."

"Any time. And I mean that." I stare down at her, noticing the way her dark eyelashes frame her honey eyes so perfectly. They're not too long and not too short and certainly not something I ever noticed on a woman before this moment.

She blinks and looks toward the different storefronts that surround us. This isn't an area of town I've ever taken the time to get to know. I tend to stick to my office and condo when I'm not out on a jobsite. The only times I ever venture to new restaurants are when I'm meeting with a client I need to impress, but those meetings are way too highbrow to include something like this.

Just walking outside, window shopping, and people watching? It's nice.

We talk about her classroom and then venture on to the tri club and what to expect for the next race in January. And before I'm ready, it's time for her to get back to school. When she climbs from my truck and waves good-bye, I have the sudden urge to find out what she's doing for the holidays this year because maybe we could do something together. But I force myself to drive away instead. I'll see her at the club workouts, and that needs to be good enough. Nobody should feel obligated to hang out with me during the holidays, least of all someone as pure as sunshine like Raven Oliver.

Chapter Thirty

RAVEN

Christmas comes and goes with nothing special to make it different from any other year. I think people look at me and they think, *that's a girl who goes all out for the holidays. I'll bet she bakes cookies on Christmas Eve*. Really, it's the opposite.

Nothing feels more hollow to me than facing another Christmas and New Year's solo, so I don't string lights outside my home or decorate a tree. I don't go to clubs or parties where everyone will kiss at midnight, and I try not to dwell on the fact that for that month and a half between Thanksgiving and the start of the new year, the whole world has found exactly where they belong. Everyone but me.

If I didn't have the tri club, I think I would go crazy. With the exception of a few days, we kept up on our work-

227

outs. Race season is coming up fast, and everyone knows that it's time to get serious. Even Briggs seems to take things more seriously, finally emailing me his food journal so I can make suggestions and showing up early to all the club workouts. He has a nervous excitement about him, the energy that everyone gets training for their first real race season. The 10k on Thanksgiving was just a taste of what's to come this year, starting with our sprint today.

"Are you ready for this?" I ask as he joins our group outside of the YMCA.

He nods, and a few of the other club members pat him on the back and offer words of encouragement.

The Turkey Trot was a primer, but this is the real deal. Today he will push himself to complete all three legs of a sprint triathlon. Granted, it's not like we are competing among strong athletes, and we certainly aren't doing a full-distance event, but he'll get a taste of the adrenaline that is swim/bike/run today, and that's something you only get to experience for the first time once.

The YMCA sprint triathlon is a staple for our club. It's the first real event in the city, and we do it every year as a way to keep in shape during the colder months when no sane race planner puts a real tri on the calendar. The first half mile takes place in the pool, followed by a thirteen-mile bike ride through the neighborhoods that surround the gym, and an easy downhill 5k run to finish it off. It'll take our crew anywhere from one to two hours, so it's nothing on a full or even a half triathlon event, but it's a chance to get our heads in the game.

"Look who showed up this year," Leonard says under his breath, nodding toward the parking lot.

A bus with one of the Texas University's logos glistens under the morning sun. Sometimes the local college teams bring athletes out to compete at these smaller events for the same reason my club does--experience.

"Competition," I say with glee and can't help but smile. This is the kindling I need to light a fire in my crew today. There is nothing like a group of young, fast kids to make you push yourself to your limits.

"Alright, everyone, gather round." The thirteen of us huddle up, and I take the time to look them each in the eyes as I talk. "Treat this like a qualifying event. When you're in that pool or you're riding your bike or running, I want you to imagine that you're this close to making it to Worlds, and you just have to shave off one minute from your personal best to make it happen."

They nod along, and I know they're all thinking of whatever that number is for them. Truthfully, most of these people will never go to a championship-level event, but that's okay. Visualizing that you can is still an important tool in getting over whatever current hurdle or plateau is preventing you from moving forward.

"You're competing against yourself. The only person whose time matters out there is your time." I pause for dramatic effect. "But that doesn't mean you can't try to beat those kids who are here to show you up."

I point to the bus and the collective consensus is that the university team has another thing coming if they think they're going to wipe the floor with us. None of us are close to their age, but a few of us did compete back in our college days, and all of us are ready to push alongside these kids.

After a few more minutes of hype, it's time to go inside. The outgoing sort immediately peel off to network, and the introverts are left to huddle together, waiting until it's time to get in line at the pool.

"How's your shoulder doing?" I ask Briggs, who is obviously one of the introverts of the group. I wouldn't have let him compete in this event if Leonard hadn't signed off on it, which tells me Briggs really must be taking the physical therapy seriously, but that doesn't mean I want him to push an injury if he doesn't feel ready.

"It's not perfect, but it's good enough for this," he says. "Leonard's really been helping me."

"And what did your doctor say?"

He sighs heavily. "That if it doesn't heal soon, I should consider surgery."

"It won't take you out as long as you think it will." Not that I've had rotator cuff surgery, and I think people should avoid surgery as long as possible, but sometimes there's only so much the human body can do on its own. "It's not that uncommon of a surgery. You should talk to Kate. She had her left side done a few years ago and will probably get the right soon too. She used to be a swimmer, it's a common injury."

He gives me a sharp look. "Look, you told me if I saw

my doctor and worked with Leonard, then I could be back in the club."

"I did say that, but--"

"And I'm doing those things. Let me see what I can do, okay?"

He stalks off, and I feel as if weeks of relationship building between us just crumbled. But he's right. I did say that and he is trying. I wouldn't be so pushy with other clients, but would he be so defensive if I was someone else?

Our relationship is starting to confuse me. It's like a puzzle, and I hate puzzles. I've always hated them, even when they were one of the few things my parents would sit down to do with me.

An announcer comes over the speaker telling everyone to line up by division, and I refocus by getting into line and watching several of the athletes push to the front. This is common--the people who are vying to win want to be up front. A couple of my club members finagle their way up with the college kids, but most of us hang back, me included. I'm more interested in soaking up the experience than standing out. Those uber-competitive days are over for me, but I can't help but feel nostalgic for that kind of passion. What's something that makes me want to elbow my way to the front? Something I care enough about to make sure I get my shot?

My gaze flicks to Briggs, and I can't help but notice the way he towers over almost everyone else here. I know first-hand that those broad shoulders are out of commission, but that doesn't seem to stop me from fantasizing about being scooped up and carried off to his bedroom. I'm not sure whether to blame loneliness or lust, but he is there, in my thoughts, all the time. Sometimes I think about those little lines by his eyes, or the shocks of gray in his otherwise dark hair. Other times I think about the way he moves, the way he commands a room, and I start thinking I might like to be a room. My heart clenches because I know my answer. I want love. And I want Briggs. I just don't know how to get either.

Chapter Thirty-One

BRIGGS

It's not like the races in the movies. The crowd doesn't swell, dramatic music doesn't escalate until you're on the edge of your seat, and your body tingles with anticipation. Nobody shoots a gun.

A horn blasts, and the first wave of swimmers dive into the pool. It's mind blowing the way these kids' arms and legs slice through the water. Some of them are deadly fast, and the water around them barely even moves. It's the way they cup their hands or some bullshit like that. I'm supposed to know. If I paid half as much attention to the words coming out of Raven's mouth during workouts as I did the thoughts tumbling around inside of my head, I would be a lot further along in this training process.

My fatal flaw is going through the motions without analyzing the why. Example, why are so many of these dudes in neon unitards? Is there a rule about neon? Does it make you faster? Did Nike run out of normal colors, and no one can afford to special order? My own trisuit is mortifying enough. It arrived weeks ago, but I never trained with it in the pool, and I sure as hell didn't wear it when we ran or cycled. Standing here today in a sleeveless one piece with shorts that end four inches above my knees and a fit that could best be described as, "package enhancing," is the kind of uncomfortable I'm going to have recurring nightmares about. At least it's all black. That is the nicest thing I can say about an ensemble I spent an unmentionable amount of money on.

Everyone says I'll get used to it, that I'll even come to like it, but I seriously have my doubts. I consider it a necessary, and embarrassing, evil. If my siblings had showed up for this race the way they did the Turkey Trot, this whole quest for personal enrichment would be over. I can't let pictures be taken.

In what feels like absolutely no time, the next division of racers take their spots at the edge of the pool. This is Raven's heat, and she turns to wave at me before putting her game face on. Now *she* looks cute in her neon trisuit, even with the sleek, white swim cap that keeps her long dark hair from dragging in the water. The idea of being so good that a few seconds extra could make or break your race is laughable to me. My aim today is to finish, not drown, not fall off my bike and roll around the neighborhood like a big useless pinball. Time isn't even on my radar.

The horn blasts again, and I watch as Raven dives into the water. She's a gazelle or a dolphin or some other water animal compared to grace and talent. A quick scan of the room tells me I'm not the only one who thinks so. Eyes chart her course down and back, down and back. She's hard to look away from, even with half a dozen college girls filling up the lanes beside her. It's no wonder that she was a professional, that she's built this thriving coaching business––*she's good*.

She pops out of the pool in third place, and I'm like every other chump in the stands, hooting and hollering, cheering her on as she whips that swim cap off and jogs out into the parking lot to mount her bike. I wish I could follow her. I couldn't keep up, that's for damn sure, but I like watching her in her element. I like it a lot more than stepping up to the water's edge and preparing to dive in myself.

Surprise, surprise, just as Raven exits, my nerves decide to make an appearance. Jaci crosses my mind. She really wanted to do this? Together? Good God, I can imagine her dying of laughter watching me shimmy into this damn suit. It's a happy thought for once. Something rare when her memory is involved. I'm smiling like an idiot, lost so deep in my own thoughts that I nearly miss the warning announcement. Everyone around me is moving into position, and my body follows along like this is dive four hundred and twenty-six and not number one.

We dive in, and just like in practice, I keep my head down, my arms ahead of me, and paddle my feet, getting the most out of that initial push. Water rushes past my ears, and I stare at the black lines on the other end of the pool. The goggles Raven recommended are every bit as watertight as she assured me they would be, so swimming blind is one less thing I have to worry about. My division isn't nearly as fast as those before us. We are a rag-tag group of amateurs and first timers. I want to turn my head to the side and survey the rest of the lanes, see how the competition is doing, and how far behind I really am, but I know if I do that it will mess with my head. It's fine to come out of the pool last, but way better if you don't *know* your last 'til it happens.

This is the hardest leg for me. I've put in plenty of hours on a bike, and more miles on the road than I care to count, but the pool has been my obstacle since the beginning. My shoulder is beginning to ache, and exhaustion is hitting me. I feel like a drowning rat, and the temptation to roll over on my back and do the backstroke for the last few laps is creeping into my psyche, but I'm doing my best not to think about it.

Leonard warned me about that during physical therapy. He said once you flip over, you're signaling to the lifeguards that you might be in distress, plus you can't see the swimmers in front of you anymore. It may be easier, but most competitors consider it admitting defeat. Besides, I want that roaring cheer when I pop out of the pool, the same as Raven, not a slow clap for the dude who took it easy the last three hundred yards.

I push myself through the pain, and when I pull out of

the water on the final lap, I can't wipe the grin from my face. There are still four men in the pool. I'm not last, not even close.

You're not last. You're not last. You're not last.

Those three words become my mantra throughout the rest of the race. It's not Dr. Thomas's, *"I am open to forgiveness and joy,"* but at least I'm not focusing on the stitch in my side, the pain in my shoulder, or the cramp in my thigh. I keep my eyes ahead and catch sight of one of my teammates as I climb off my bike to park it in its designated spot. Rob has already started his run, and I make it my mission to catch up to him. Soon we're side by side, egging each other on to go faster. Several others who aren't in our club join us, and an easy camaraderie swells between the group with each step forward. We push ourselves hard while simultaneously laughing at ourselves and ribbing each other. Maybe it's the endorphins, but this feeling is something I haven't experienced in years, and it makes the rest of the race enjoyable.

When I pass through the finish line, a startling thought pops into my head: this is fun. Never in a million years did I think a triathlon would turn out to be fun, not even a shorter sprint one like this. Half the reason I signed up for the club was because triathlon was another thing I could torture myself with. It's too much cardio, too much training, too expensive, too competitive, too . . . everything I'm not.

And yet here I am, a finisher. Smiling. Enjoying myself. My gut instinct is to shut it down, to tell myself that I don't deserve this, but for once, I push that instinct aside and let myself be happy.

The honkey tonk is ungodly loud and boisterous, overflowing with dancers and drinkers--most of whom are far too young for me. Not at all my kind of place for a Saturday night. But Raven invited the tri club to come out and celebrate after our sprint, and I'm ready to release the feelings I'd collected along that race route today. So I show up at The Pink Pony Saloon a half hour late, trying not to feel out of place without a pair of cowboy boots or a ten-gallon hat. Again, not my thing. A lifetime spent in Texas, and I still never thought I'd be caught dead in this place.

I scan the crowd and find our crew huddled around a table next to the dance floor. I'm glad they have a table because that's where I plan to spend the evening. If they'd all been out dancing, I might have turned around and gone home. I'm not in the mood for dancing. My muscles are sore, I have no rhythm, and if I am going to make a fool out of myself, it won't be in pursuit of the perfect line dance.

"There he is," Leonard hollers as I approach the group. His arm is slung around his husband's shoulder and the two of them are dressed up like they just stepped off the set of a western movie starring Dolly Parton. The bolo ties pain me but good for them.

Raven motions to the almost empty pitcher of beer on the table. "Want a drink? We've got more coming."

I pour myself a watery glass of what's left and take a long drink. I'll have one but that's it. I don't get drunk anymore. It's a personal rule of mine.

The music switches over to the most obnoxious song ever created--*Cotton Eye Joe*. The crowd squeals in delight and everyone rushes to the floor, but I hang back. I don't line dance, and I don't trust myself to be out there with Raven, especially not with alcohol in the equation. She looks gorgeous tonight in her black cowboy hat and boots, but it's the tight blue jeans hugging her ass that make me uneasy. A pang of longing runs through me as I watch her move to the music.

"You doing okay, cowboy?" Leonard appears next to me, downing his drink and eyeing my shoulder. "Are you in pain?"

"My shoulder is fine." I'm tired of talking about it, and even though he's my physical therapist and is fast becoming a friend, I don't want to go there.

"Then why the long face?" He's clearly tipsy by the way he elongates his words. I could probably say whatever I wanted, and he'd forget it by tomorrow.

I set my drink down and I sigh. "I just don't like going out. It's not my thing."

He nods like he gets it, but I think he's just being friendly. How could he get it? He's here with the love of his life, having a great time. I'm here because I wanted to celebrate the race today, but the second I walked through those ridiculous, pink saloon doors and felt the vibrant energy of the crowd and heard the country twang of the blaring music, heady guilt swept through me.

I don't get drunk anymore because when Jaci died, I relied heavily on alcohol to stay numb. One night, I went to a seedy bar and got shit-faced. When I got up to leave, I fully intended to drive home—I even walked out into that parking lot and fumbled for my keys at the truck door. I didn't end up driving, but I was close enough to let self-loathing course through me as I called an Uber instead. That moment rattled me to the core, and I decided then and there that I couldn't be trusted with alcohol. Here I was, close to drunk driving, when only two months earlier I had killed Jaci in a car accident I caused. How could I ever trust myself not to put others at risk?

"Maybe dancing will cheer you up?" Leonard says, dragging me out to the floor with the rest of the tri club and their guests.

The song switches over and it's some other country line dancing monstrosity I have no business attempting, but I follow along with the steps as best I can anyway and try not to bludgeon anyone's feet.

Halfway through the song, I catch Raven's watchful gaze--it's shadowed in something sensual that I shouldn't want to reciprocate, but I do. And then I fumble with a stupid boot stomping move, and she laughs at me, her eyes lightening and her mouth going wide and joyous.

"You've got moves, Briggs," she calls out.

My cheeks prickle when I tell her to shut up so I can concentrate, and she laughs harder. Something within me releases and I find myself inexplicably laughing too. I do look ridiculous, I knew I would, but maybe how people look isn't why they go out country line dancing with their friends. Maybe they do it to get lost in the crowd and the music and themselves, and if they're lucky, to get lost in someone else.

Chapter Thirty-Two

RAVEN

It's our Saturday morning workout, and today I scheduled a long run with a focus on heart rate zones. The goal is two hours at a zone three heart rate, which is a great competitive pace to increase blood flow to the body without losing oxygen. For most of my members, that means twelve miles, for a few, it's closer to nine, but my fastest members could make it as far as fifteen. The key here isn't distance, it's maintaining a healthy heart rate.

"I'm so glad January is almost over," Briggs says between short breaths as we maneuver between a group of stroller moms and press forward.

We're on an outdoor track today, and even though running in circles isn't my favorite, it's great for this kind of group heart rate exercise. It also means we have to play well with others, even the moms with strollers who tend to take up a lot of space, or the old guy who runs with a radio speaker instead of headphones, blasting staticky classic rock. And especially with the people who will come out here one time, dressed in brand-new Nikes and Lulus, never to return again. Truth is, they all have as much right to be here as we do, and I hate the elitist attitude a lot of coaches and athletes have toward people who don't fit into their boxes. I hate the attitude, but also, I hate wiggling between the crowds. The coach in me wants to cheer them on and declare that a New Year's resolution is as good a reason to change your life as any other, but years of experience has taught me that two-thirds of these people will be gone by February.

"Don't let Raven hear you say that." Damien laughs, running a few paces ahead of us. "She loves January. Can't get her to shut up about it."

"It's true," I say, looking down at my heart rate monitor to see that I'm below where I should be if I were in zone three. I'm not sticking to a zone today because I need to chat with all the club members, some as they pass me, and others as I slow down for them. Right now I'm pacing with my slower crew, feeling proud to see how much my newest member has improved in the four months since I met him. If Briggs didn't look so annoyed, I might even think he's enjoying himself.

"Don't you hate the January crowds?" Briggs asks incredulously, his frown deepening. "I went to the gym last night for my weight training and could barely get a hold of free weights, let alone use the machines I wanted."

"Tell me about it," Damien says, "that's why I go at three in the afternoon. Nobody's there at three, they're all at work or picking up their kids from school."

"At three in the afternoon, I'm definitely at work," Briggs grumbles.

Gosh, he's grumpy today. How anyone can be so grumpy on a beautiful, blue-skied Saturday morning, I'll never understand. I smile for a long second, taking in the paved track with at least four times the typical amount of runners on it, spotting my clients dotted among them.

"I actually love it when it's busy," I confess. "Not when I have to fight over weights, of course, but running among crowds is good preparation for our races, and I actually love to see so many hopefuls trying to get in shape."

Briggs hums to himself. "You know that most of these people will quit by this time next month?"

I sigh. "Well, it's not easy to work out like this consistently. If it were easy, everyone would do it."

Briggs hums to himself, and I wonder what he's thinking. "Well, not everyone has a coach like you."

My cheeks warm.

"It's true," Kate says as she comes up right behind us, giving me a little wink. "I wouldn't be here if it wasn't for you, Raven."

Kate pushes ahead as Briggs nods, our eyes locking for an electric moment, something that's been happening between us more often than not lately. Something that I can't make heads or tails of. I wonder if he is thinking, like I am, that not too long ago he *did* quit. The gym may be dead in a month or so, but that's a little heartbreaking when you stop and think about it. Right now everyone there and everyone circling this track wants to make their life better, and that's what I'm choosing to focus on today.

A sense of pride wells through me at the compliments. This is why I do what I do. I could choose to live off my private school teacher salary and train for races on my own without all this added work, but pushing people to achieve something they badly want, that's a drive so much bigger than a paycheck.

"Thanks, guys."

"Your way of spreading happiness to the world is one grueling cardio workout at a time," Damien says with a laugh.

"I guess you could say that."

"You know there are drugs you can get that take a lot less time and energy. Possibly even cheaper," says Leonard.

He's managed to lap the slowest group and catch up with us on the straight away. It's just like him to absorb only the last thirty seconds of a conversation, then offer the perfect quip to make us all laugh.

Even Briggs is smiling now. I haven't seen him smile all morning. It makes my own smile grow even bigger. It's a good thing my cheeks are already flushed, or he'd see my feelings written all over my face.

We finish our run, and while half the group heads off

to finish the weekend with their family or significant others, a core group of us hit up the coffee shop where Briggs and I first met. There are definitely days I wish I had somewhere else to be. It can feel like the island of misfit toys, each of us going off about how we'll spend the rest of the day, some of us not having any obligations worth talking about, but with Briggs in attendance, it's different. It's something I look forward to. The best part of my week, and I'm pretty sure that means I am building myself up for one hell of a fall.

Nicky brings all of our coffees to the table, and Briggs smirks when he reads the Sharpie scrawl on the side of mine.

"Hot Buttered Rum, minus the rum. What could possibly prompt you to choose that?"

Nicky answers for me, "Haven't you learned yet? This girl orders whatever the special is."

I shrug. It's true, and I'm unashamed.

Nicky fans himself with our stack of napkins. "She needs one of those men in her life who picks everything for her. You know, like the jerks in rom-coms who lose the girl to farmers or coffee shop boys." He waggles his eyebrows.

"You can leave your boyfriend for him," says Briggs, giving me a long serious look as Nicky sets the napkins in the center of the table and heads back to the front counter.

He's joking, but I remember his reaction to Andre when we ran into one another at the club, and I get the impression Nicky being clearly gay is the only thing making the statement even remotely funny.

I've been looking for a subtle way to mention that Andre and I are no longer together since Thanksgiving, but every time an opportunity comes up, I chicken out. It's not like I can say, *Hey, you might be wondering if I'm single. Well, lucky for you, buddy, I am!* Again, I let the moment pass, mentally kicking myself the whole way home.

I'm hopping out of the shower, fully intent on climbing into my favorite hoodie dress and pajama combination to order takeout from the Thai place down the street when Briggs' number lights up my phone. At this point, I consider us two people with a decent relationship. Friends, but definitely not emergency contacts. He has never texted me without it being to cancel a workout or let me know he will be late, so curiosity has me launching toward my phone like a mountain lion in hot pursuit.

I'm going to try eating at that new place on 3rd. The one Rob mentioned at coffee. Do you want to join?

My heart rate has left zone three. Zone three is a distant memory. I'm near cardiac arrest. I don't want to look like the kind of woman who has a better relationship with the Thai delivery driver than she does her own mother, so I count to thirty in my head before typing back.

Sure, what time?

He does not count to thirty. He apparently does not worry about looking like a hoodie-dress-wearing loser with no plans on a Saturday night.

7:00 p.m.?

Cool as a cucumber, I send back a thumbs up emoji, then fling open the doors of my closet. I have an unchaperoned dinner with Briggs Lawson. I will take no prisoners. Full scale hotness is about to commence. That little voice in my head, screaming, *caution, caution, you don't know what this is,* gets the silent treatment as I pull out my best pair of not-just-friends shoes.

Chapter Thirty-Three

BRIGGS

I could have asked Turner to go. His schedule is about as void of activity as it gets these days. He either has Charlie, or he has a bad app-date lined up, and given how much he complains about those, it's not difficult to imagine he would cancel if I asked. Except there is this wall between us now because I'm a jackass and still haven't apologized for the argument in my apartment after Thanksgiving.

We get through work. I double check his numbers and hold him accountable. He's no longer slipping under the pressure of balancing his new normal with the mounting pressure at work, and when Mom invites us both to dinner, we play nice, but the easy nature of our relationship has dissipated. I need to fix it, but I have yet to figure out what that conversation will look like.

That's my excuse for inviting Raven to dinner tonight. There was no one else, and going alone as I usually do feels pathetic somehow. I didn't allow myself to overthink it. We are friends. We've been to dinner parties together, we meet up for coffee on a regular basis, and we share a common thread with the race season ahead. What I conveniently ignored is how all of those activities have involved other people or have been paid interactions.

Now I'm picking a shirt to match my trousers while trying to figure out how to casually drop lines like, "I'll grab dinner if you want to cover drinks." Or should I pay for everything since I asked her to come? Do friends pay for other friends?

She's got that miserable boyfriend to prevent this from being an actual date, but that doesn't mean I want it to look and feel like one. That would be a real disaster, taking everything I've built with Raven over the last four months and turning it into an ill-fated evening out in which I learn she's a cheater, or she goes home thinking I'm the kind of asshole who makes a move on a taken woman. That is not me, and anyone who tried that kind of bullshit with Jaci would have met a version of me that hits first and considers bail later.

Tonight's about walking a line and walking it well. I already one hundred percent regret the entire decision to text her. This is the shit that loneliness does to you. This is why processing your feelings is a bad idea. The me who isn't working on himself didn't have time for loneliness or any of the dumb decisions that spawn from it. The me who is working on himself questions if paying for drinks signifies something more than simply paying for drinks.

I land on a dark-blue button down with white polka dots so tiny they could be pin pricks, and a pair of tan chinos that look nice with my favorite dark-brown leather belt. Standing in front of my bathroom mirror, several thoughts cross my mind. For starters, I recently played Santa *and was convincing*. It's a damn good thing I joined the tri club, and also, I don't know what it's like to go to dinner like this without Jaci straightening my collar or reminding me that cufflinks haven't ever been cool or necessary. More often than not, I hear her voice in my head when getting ready to leave the condo. Tonight she's silent, and I don't *want* to know what that means.

The restaurant has valet parking, and it feels very strange tossing the keys to my truck to a teenage boy, but this is the place I picked, and those are the rules. I can see it in his face when I'm reluctant to let go—he thinks I'm one of those guys obsessed with my truck, worried he's going to put a dent in my baby. What I'm really worried about is whether or not his feet will reach the pedals and if he knows how to safely operate a vehicle of this size. I briefly picture his foot slipping on the gas as he plows through the outdoor seating area and goes flying through my windshield. Intrusive thoughts––that's what Dr. Thomas calls these. I didn't really have these before the accident, but now they seem to slip their way into everyday situations, filling normal moments and interactions with the keyed-up anxiety of standing on a high ledge with no guard rail.

My heart races as I walk into the restaurant, until my eyes land on Raven and it slows again. Calm washes over me the way it does a child who thinks they've been lost in a crowd only to feel their mother's hand tucked neatly in their own. She's standing to the right of the hostess stand, and she looks the way I would want a first date to look. Her dark hair has been pulled back into a loose ponytail, with just enough left out to frame her face. She's not the type of girl that needs makeup, but when she wears it, it's hard not to be completely sucked in by the sweetheart shape of her mouth and those wide honey eyes that hold such a unique blend of sexy and curious.

Even thinking the word sexy in correlation with Raven makes me feel like a perv, so I push her appearance from my brain and focus on letting the hostess know we need a table for two, preferably inside, where no teenage valet will mow us over.

The atmosphere is far more romantic than I expected, and seeing that Raven and I both took care with our appearances makes me wonder what she's thinking. I pull out her chair and settle in across from her at the intimate table. I should focus intently on the menu, but I can't stop looking at the way the candlelight flickers across her face.

"It smells amazing in here," she says. "I love Italian food, but it's a shame there's not a grocery store attached and people yelling across the room in fake accents."

Her reference to our *Polar Express* Day *not-a-date* lunch makes me chuckle. "I'm not sure if anyone can top that."

She nods to a table near us where a worker is busy lighting a cheese wheel on fire. "Ah, but these guys have pyrotechnics."

I eye the scene with amusement. "I don't know what they're making over there, but whatever it is, I'm getting it."

"It" turns out to be table-side carbonara. After our salad bowls are cleared, the cheese wheel guy maneuvers over his stand to us with its massive cheese wheel perched on top. The inside is hollowed out to create a bowl, and he promptly squirts some alcohol in the bowl and lights it on fire. It blazes a foot in the air for all of two seconds, and Raven squeaks in amusement, her smile growing radiant. The cheese wheel guy notices, giving her his full attention while he prepares my meal. He's clearly an authentic Italian, and the dimples in his cheeks deepen as he retrieves separate bowls of pasta and bacon, mixing them together in the melted cheese.

"That looks amazing." Raven's eyes beam over at the bowl and a hole opens up right smack dab in the middle of my chest. I just haven't decided if it is lust or something else that hole is about to unleash. She doesn't seem to notice any change. "Briggs, you're totally sharing that with me."

I nod because I'd share anything with her.

"What did you order?" the guy asks Raven, and the two begin a lively discussion about varying types of Italian cheese present on the menu. He goes into the process of making and aging it, bragging about how the restaurant sources directly from Italy.

"It's such a *pleasure* that I get to make the carbonaras," he says in his thick accent.

I roll my eyes at the way he puts added inflection on the word pleasure, adding double meaning to his words as he stares at Raven like there are other forms of pleasure he'd like to show her. I kinda hope he makes minimum wage because that accent isn't fair. Her cheeks flush immediately, the pink prickling across her face and down to the neckline of her dress. Is the guy really turning her on with talks of *cheese*? I've been told all women love cheese, but good hell, this is ridiculous. I've never been jealous of a food service person before, but I'm about two seconds away from ripping this guy's head off.

"One wheel can bathe a hundred orders of carbonara." He tongs the pasta onto a plate and sets it in front of me while keeping his eyes on Raven.

"Okay, that's enough, Romeo," I snap. "She has a boyfriend."

Both Raven and Cheese-Freak shoot me startled expressions, but he nods once and wheels his little cart away.

"Good riddance," I mutter, then hold out the plate to her. "I'll trade you for your lasagna if you want."

She raises a questioning eyebrow. "No thanks."

"Really? Because you seemed unusually interested in this carbonara."

She laughs then, her eyes wide with mirth. "Calm down, Briggs. I just want a bite."

Seemed like she wanted more than that considering her blatant flirting with the Carbonara Don Juan.

"I really am happy to trade. Don't you realize by now that I have a problem saying no to you?"

Silence descends over us, and we both go still. I can't believe I just said that. I wouldn't have if I'd been able to keep my cool.

She swallows hard and sits up taller, her voice a soft whisper. "That cheese was on fire, Briggs."

Her response lightens the mood and I chuckle, rolling a spoonful of the pasta onto my fork and pointing it toward her like she's a kid waiting for me to make a choo-choo noise. She pops her perfect mouth open, and I carefully slide the noodles onto her tongue. She closes her mouth and audibly moans, her eyes flutter closed, and my body goes hard.

"So good," she murmurs, swallowing and licking the tiniest bit of sauce from her lower lip.

I'm no longer jealous of the Carbonara Don Juan, I'm jealous of the damned cheese. I suddenly have visions of other things she could do with her mouth, and I have to tug at my collar to keep from overheating. This isn't okay.

I clear my throat the same moment she says, "I don't have a boyfriend anymore, by the way."

I blink at her, then I shove too much pasta into my mouth because I don't trust what I'll say next. She's right, the food is amazing, but the dopamine hit from cheesy carbs has nothing on what her words just did to me. *She's single.* And we're here together in this romantic restaurant. Surely, she thinks this is a date. Do I want it to be a date? I could make it one. Right now, I could turn on the charm. I see the way she looks at me. The longing that's been there, longing that I haven't let myself think about during my days but has been eating up more and more of my nights lately.

When we leave here, I bet she'd let me kiss her.

"When did you break up?" I ask carefully. "Are you okay?"

She stares at me for a long moment. "I'm fine. I broke up with him right before Thanksgiving."

Thanksgiving. When I made her the cake. When she hugged me at the finish line of the Turkey Trot. When she had dinner with my family, and I left her there because I was starting to develop feelings. If Raven broke up with her boyfriend right before Thanksgiving, then I've been reading our friendship all wrong for months, and *this* is definitely a date.

Chapter Thirty-Four

RAVEN

Briggs is hard to read. His outfit and his demeanor scream date. His choice of restaurant and his obvious jealous reaction to my conversation with the waiter? Those are date things. Those are man-who-wants-you things. But then he says things like, "she has a boyfriend" and asks if I'm okay about the breakup.

I should have told him about Andre earlier, but if I had, I don't think we would be sitting here now. My guess is he would've dodged all non-training related contact with me, and even thinking about that makes my heart feel like it's plummeting to the bottom of some deep and bottomless cavern.

I order myself an extra glass of wine and he doesn't. Maybe I'm a terrible person for hoping he would drink enough to relax, but it would be so much easier if there were a way that I could strip him of the barriers he throws up whenever there is a moment of connection between us. By the time I hit the bottom of my glass I'm feeling like there are no barriers on my end, like now would be an especially good time to tell him I really admire the way the fabric on his shirt pulls tight across his forearms. Thankfully, I'm sober enough to realize those are inside-your-head thoughts, not speak-out-loud thoughts.

The conversation has been seamless, from carb talk to thorough evaluations of the tiramisu. The night is young, and we could go out dancing. I'm close to dancing in my chair, but when the waiter—not hauling a giant wheel of flaming cheese—returns with the check, Briggs slips his credit card into the black leather folder and thanks me for trying the place out.

"I've been wanting to come, but this isn't really Turner's scene, and I would feel out of place eating at a sit down Italian restaurant solo."

He's breaking out all his tricks. Not seduction tricks, but deny-you-have-loins tricks. I'm not willing to let him off so easy.

He walks me to my car, the valet placing the keys in my hand before shuffling back to his stand. I should slide in but I linger by the door instead. I peer up at him, desperate to find something in his expression. Anything to mirror what I'm feeling inside. But he's guarded, that finely tuned CEO mask of his firmly in place. Frustration crushes me. I can't keep doing this, this pretending that we're not stealing looks every chance we get, acting as if we're not keenly aware of each other's presence at all times. We're only supposed to see each other three days a week at club training, but then things like today keep happening to make it four. Because what man invites a woman to a romantic dinner if it's not supposed to mean something?

His eyes travel to my lips and his mask slips, longing flashing across his face. Longing and anguish and desire and pain. Adrenaline burns me up as I inch toward him.

He leans down and wraps his arms around me. I think this is it. The angsty moment before the kiss, but he pulls me into a warm tight hug instead. The hug doesn't feel like an apology or a diversion, it feels like exactly what Briggs needs.

"Thank you," he murmurs against my ear. "For everything."

"There's nothing to thank me for." My voice sounds hollow and wooden.

He shakes his head, still holding me too close for friendship. I wish I could see his face when he says, "But there is."

HE DOESN'T ASK me out again after that. February rolls into March, and we continue on as friends, friends who still stare at each other, but also friends who don't go out alone anymore. It's enough to get me back onto the dating apps, and by the time spring break arrives, I'm chatting with three new guys, although I haven't agreed to meet any of them yet. I'm still waiting for that spark. Meeting Briggs has changed the landscape. I'm starting to fear I'll never find the same electricity.

"I don't know about you, but I am so ready for this trip," Leonard says as he carefully loads the last of the bikes into the trailer.

Most of the tri club is flying to Phoenix, Arizona and driving the two hours north to Sedona. Because it's a long twenty-hour drive to get there from Austin, Leonard and I volunteered to transport everyone's bikes over. The club does the majority of our races locally, with three travel races every year. Everything is optional, of course, but all of us travel at least once. We're always sure to pick one fun destination race that's more of a vacation than anything else. This year, Sedona is that race.

We're only doing a half-marathon, but we're bringing bikes because I've got a long ride planned for us as well. We could've shipped our bikes, but since it's my spring break, I offered to road trip over. It will save my clients hundreds of dollars on shipping fees, and it will be a little fun, because alone time with Leonard is always a good time.

As he pulls onto the highway, I have a flash of fantasy that it's Briggs going on a road trip with me, his hands on that steering wheel and body a foot away from mine. My cheeks go hot.

"Good choice, by the way," Leonard says. "I've always wanted to go to Sedona. You know I love all that meta-physical stuff. I can't wait to get my tarot cards read, and you know I'm going on the vortex tour."

"Vortex tour?"

"They say that the pine forests mixing with the red rocks create healing vortexes of energy," he replies, totally serious. "People travel from all over the world to hike to them, and I'm going to find them all."

Well, okay then.

"Sounds a little woo-woo, but I'm totally in."

I smile to myself, wondering about what all Sedona has to offer and how the tri club will fare there, then I sigh wistfully as I think of the three full days I'll have with Briggs once he arrives. It sucks that he can't stay the whole week with us, but with his demanding work schedule and his commitment to never having a good time, I feel like we are lucky he agreed to go at all.

"Out with it," Leonard says. "You're never this excited for a race."

I scoff. "Excuse me? Yes, I am. And I haven't been to Sedona before."

"Your enthusiasm wouldn't have something to do with Briggs deciding at the last minute to register and fly out for the race, would it?"

I blink rapidly and sink into my seat, knowing I've been caught. But Leonard is one of my closest friends, and I've been dying to talk to him about Briggs for months. I didn't know how to bring it up without seeming unprofessional, but he nods at me encouragingly, and the confession comes pouring out.

We spend the next twenty hours bouncing between pop music, crime podcasts, and an extremely thorough dissection of my relationship with Briggs. By the time we hit Sedona, one thing is clear, there is no shoving this secret crush back in the bag. Now that Leonard knows, I pretty much have to do something about it or deal with the consequences of stern judgment every time I chicken out in his presence.

I have no strategy for getting Briggs to give in to what he obviously thinks is a really bad idea, but I do have a secret accomplice now, and that's almost as good as a plan.

Chapter Thirty-Five

BRIGGS

I always feel a little excessive flying by private jet, but Lawson Construction pays for hundreds of flying hours each year. If I *don't* use the jet, I'm wasting company cash. It's normal for me to travel this way, but it's obviously an extravagance for Chris and Richelle, who immediately canceled their commercial tickets when I offered to bring them along in the jet.

We're twenty minutes into our flight, and my team-mates are still gaping at the luxury that is privatized air travel. I have a hard time getting into the conversation with them, keeping my eyes focused out the window instead. Flying over Texas isn't as scenic as a trip over the mountains of Montana or a flight up the coast of California. The landscape is mostly brown, and it feels like the state goes on forever, but that doesn't quell my excitement for the trip. I've never been to Sedona.

When the attendant brings out trays of extravagant catering, my companions go wild, and I try to remember the last time I traveled for pleasure and not work. It doesn't take long to dial in on the fact that I haven't been anywhere since the accident. When I do remember the last trip, I'm surprised to find that my memory isn't all sunsets and champagne brunches.

I wanted to go to Hawaii because everyone wants to go to Hawaii. It's supposed to be one long cocktail in paradise, but Jaci didn't want to go. She'd mapped out her own dream vacation. Four nights in a bed and breakfast on the Oregon coast. The place had a literary theme that she'd read about in a travel magazine, and she was dying to sleep in the Edgar Allen Poe room. I hated the idea and told her as much, but that didn't stop her from booking the tickets and plotting out all the places along the coast we absolutely had to see. She even bought an expensive camera to document the vacation.

We saw the house where they filmed *The Goonies*, ate in restaurants *Food & Wine* called local treasures, and built a bonfire on the beach. Only the beach was no tropical island. It was windy and cold. Instead of reveling in the way the waves crashed on the shore, I bitched about not being in Hawaii. By our third night there, I'd managed to make Jaci cry, and rather than own the fact that I'd been an ass, I stuck to my guns and wasted the final day of the trip frequenting the hotel gym, fueled on testosterone and self-ishness.

We were young back then, and I was too immature and stressed out about stupid shit to be the husband she deserved. No relationship is perfect, but when someone dies you don't just forget about the fights you had. I'd give anything to go back and redo that vacation with Jaci.

Part of me wishes I hadn't remembered Oregon at all. Knowing Jaci and I weren't perfect—that I didn't make her as happy as she deserved, that she harbored secret dreams she never told me about—it doesn't make it any easier to not have her here. It highlights how much time I wasted focusing on myself. It's a long-ago memory that I'd pushed to the back of my mind, and I'm not sure I'd have ever thought about it if I weren't flying out to spend the weekend with Raven. And the tri club, of course, but Raven's all I can think about lately.

And I shouldn't be thinking about her. I shouldn't, because I know I'll never be able to love her. Love is not something I'm capable of anymore. Which is exactly why I don't think I can do another relationship. I'll never be good enough to treat someone the way they deserve, to give them what they truly need. If, by some miracle, a relationship does happen, I refuse to be a source of pain in another woman's life.

Raven's face pops into my mind at this, and my stomach hardens. If I can't guarantee I'll make her happy, then what's the point in trying?

I don't think I *can* try.

I don't know.

Maybe . . .

Maybe I should express these concerns to Raven and let her decide. When I let my negative mindset take over, I have the ability to do real damage to the people around me. If races are what it takes to make Raven happy, then I could get behind races. I'd saw my right arm off to be able to curl up beside Jaci in the Edgar Allen Poe room or watch her watch the waves in silence. There's no going back, but I could be better moving forward. I could be the guy that runs the race at Raven's side.

"You okay there, cowboy?" Chris asks, snapping me from my thoughts. I put on a fake, albeit charming smile, and engage in small talk for the rest of the flight. I like Chris and Richelle, mainly because they're the slow ones in the club like me. They make me comfortable and they never judge.

When the pilot announces our drop in elevation, the three of us turn to the window, watching the clouds thin until the ground comes back into view below us. Deep-red clay stares back at us from the tops of rock formations that look more like a painting than real life. Racing here will be a privilege, and I can see why the club picked it for their annual destination event.

The private airport is tiny and located on top of a bluff in the middle of town. When we descend, visions of us crashing into the mountain flash through my mind, but we land without incident and the pilot and co-pilot come out to greet us. I slip them each a tip, and go to help them retrieve the bags from the undercarriage anyway. I don't have to, it's not my job, but I'm antsy and need something to do with my hands.

We roll our bags to the airport entrance and are met by Leonard and Raven, who'd insisted on picking us up in Leonard's truck. I planned on getting a rental car, something big and safe and brand-new, but I was shot down. The club carpools together at these things, all of us crammed up into three or four vehicles to make it easier to find parking. At least Leonard has a decent truck.

"How was your flight?" Leonard asks, giving hugs to each of us.

"Bougie and amazing," Richelle says, patting me on the arm. "I could get used to that. You know I'm an old lady compared to the rest of you. I don't think my bones can fly commercial anymore."

Raven snorts, but then eyes me with curiosity. "Do you always fly private?"

I scratch at my throat and nod, wondering if that's a problem for her. Most women would love that about a man, but I have the feeling she's not like that. She's so down to earth, and probably thinks I'm purposely flaunting my money. I've never cared what anyone thought of my wealth or what I did with it before this exact moment, and I don't know what to do about that.

"Where to first?" Chris asks.

"We're meeting the rest of the club for lunch, dropping bags off at the hotel, and then we have a special hike planned for this afternoon," Raven says. She's been here all week planning things out, and she seems more than a little excited.

"What's a special hike?" I ask.

Her eyes light up when she grins at me. "Just you wait and see."

THE BREEZE MAKES up for the late afternoon heat, and the intermingling scents of the desert and forest are unlike anything I've experienced before. Sage bush, cacti, and thin, twisting pine-like trees dot the landscape as all thirteen of us hike in a long line up the winding dusty trail. It's busier than I expected, and we're passing groups of friendly hikers every few minutes.

When I looked up the Sedona trail system last week, I was surprised to learn that there are over two hundred hikes out here. No wonder it's such a beloved tourist destination. Cathedral Rock must be one of the more popular spots with all these people out here, but even the other hikers can't take away from the beauty of the expansive orange-and-red desert with its deep-blue sky.

It's supposed to be a short hike, which I'm grateful for. Work has been crazy lately, and I'm looking forward to a good night's sleep. Tomorrow we're going on a long bike ride and exploring the downtown area, then Saturday is race day.

We gain elevation as we approach the looming spire-like shapes, and I'm struck by a grand sense of awe. It takes a lot to amaze me, and I'm not easily ruffled, but this place is nothing short of extraordinary. Jaci would've loved it, and I wish she could be here, but I'm grateful to be with friends. To see their faces mirroring mine offers me a sense of belonging. I haven't had that in so long. It's strange to have people outside of my family that care about me, and that I care about too. I had shut myself down so completely after Jaci's death that I lost my friends one by one. And yet here I am again, slowly launching into new relationships.

I have a feeling this trip is about to crack me wide open.

Once we reach the base of Cathedral Rock, which is more like a mountain by Texas standards, Raven gathers the group together. "The climb to the top is challenging but worth it. This spot is famous not only because it's beautiful, but because it claims to have one of Sedona's healing energy vortexes." We exchange nervous glances and Leonard nods enthusiastically as Raven continues. "The land is rumored to bring peace and emotional healing. I ask that you climb this rock in silence and take some time to meditate at the top. After a while, I'll gather everyone together, and we can take some photos with the sunset."

She peers up at the sky with a pleasant smile. "It's scheduled to set in an hour."

It amuses me to no end that Raven has googled the exact time the sun will set. The woman doesn't hope experiences will happen, she *makes* them happen.

From the looks of things, we will be hiking back to the

cars in the dark, and maybe I won't be getting as much sleep as I planned, but I suddenly don't care. I want to do this. I don't know if I believe all the energy vortex stuff, and I definitely wouldn't believe it if I wasn't standing here, but there is something special about this trip. I'll take whatever it has to offer me.

We take off in silent contemplation, and Raven's right that the climb to the top is challenging. She's also right that it's worth it. I hadn't anticipated having to scramble up the face of the path, my palms digging into red rocks, still warm from a day of baking in the sun, but it doesn't take long, and the view is stunning, offering vistas of the whole valley. The sun has already begun its descent, and the sky is the slightest of pinks. Soon, the entire desert will be aglow in reds and purples.

I find a secluded spot on the edge of the rock, away from all the people, and sit. I don't like to meditate. Dr. Thomas has asked me to do it on multiple occasions, and I've tried, but I can't get my mind to slow down. When I close my eyes, it's Jaci's death that runs on a loop behind my eyelids. You can't meditate your way out of that. Maybe it will be different here. Maybe this time when I take a deep breath, I'll go still, the way meditation is intended to be.

But it's no use, the moment I close my eyes my heart speeds and my palms begin to sweat.

Thump, thump, thum-thump--I'm startled by the pounding of drums, turning to find a group of three people further up on the rock. They're each holding a large deer-skin drum with beads of vibrant blue and orange strung around their necks. As they play, everyone on the rock goes reverently silent. Right now, being here, it feels like a gift, and I close my eyes to receive it.

I'm shocked to find that the drums actually help me calm enough to meditate. Or try anyway. They're a steady rhythm, like a low, earthy heartbeat. I get lost in the song, grounded by the music, and I swear I actually understand what Raven means when she says this land has healing energy. Not that I will be saying that out loud anytime soon. Jaci comes to my mind as she always does when I try to relax, but this time I don't stop myself from letting thoughts of her through. Her death, our life, I see it all, but somehow, I'm removed in a way I've never been before. This time it's like she's standing next to me watching these memories, watching her death, and she's not angry. She's not even sad––she's just there.

Please forgive me, I silently beg her. *I'm so sorry.* I have whispered these words inside my head a thousand times, but this time it's different. This time I feel heard, and maybe it's the drums or whatever this vortex thing is, but I swear I hear her lyrical voice whisper in my ear.

There's nothing to forgive. It was an accident.

That bursts my floodgates wide open, and I don't even try to fight the tears. It's all too much. I open my eyes and blink at the horizon of the most beautiful sunset I've ever seen. I don't know how long I've been in meditation, but long enough for the sky to completely transform. It's pink. It's purple. It's nearly blue in places and the gold of the sun setting behind the rock lights everything from behind in ways no camera can capture. I always thought Texas had the best sunsets, but this one is better. It's a stark reminder that I don't know everything, that life has so much to offer, even to someone like me.

Chapter Thirty-Six

RAVEN

I don't say anything to Briggs. No one does. But we get it. We all get it. Whether it's mid-race or mid-life crisis, we all find our breakthrough at some point. I know that moment at the top of Cathedral Rock means something unquantifiable to him. I wish I could ask him to tell me about it. The same way I wish I could ask him to tell me about any number of things in his life, but I don't want to push, not when it feels like we are so close to bringing him back from that edge of self-punishment and grief he's so stuck on living in.

After one spectacular photoshoot with the sunset at our backs, the nine of us head back down to the trailhead and pile into our cars. I know that Briggs is used to private jets, and I'm guessing he and his wife enjoyed a luxury vacation every now and again, but I'm pretty confident that our accommodations are going to blow his mind. Leonard and I have both been doing destination races for years, and that didn't stop our jaws from hitting the floor when we pulled up to the place.

It isn't one of those enormous, multi-floor hotels with too many windows and granite everything. The buildings are red stucco and shaped like the plateaus that form the backdrop surrounding them. The place has three colors. A smattering of green trees with small delicate leaves, lilac-colored bushes that form a barrier between the buildings and the walkways that connect them, and red. Red is everywhere in every shade, from the scarlet trees, to the benches, boulders, sunsets, and most of all, the vista views. I started my morning with a dip in the pool, and to say that it felt majestic is one hell of an understatement.

Our hotel is basically a hidden spa right below the hustle of the touristy main street, and I can think of no better place to prepare for and recover from a race. It's no surprise when we head up to our block of rooms and all I hear behind me is shock and awe.

"This beats the Hilton."

"And the time we went camping," adds Allen.

Everybody laughs, except Briggs, who can't possibly understand the pain and anguish that comes along with that particular set of memories.

"We were young. We were impressionable," says Leonard.

"We were idiots," I say, then turn to catch Briggs' eye. "Someone whose identity shall remain anonymous thought it would be a good idea to camp near the starting line of a full-on triathlon."

"In July," Leonard adds.

"In an area they recommend you bring a bear can to." Allen laughs.

Briggs shakes his head. "I don't even know what that is."

I can't not smile at the memory, despite the fact that it was single-handedly the worst race experience of my life. We're talking two and a half miles swimming, one hundred and twelve miles on the bike, and then a full marathon, after sleeping on the ground in a hot tent.

"It's a can you put your food in and hang from a tree so a bear eats it instead of you. No one slept, and everyone performed terribly."

"I like to think we bonded that night," says Leonard. "But I think that's mostly the PTSD speaking. It's the one and only night I ever spooned with a woman."

Everyone laughs. Every trip is full of memories like that. This one won't be any different. Except I hope we all remember this as Briggs' first destination race with the tri club and not his only. It feels so right to have him here that I can't picture going back to life before his surly ass joined our crew.

We agree to shower the stench of travel and hiking off ourselves before meeting up for dinner on the back patio where the hotel restaurant is ready and waiting. We usually try to go easy on the restaurants when we go out in packs. A table of nine is no easy feat, and the last thing we want is to tick off the staff at meal one of a three-day stay. This place makes it easy on us though. Wood-fired pizza is the entrée, and there are only a few other couples dining out. We score the best table, if you ask me. Instead of being seated in patio chairs like the others, our group scatters around a massive outdoor sectional with a fire pit in the middle and a view of the nighttime desert.

Leonard and Allen are the first to arrive and they have secured us all a bucket of chilled white wine to get us started. We don't get drunk at these things. No one is dumb enough to pay a race fee only to dehydrate yourself before it starts, but we do enjoy one another's company, and a glass of wine is a great way to break the ice, not only for new members, but for those who haven't been social outside their everyday lives in a while.

Pizza has been ordered and the cool breeze wrapping around us has everyone laughing and sharing stories of the races and trips we've shared in the past. I should revel in this perfect evening, but my eyes keep drifting to the open pathways that surround the restaurant. We're missing one important member of our party, the one who broke down during the hike and hasn't said a word since.

Leonard pats my knee. "We're in the middle of the desert and room service is limited to fancy nuts and charcuterie. He'll be here, relax."

I'm wearing the world's cutest black shorts with a white silk blouse that ties around the neck and leaves my shoulders on full display. Someone once told me I had nice shoulders and ever since I've been dressing to highlight them, like scoring a husband is one sleeveless top away. I take a deep breath, trying to relax as Leonard suggests, but it's harder than he makes it sound. Something about Briggs makes me feel like I'm seventeen again and Aaron Michaels is standing across from me at track practice. It didn't matter how much I trained, if our eyes met, I was done for. I was Jello. He was a full assault on my nervous system. To feel that way again at thirty years old is both incredible and awful, just the way I remembered it.

Leonard clears his throat and jerks his chin toward one of the paths. "Damn."

Damn is an unfair assessment. I nearly drop my glass of wine. Briggs Lawson might as well be walking in slow motion; the desert looks so good on that man. His dark hair glistens from his recent shower, his body fills out his clothes like they were tailored for him, and those hazel eyes possess that steady, take-no-prisoners gaze he exudes so well. But none of those things are new, none of those things hold a candle to the visible relief on his face. He looks like he feels ten years younger, and even his movements seem more fluid.

He sits down in the empty space across from me and slides into the group conversation as if he were a part of our club all along, and by the end of the meal, I almost forget that it's only been six months since I met him.

THE POOL IS HEATED like bathwater and lit from below in soft aqua hues. I back float listlessly, cradled by the warm water while staring up at the expansive black sky with its swaths of glittering stars. Although Texas has incredible night skies, the city lights pollute the view. It's rare that I get to partake in star gazing like this. I couldn't resist the temptation to come out here instead of going to bed when everyone else did. We have one more full day tomorrow to be tourists before the race on Saturday, so I let myself have this chance to gather my thoughts.

Only the opposite is happening, and my thoughts drift away on the chilled breeze as I sink deeper into my emotions. I can't deny it anymore. This isn't a crush, it's a beginning, and maybe an undoing.

"I thought that was you." Briggs' deep voice pulls me to the present, and I flip over, my feet searching for the bottom. When did he slip in? The pool is now empty except for me and Briggs. Even the couple making out in the hot tub earlier has found better things to do.

My mouth pops open to say hello but I lose the words. I wasn't expecting company, and this particular company has a way of making me forget things, like apparently how to tread water.

Briggs slips his arms around my waist and pulls me to him. "I've got you." His voice is gravelly and strained.

Every nerve in my body fires. This man is holding me in the deep end, not only literally, but figuratively too. The night is peacefully still, everything quiet save for the trickling of the nearby creek, chirping of the crickets, and catching of our shared breaths.

I'm a swimmer, a runner, and a cyclist. I've been active

my whole life, but right now, I can't breathe. Briggs is in swim trunks, I'm in a bikini, and we're holding each other, skin on skin, our heads barely above water. I say nothing as I lay my body against his, and he swims us to the edge of the pool.

This is it. He's going to kiss me.

Anticipation is both sweet enough to save me and cruel enough to kill me, because I won't make the first move. I deserve to be pursued. And he deserves to *choose* to move on.

He takes me into his arms, holding on tight, chests pressed together, heartbeats as one. I wrap my legs around his waist and his forearms slide down to tighten on my low back. I'm pressed against the side of the pool, heat flooding my system, my mind going blissfully blank. I keep waiting for his head to dip, for his lips to find mine, but they don't. Instead, we stay there against the wall of the pool, all heartbeats and heavy breathing and anticipation.

Eventually, he releases me and walks me to my towel, draping it over my shoulders without a word. I'm deeply disappointed, but not ready to give up, not when we were so close to kissing. He walks me to my door and waits while I slip my keycard in and the light blinks green.

"If I asked you to come in, would you?" I almost can't believe my courage, but I hold his gaze and wait for his reply.

He stares at me like I'm the most desirable woman on the planet. "Do you want me to come into your hotel room, Raven?"

I nod boldly and his gaze darkens. All I can think about is how it would feel to close the door behind us and let his hands do all the things his body signaled they wanted to while we clung together out there under the stars.

"But I'm going to say goodnight instead," I say, and he nods because he understands.

This isn't a rejection. It's patience. It's me waiting for him to make the move, because I deserve that much.

I quickly close myself in my hotel room and lean back against the door, clutching my towel tighter to my body and inhaling quick gasps. I've never wanted anyone like I want Briggs, and I have half a mind to rip the door open and drag him in. *Except* he never kissed me. If he was ready, he would have, and I don't want to tempt him with sex if he's not ready for *everything* that comes with it.

Tonight wasn't about kissing, or all the things that happen after you cross that boundary. Tonight was just as I thought--a beginning. Maybe even a promise. When I finally drift off to sleep, it's with a goofy grin on my face, and dreams of tortured hazel eyes.

Chapter Thirty-Seven

BRIGGS

There are lines that you cross and regret, and lines that you cross with so much enthusiasm it hurts. Taking Raven into my arms tonight, the warm water surrounding us and only an inky black sky to bear witness is something impossible to regret. The pang of guilt I should have at another woman's body pressed up against mine was so fleeting, I barely had time to register it.

I'm not superstitious. I'm barely even spiritual. It's not like I actually believe Jaci was with me at the top of Cathedral Rock. I know the voice I heard allowing me to move on came from within me, not beyond the grave, but I feel changed all the same.

I can't stop smiling as I lace up my cycling shoes and toss on shorts and a t-shirt for this morning's bike ride. The automatic mood boost that comes from getting a good workout in has rewired my brain so that, instead of dreading working out, I crave it. It's laughable now to remember jogging that first morning back home, hurling all over the sidewalk, and breaking down in the shower. It's only been six months, but nowadays I need the run *not* to break down in the shower.

I meet the club in the hotel lobby where everyone is engaged in their pre-workout rituals. Some swear by the caffeine in coffee, while others claim it dehydrates you and adds unnecessary bathroom breaks. Leonard is my favorite because he one hundred percent knows better, but loads up a bagel with cream cheese and bananas anyway.

"It's free," he says through a mouthful. "Stop looking at me with your judgy eyes."

I hold up my hands in surrender, but refuse to stop making exaggerated judgy expressions in his direction as I snag an orange from the breakfast bar. Across the room, Raven is avoiding looking at me. She's got embarrassed, shy girl, written all over her, and it's so out of character that all I want to do is be a jerk and make her blush. So while she's deliberately talking to everyone but me, I'm doing everything possible to get her attention, including blatantly checking her out while I peel my orange over the garbage can.

"Clearly I missed something," Leonard says, filling the space beside me.

I raise my eyebrows suggestively but remain silent long enough for him to shake his head. "You know I'll get it out of her eventually anyway, right?"

I shrug. Apparently, being insufferable is my plan for the day.

The nine of us line up outside the hotel, and Raven leads us through the usual stretching routine, with reminders to fill up our waters. "The desert can sneak up on you," she says.

We wheel our bikes up the little hill in front of the hotel, main street tourists already out in full force despite it only being eight a.m.

Allen takes off first, since he's the fastest of our crew. In the beginning, I was content to get through a workout without wanting to die. Now, I like the idea of improving my speed. I'm not an idiot, though, so I'm not trying to keep up with a guy like Allen.

Raven is taking the rear for today's ride. We're going on a thirty-mile loop through all of Sedona known as Red Rocks, getting a chance to see the different areas, which I've been looking forward to more than the race tomorrow. The whole thing should take a little over three hours, faster if we were in a race, but as we're not, we have to account for traffic lights and we're keeping the group together. As I snap my shoes into my pedals, a surreal sense of awe comes over me. I'm shocked that I can keep up with these people, that I'm even here doing this at all. When I started, I would've thought biking five miles was an accomplishment. Now I'm doing thirty without a problem.

We quickly leave the busy main street behind and head uphill near Munds Mountain. One of the most challenging elevations of the loop is first, which my muscles are none too happy about, but it'll be worth it when we get to coast down the hill and head over to the other side of town.

I make a point to stay near Raven. I'd be one of the back bikers anyway, but I want her to know that I'm purposely sticking close, that I want her as my companion in this. My choice pays off, because I get to see her smile when we reach the different landmarks throughout the area. And it truly is something spectacular. Not even the toughest elevation climbs can ruin the beauty that is this desert forest in the springtime.

The blue sky stretches out seemingly into eternity as we wind our way through Sedona, sticking to bike lanes as often as we can, but sometimes having to ride in the road with the traffic. It makes me edgy, but the cars must be used to driving by cyclists out here because everyone gives us a wide berth. That and we pass several other biking groups as we go, everyone nodding to each other in camaraderie. We're like this exclusive club with the best kept secret. Why explore by car when you can do it like *this*?

A few hours later, we reach the twenty-fifth mile. We're on our way back in through town, and the traffic has picked up considerably. We've left the wonders of the more secluded roads behind and are on one of the main thoroughfares in town, busy little restaurants and hotels dotting both sides.

Raven is now about ten feet in front of me. We keep toggling each other so we can point out the different landmarks. If it weren't for all the others here, it would almost feel like a date. I'm about to catch up to her to trade her again, when she begins to slow ahead of me. I press down on my pedals harder because it feels like she's waiting on me, that or I want her to be. Either way, this is my shot to steal a moment alone with her, so I forgo all training advice and kick it into high gear. It's worth it when I pull up beside her and she smiles.

"Having fun?" She beams.

I nod. "It's amazing." And it really is. Even the cars aren't making me nervous. I didn't think I'd ever feel this good on a road again. "Good job, Raven," I add. "You've outdone yourself with this trip."

She replies with a shy thanks and then slows to take the rear again. I look back for a moment, our gazes locked, when everything seems to go into slow motion. A blue car swerves into the bike lane.

I yell at her to look out, and she turns her handles hard, jetting her front tire toward the sidewalk. Her bike goes careening over the curb and flips, her whole body flying over the handlebars and into the grass on the other side.

The car honks, tires squealing, as it speeds away.

Chapter Thirty-Eight

RAVEN

It happens in a flash. One second, it's just Briggs and I smiling at one another across one hundred feet of road. The next, the car is in my peripheral, the smile on Briggs' face is replaced by a look of sheer terror, and I'm lying in a crumpled mess on the other side of the curb.

God bless grass is all I can think when the world stops spinning. Nothing is broken, and it doesn't feel like anything is even sprained. Except maybe my pride. If I had been paying attention to my surroundings, the way I train each and every member of the tri club to do, I never would have let the car get that close to me. But I wasn't paying attention. I was staring at Briggs, and now he's hovering over me, his face so lined with worry that I feel like I should apologize even though it was me that almost got hit with a car.

"I'm okay," I breathe out, carefully unstrapping my helmet. It's just Briggs and me, the other bikers are further up and have yet to come back for me. It's no matter though, because the look on Briggs' face is pure horror. His eyes are watery, and his mouth is tight as he runs his hands over my body, looking for injury.

His hands are shaking.

I'm not even shaking the way he's shaking.

"Really," I say. "I'm okay. It was just a fall. The car didn't actually hit me."

His breathing grows heavier, faster, labored beyond anything that I've experienced, even in a race. This is a panic attack. I've never had one, but I instantly recognize it.

"Briggs," I try again. "I'm fine. Look."

I sit up and squeeze his hands with mine, then pull them to my heartbeat. "See? I'm okay, breathe with me."

His eyes glaze over, and I swear I hear him breathe her name. *Jaci.* Recognition hits me. Guilt rises in me. He just saw me almost get hit by a car, maybe even thought I was hit, and his mind returned to the worst day of his life.

"I'm not Jaci," I say carefully, squeezing his hands even tighter. His eyes lock on mine and the haze begins to clear. The pain is still evident there, but he's starting to calm down. "Come back, Briggs."

He blinks several times, his breathing finally slowing, when he squeezes my hands back.

Suddenly Leonard is kneeling in the grass beside us, the other club members huddling around us. "A hundred to one, that guy was texting," he growls. "They're always texting when they don't see us. Damned distracted drivers. He could've killed you."

A look crosses Briggs' face that I can't identify. I nod in agreement with Leonard and the quick movement of the nod sends my vision into a sudden tailspin. Things start spinning again, and it occurs to me that while my body might be no more than a little bruised from the neck down, something is definitely not right with my head.

"How many fingers am I holding up?" Leonard asks.

I turn and puke into the grass.

Briggs' eyes go wide with shock. The sun is too bright, the street is too loud and then fuzzy edges and an over-whelming desire to let sleep erase all my problems.

"You can let her sleep now. Good news is, it's not a concussion."

"She puked." I hear Briggs' voice. "And she passed out."

"It's hot out today. How many miles had she ridden before the fall?"

My head is exploding with pain, but I blink my eyes open to find a man in a white lab coat over blue scrubs standing beside my bedside. It all rushes back to me then, the accident, vomiting, passing out, Leonard calling for an ambulance, and Briggs insisting on riding in the back with me to the hospital. Then arriving here, the flurry of activ-ity, the waiting, the tests, Briggs trying to keep me awake.

Me falling asleep anyway.

I carefully gaze up at the doctor, not wanting to move my aching neck. This man doesn't look like he wants to give me drugs with the same fervor that I would like to be given drugs. He looks calm and responsible, like he knows what he is talking about.

Meanwhile, Briggs looks like he has actually been hit by a moving vehicle. His hair is standing up in every direction, his eyes have that haven't-slept-in-days look, and his shoulders are hunched.

I want to tell him to relax, everything's fine. I've fallen off a bike before. I've even almost been hit by a car before. Heck, once I was coasting down a long hill and some idiot parked on the side of the road opened his driver's side door and clotheslined me so hard I had to wear a sling on my shoulder for a week.

"Twenty-five miles, give or take," Briggs answers.

The doctor nods knowingly. "That distance in weather you aren't acclimated to and a tough fall will leave you with a nasty dehydration headache, not to mention the bump on her head, but CT scans don't lie. She'll be okay. The IV fluids and that Tylenol are going to have her feeling better quickly."

Tylenol. I grimace. Somehow it feels like Tylenol isn't going to touch this headache.

"How about Tylenol plus," I mutter, and they turn to look down at me with completely opposite expressions on their faces.

The doctor laughs. Apparently, he thinks I have a sense

of humor. I do not. Not at the moment anyway. And Briggs doesn't either, in fact, he looks like he wants to rip the doctor's head off.

Instead, Briggs slips his hand into mine, and the doctor reassures him one more time that I'm going to be fine. Judging from the look on Briggs' face, he doesn't believe it. According to his face, I've got stage four cancer and the long goodbye is imminent.

"Triathlon rule number one: no flirting on bicycles," I say, trying to lighten the mood after the ER doctor takes his leave of us.

The discharge nurse will be in soon, and I can't wait to go back to the hotel and rest. Well, that, and to check on my bike, which I was promised would be taken back to the hotel for me. My poor baby.

"I don't know what I was thinking." Guilt laces Briggs' tone and my heart drops.

I wanted to make him laugh, but I'm clearly not doing a good job of that. It doesn't help that the pressure in my head makes laughing feel like a real bad idea.

"I'm kidding, Briggs. I'm fine. It was no big deal. If I must go, I'm content for it to be while I'm locking eyes with a hot guy."

Personally, I think this a very clever line, but the reception is still icy cold.

"You could have been killed. He could have hit you, and in twenty seconds, maybe less, everyone you know and love would be getting that call everyone is terrified of getting." There is a tremble in his voice. A shake of his hand in mine.

"But he didn't. I'm fine. You heard the doctor, not even concussed." I squeeze his hand. "Close calls happen."

"They shouldn't though. They can be avoided."

And just like that, that infamous Briggs-barrier comes roaring up between us. The difference is, I won't let it stick around this time.

"Briggs, tell me about what happened to your wife?"

He grimaces and his eyes roam my face, as if searching for something. Does he think I'll judge him for her death? Blame him? He accidentally called me her name on the roadside—it's high time we talked about her.

He sits down on the edge of the bed, and I press the arrow on the control panel to sit up. I want to look him in the eye when he tells me whatever he's about to tell me, because I can feel that it's important. My headache is still roaring, and my neck still hurts to high heaven, but none of that matters to me right now.

I reach out and grip his hand into mine, threading our fingers together. "You don't have to tell me anything if you don't want to, but you were so scared for me when I fell. I want to understand."

His face goes red, and I can tell he wants to argue with me, but instead he lets out a short breath. "Jaci died because I fell asleep at the wheel."

My mouth pops open. I don't know what to say. This is news to me, but so many things make sense now. Why he has so much self-loathing, why he blames himself, why moving on has been so hard for him, why we've had to take it slow between us.

"You can tell me about it," I say softly. "I won't judge you."

I'm still gripping onto his hands like they're my life-line, my tether to Earth, or maybe it's the other way around. Maybe I'm his.

His eyebrows furrow at that last line, a flash of anger lighting his hazel eyes. "You should judge me. I knew better. I was going on thirty hours of no sleep because I was obsessed with a deal we were trying to close. She offered to drive us home from work that evening, but I insisted because of the baby."

I try not to let my face show that I don't know this part, but Jaci being pregnant is a dagger to my heart. He's faced the worst pain imaginable. How is he ever going to move on if he's already lost an entire family?

His lips thin, and he breaks my gaze but hangs onto my hands. "My truck was in the shop. We were in her shitty little sedan. She should've had something nicer, safer. She was the CEO's wife. We had money. But she liked that stupid little car, and I didn't care." His voice cracks. "I didn't care."

"Of course you cared––"

"And she's dead. They're dead, because I fell asleep and drove us headfirst into a highway underpass." He looks back at me, his voice haunted and utterly devastated. "You wanna know the sickest part? I was fine. Walked away with a partial tear in my rotator cuff, but that was it. Not Jaci. Not the baby. They died on impact. I woke up and saw Jaci like that, her skull crushed, blood everywhere. She was alive and then she was dead in an instant, because of me."

"It's not your fault."

"It is. Please don't say that it's not because I know it is." Tears are running down his face now. Mine too. Terrible, heartbreaking, unfair tears. "I've made peace with that. I'll always blame myself, never forgive myself, but I know Jaci would forgive me. That's who she was. It should've been me, not them."

The *them* strikes me. I've spent all this time thinking he is mourning her alone, when he's been grieving both the life they had, and the one they were going to bring into the world.

"Don't say that," I whisper. As messed up as the world is. I can't imagine mine without Briggs in it.

He drops my hands and leans forward, the rough pads of his thumbs swiping the tears from my cheeks. I do the same for him, wishing more than anything that I could take this pain from him.

"Why not? It's the truth."

I don't know what else to say. I wish nobody had to die that day.

He takes a deep breath. "But I've also realized that she would want me to move on." Our eyes lock. Red rimmed. Full of hurt. Full of hope. "So that's what I'm going to try to do. I don't know if I can, but I'm going to try. If there was one thing Jaci wanted, it was for me to be happy, even when I didn't deserve it."

"You *do* deserve it."

He shakes his head slightly. "I don't, Raven. I really don't."

Chapter Thirty-Nine

BRIGGS

In all of my years on this planet, I've never touched a
tarot card. I've never cared to, and to see them
splayed out in front of me now feels like a party
trick.

"Pick three cards," the wizened man sitting across
from me says in a matter-of-fact tone. He looks like he
stepped out of a Renaissance Festival, and I'm not sure
what to think. Is he faking it? Is this real? Is it fake, but he
thinks it's real? Maybe it doesn't really matter, because it's
not as if I'm going to be making life changes based on a
few tarot cards.

"Any cards?" I ask. "Or left to right? Right to left?"

His crinkly eyes narrow on me. "You can't mess
this up."

Oh, is my unhealthy perfectionism so obvious? I hold

back an eye roll as I slide three random cards from his spread. He puts them to the side, then gathers the other cards back into a neat pile. He flips over the first card, and a frown drags his features down. All I can think is, thank God I'm alone in this shoebox of a room with him. I'm not fond of the idea of my fortune being read in front of everyone in the tri club.

Raven booked us thirty-minute sessions at Sedona's most famous metaphysical shop, taking whatever they had available so everyone could participate. Some of us are doing card and psychic readings, others are meditating in a futuristic-looking machine called a crystal light bed, and Leonard boldly went upstairs to meet his spirit guides.

Whatever that means.

I have no idea about anything here, let alone the massive crystal shop we walked into to meet the "energy workers," but after yesterday's events, I'll do whatever it takes to make Raven feel happy with this trip. And right now, our foray into this Metaphysical Disneyland is top of her list.

At least it's something to keep us busy before our race tonight. I was afraid she would want to get back on her bike this morning for another ride. I'm making her buy a new helmet before that happens, and if she won't buy one, then I'm buying it for her. Preferably a techy one that calls an ambulance the second it detects an impact.

"In your past, you experienced catastrophic change," the card reader says. My heart rate picks up, and I lean over to take a better look at the card. 'The Tower' is written across the top of a cartoon depiction of a stone tower being struck by lightning, men and women falling out of it. Or maybe they jumped, considering the tower is on fire.

"This would've been something massive and probably painful, like a divorce or a death," he says.

I click my tongue. "Okay, you got me there." That's all I'm going to say, and if he prods me for more information, I won't say a thing. That tower card could've been a coincidence. "Let's see what else you've got for me."

"This is your card for the present," he says, moving on to the second card I drew. "The Moon is here to warn you that things are not as they seem, and you may be lying to yourself about something. It's a call to trust the universe to help you through your life instead of resisting change."

I stare down at the card, glaring at the bright yellow sun with the grinning moon character inside of it. Two doglike animals are barking up at it, and a crab sits at the base of a stream. I have no idea how to decipher what any of this means, but I don't like the look of it.

The man's eyes narrow on me. "Is there something in your present that you could be missing?"

My gut hardens and I wave my hand. What a dumb question because if I knew what that was, I wouldn't be missing it in the first place.

"And what about the third card? Let me guess, that's my future?" I ask dryly.

"Indeed it is. But you must know, the cards reflect where you are at when you do a reading. Not much in this life is completely set in stone. You're in charge of your own destiny."

Tell that to the people who lose their lives early in senseless accidents. I lean back and level this guy with my CEO-stare. "If that's the case, then why read tarot cards at all? It seems self-indulgent."

"They're a guide," he says. "They won't tell you anything you don't already know, but they'll help you to gain clarity when you're feeling conflicted or unable to see the forest through the trees."

I guess that makes sense, and I'm not really here to be a dick and insult this man's profession, so I backpedal. "Fair enough. Let's see my future card."

He flips it over to a depiction of a man and woman standing hand in hand with the words 'The Lovers' written across the top. Raven instantly flashes to my mind, which in turn sends a wave of guilt through me for not thinking of Jaci first. But it's impossible for Jaci to be in my future, even if I know I'll always carry her memory with me. Raven . . . she could be another great love of my life. It's so strange to me how much my thinking has shifted in the past few weeks. *Another* great love, not *the* great love. Somehow, I've gone from Jaci's end being the end of all love for me, to accepting the possibility that there might be other loves left in my life.

I reach for the card and accidentally bump the stack of cards next to it in the process. A card slides off the top and the card reader flips that one over as well, but I'm too busy looking at The Lovers to notice.

"There is new love on your horizon," he says with a smile. "But it comes at a price." He slides over the extra card for me to get a better look. It's upside down and I tilt my head to read 'The Hanged Man'.

"I don't know what any of this means." I toss the lovers card back onto the table and lean back in my chair, the start of a headache coming on.

"The Hanged Man represents a stuck and unhappy situation, but when you get the reversal as you did, it means something else entirely––it's telling you to be willing to see this relationship in a new perspective, but it's also warning you not to rush into things before you come to this new *and positive* perspective."

Okay, I see what he did there, adding emphasis to the word positive. I must carry around a metaphorical sign that reads, 'Beware: I'm a grumpy asshole.'

"And what's the new perspective I'm supposed to take in this new relationship?" Because I'm pretty sure Raven has changed my mindset tremendously over the last six months, and I don't know what I'm missing.

"I can't answer that. Only you can." He nods to the cards. "Unless you'd like to ask for further clarification?"

I almost give into the ambiance of the dimly lit, incense-filled room, the confident attitude of the card reader, and the seductive idea that tarot can answer all my questions. Particularly troublesome questions having to do with this new woman in my life that I can't seem to stop thinking about, that I'm not sure I'll be able to love the way she deserves to be loved.

But I temper myself. No matter how accurate this reading has been so far, I'm the one making decisions for my life, not a stack of cards.

"I think this is good enough for me. You've given me a lot to think about. Thank you."

"Do you have any other questions? We still have ten minutes."

I take a look at the reading one more time, committing the four cards to memory: The Tower, The Moon, The Lovers, and the reversed Hanged Man which he's laid across The Lovers card like a warning.

"These are all major arcana, which are significant cards in tarot. When someone pulls even one of these in a reading, I give it more weight than the lesser cards."

"So, does that make me special?" I'm not mocking him, I'm mocking myself.

"We're all special," he says sagely. "But the messages of these cards hold importance in your life right now. You came from troubled times, you're in the middle of change, and you have a new romantic relationship on the horizon." He taps the reversed Hanged Man. "But you must remember to look for a new and positive perspective if you're going to make that relationship work."

"So being a self-loathing asshole isn't attractive?" I joke.

"It's not." He laughs. "Please be mindful that there is something important you're denying yourself right now." He slides the moon card closer to me. "Figure it out and change it." He picks up the lovers card. "Or jeopardize this."

I blink at him. Coming in here, I was apprehensive. During the reading, I was cautiously optimistic. But now? I'm confused. And a little frustrated. Because what is he talking about? What could I be doing wrong?

I don't like it when people get in my head like this. It's not something I allow. Not in my career. Not in my personal relationships. Not ever.

I tell the guy some bullshit about remembering this reading and putting it into practice, then I get up to leave and he walks me back into the main area of the shop. He puts his hand on my shoulder. "You said so yourself that being a self-loathing asshole isn't attractive. Perhaps you already know what you need to change?"

And then he's gone, leaving me alone with my thoughts and about ten-billion crystals lining the walls. They're everywhere. So are the tall witchy-looking candles, and the hoards of knickknacks that aren't my thing but I admit have a certain draw to them.

I head out back to the gravel parking lot and walk down to a park bench that faces the red rocks in the distance. A sense of calm washes over me just from being out here instead of back in there with tarot cards trying to tell me how to live my life. I take a seat and allow myself to think about what happened objectively.

Objectively, a lot of it made sense.

And a lot of it didn't . . .

So what's the point of worrying about it? Except that

maybe he was right, and I nailed it on the head the first time. If I go into a relationship with Raven while beating myself up the entire way, she's going to be brought down by me. She's going to get tired of it. She's going to leave . . .

Raven's voice trickles over from the parking lot, and I jump up to go find her, to ask her how her reading went, to maybe tell her about mine. She wasn't doing a card reading, she was sitting down with someone who actually claimed to be a psychic, and I have no idea what the experience would've been.

"She immediately picked up on my desire for a family." I hear her say. "She knew I was a teacher, if you can believe it, and she said that I'm such a good teacher because I'm maternal by nature."

"And what did she say about children?" Richelle asks enthusiastically. "Any in your future?"

"It was a maybe." Raven's voice is raw with emotion, and I step back. I shouldn't be eavesdropping on something like this.

I didn't know Raven wanted to be a mother, but it makes sense. She'd be an amazing mother. People don't become kindergarten teachers if they hate kids, and training our sorry asses takes a mountain of patience.

What does that mean for me though? For us? I'm terrified of seeing someone through another pregnancy. I stopped picturing myself as a father when I lost them. What if I can't be that person again? Raven deserves much better than a self-loathing asshole dragging everyone down.

Maybe this is part of why I don't want to try to read

the future. Hoping for these things can hurt people. You think things are going to go a certain way, and it seems like a guarantee that your life will follow the map you created for it, but then something happens and everything changes. Your map is out of date, and you're headed in the wrong direction--right over a cliff into shark-infested waters. So what's the point of trying to plan the future when nothing is guaranteed? I was going to be a father once and it was ripped away. I catch Raven's eyes across the lot, and she smiles at me, so full of hope, so oblivious to the fact that I'm not the compass she thinks I am.

Chapter Forty

RAVEN

When I planned this trip, a nighttime swim spent wrapped in Briggs' arms and an afternoon lying in the emergency room were not included. I wouldn't change it though. Not even the part where a car nearly wiped me off the face of the earth. If it weren't for that driver, I might have spent the next three months dancing around the skeletons in Briggs' closet. Lord knows I wasn't getting any closer to asking him for the truth.

This race, though, it's not going in any record books. I won't be getting a PR or pushing myself the way I intended to when I plunked down the hefty race fee and opted for the fancy t-shirt and baseball cap combo that only the early registrants get.

The truth is, concussion or no concussion, the headache from yesterday's fall comes roaring back to life whenever I exert myself. And as much as I would love to be a competitor in my age division, I don't want to spend any more of this trip in the emergency room. I barely got through my psychic reading this morning, and it was completely uplifting. One hundred percent my type of activity.

It's not so bad though, running a little slower means I can pace Briggs, and it's a fun thought, crossing the finish line with him in his first half-marathon. Those first-time finishes have a way of locking themselves in your memory. As Briggs' coach, my goals for him have changed from completing races and improving times to overcoming his own self-loathing. Replacing the memories that haunt him with something to be proud of is my secret strategy, and tonight's race is step one of the process.

Night races are a whole different animal. You have to shake up your routine a little. For some it's an easy fix, for others like Allen, it messes with your head. He will no doubt spend the thirty minutes before the race stress pooping in the porta potty. I'm not sure how Briggs will handle the change, but we've discussed it in training, and as long as he was listening, we should be in good shape.

The club grabs a light dinner at a soup and salad buffet in downtown Sedona before returning to the hotel to get into our running gear. I can't help it, my chest purrs at the sight of Briggs with a race number pinned to his chest and a nervous smile. I know he is ready, but he doesn't, and the concern on his face is adorable. I eye the fuel belt strapped to his waist. He hates the thing. It looks like a seatbelt with six little water bottles strapped to it. Each is shaped like a flask and holds no more than six ounces, but we runners swear by them for good reason. Nobody wants to find themselves in the middle of the desert with no water.

"You've got this," I assure him. "It will be like a Saturday session, long and arduous, but not impossible."

"Saturdays end with coffee," Briggs says. "And no one takes pictures of you or posts your mile times on the internet for the world, and siblings to see."

"You think Turner is going to waste his time googling your results?"

Briggs lets out a hearty laugh. "Are you kidding me? Turner has probably invested in one of those apps that tracks your runner the whole distance of the race. He's probably at home right now, staring at his phone. Waiting for me to get started so he and Griffin can have a good laugh later."

"That's dark. And I don't see Turner out here, do you?"

Briggs shrugs. "Brothers are born competitors, so don't be surprised when either one happens."

I know that Briggs is joking, and he loves his family, but I wish he knew how incredibly lucky he is to have them. I'd give anything to have a sister to race with, or even hold doofy signs at the finish line. Growing up an only child was lonely and not much has changed. If my biological clock doesn't stop me, and yesterday's psychic was on point, I am definitely going to fill my household with children. I want them to grow up with all the things I never had, including bickering.

The cloudy sky is lit up in streaks of neon when the race finally starts. We'll be lucky to get an hour of light before we have to turn on our headlamps, but that's part of the fun. It gets incredibly dark in the desert. The night sky will be amazing once it's all that is left to light our way.

The runners take off, but I stick to the back, barely at a jog. I've got my club separated into three pacing groups, and I watch the fastest group leave the rest of us in the dust, Allen leading the pack. They're all fast, but I expect Allen to break away toward the end of the half and go for the win. He's been the fastest on the team for a while and has a real chance at making a name for himself as an amateur triathlete if he wants to. He insists that he doesn't care about that stuff, but I suspect he's just being loyal to our club. We're like a second family to him, and we always will be, but anyone else as good as Allen could've ditched my club for one of the more competitive ones years ago. We don't have big sponsors, and he's good enough to get placed with a team that can connect him to amazing opportunities.

Not for the first time, I vow to have a mama-bird conversation with him about it. We've had the same conversation twice before, but I really think next season he needs to give himself that chance to fly. I frown, my heart already aching at the thought of losing one of my favorite longtime clients.

"Are you feeling okay?" Briggs asks.

"I'm fine." I nod toward the pacing group ahead of me. "Go up with the others. I'll see you at the finish line."

He gives me a dark glare. "Do you really think I'd leave you back here? You have a head injury."

"I do *not* have a head injury."

"And this is a night run. It'll be pitch-black within the hour out here."

We round a corner and begin to descend the steepest incline on the route tonight. Right now we're still in town, but a lot of this race will take place on a dirt road through a nearby ranch. It's part of why the club picked this race—we really get to be out in the elements. When Kate said she hoped for an alien encounter, I thought she was joking, but then she proceeded to tell us all about the people who believe aliens frequent the area at night. I wonder if she's up ahead somewhere with her arms wide open yelling, "beam me up!"

"I'm not leaving you alone in the dark," Briggs says. He's being dead serious about this, and while I can see why Briggs might be concerned, these race committees do a great job of keeping people safe. There will be aid stations along the route and reflective markers to make sure nobody gets lost out here, alien abductions included. Not to mention, there are people of all levels racing tonight. I'll never be alone.

But I can tell by the concerned and slightly pissed-off look on his face that there's no arguing with him about this. I release a long sigh and nod. "We can stick together."

His eyes drop to my mouth for the briefest of seconds and my insides jump. "Don't sound so disappointed."

Oh, I'm not disappointed . . .

We run side by side from there, sometimes chatting with each other or the people around us, but mostly listening to the sound of our breathing and the slap of our running shoes on the pavement. By the time we turn onto the ranch's dirt road, we're on mile five, and it's time to turn on our headlamps.

Something about the bright beams flashing over the landscape makes my headache flare, and I slow down.

"I've got to walk for a minute," I mumble.

I don't point to my head, but he gets it. When has Briggs ever seen me slow down? We fall back from the other runners, edging along to the side of the gravel so that others can pass. When our hands brush, he slips his long fingers through mine.

We've held hands before. In the hospital, in the pool, but there is something different about tonight. Not for the first time, I wonder what his tarot reading revealed. The fact that he participated at all left me reeling. I shouldn't ask, but we're walking, racers streaming past us, no one to overhear the conversation, and I want to know what he experienced. Every moment of this trip has taught me something new about Briggs, and I feel like he's been learning just as much about himself as I have.

"So uh, past, present, future. Anything I should know about?"

It's dark, and I've turned off my lamp to keep my head from exploding. Still, I can see the corners of his lips turn up in a reserved smile.

"I shared my past with you in that hospital bed. I know you hit your head and all, but I like to think it was memorable."

"Spill," I grumble.

"There was a lover and a hanged man and something about imminent death."

I can feel the color draining from my face. Suddenly the desert doesn't feel so safe, aid stations or not. If Briggs gets bit by a rattlesnake, could I get him to safety before poison ravages his body?

Briggs grabs me by the shoulders and turns me so that his headlamp shines directly into my eyes.

"That was a joke, Raven. You were supposed to laugh."

It's not funny to me though. I've had enough tarot readings to know that big ideas come from them, life altering ideas. He must see it on my face because he shakes his head and places his hand back in mine.

"Look, I don't know what to believe. The desert is a weird place. I've got drummers making me cry on top of a plateau, dudes I've never met before telling me what lies ahead, and you."

"And me?"

"Yeah, and you, making me want to kiss you every time we stop long enough to think straight."

It's a bold move and I know it, but I stop right then and there, planting my feet on the dusty road. I reach up and snag the headlamp from his forehead, click the light off.

And then I wait.

The two of us stand there unmoving, everything around us pitch-black, save for what little light the moon casts on the edges of trees, boulders, and Briggs' cheekbones. I can feel his sharp eyes studying me, the way mine study him. His hands slide from my palms to my forearms and continue upward, leaving a trail of goosebumps on my skin as one hand slips free and wraps around the small of my back to pull me closer to him. So close that I can hear his soft, ragged breathing and feel his heart pounding from inside his ribcage, a nervous insistent hammering that has nothing to do with the fact that we are six miles into this race.

All that remains is the gap between our lips. I badly want to reach up onto my toes and bring his mouth to mine, but just like outside of my hotel room, my brain warns my body that I can't be the one to make the move. I can't force Briggs to move on. He has to choose to do it on his own.

The light from another runner's headlamp flashes in the corner of my eye. I expect Briggs to step back and continue walking like the last thirty seconds weren't one big bag of sexual tension, but he doesn't. He grips my waist and hefts me off the ground like I weigh nothing, and before I know what is happening, the two of us are hiding behind the trunk of the nearest tree. My back presses against the bark as his lips crush into mine. There's so much urgency in his kiss, so much passion, so much *everything*, that it steals my breath, and I have to wrap my arms around his neck to keep from falling.

Chapter Forty-One

BRIGGS

She's perfect. Her plump lips, her grasping hands, her warm body, her soft breath, her honey scent—alone each of those would make me want her, but combine them together, and I need her. I thought I'd buried this feeling three years ago, but it's consuming me now. I'm underwater, drowning in her. If Raven is the ocean, then I never want oxygen again.

She tightens her arms around my neck, and I deepen the kiss. A moan escapes her lips, and my body goes hard, aching for her. I'm not about to have sex with her up against the tree with so many people running past us, but if we were alone, I wouldn't hesitate to take this as far as she'd let me.

"Tell me what you want." I lean in, whispering against her ear. My lips brush the velvet soft lobe of her lower ear, and I fight the urge to take it into my mouth and tease another one of those moans from her lips.

Later. I'll do that later, when we're really alone.

Her voice catches when she says three small words. "This. You. Us."

"I want that too." My lips travel to her collarbone. It's a delicate bone, nothing like her. She's so strong, so powerful. But I love this spot on her. It's something that others don't get to experience. I run my tongue along it, tasting her salty skin, and briefly suck on her neck. I have the sudden urge to mark her, which makes me feel like a teenager again. That surprises me.

She squeals and pulls her neck back, her hands sliding down under my shirt to press against my stomach, her nails biting into the flesh above my shorts. Thank God I didn't wear that awful biking leotard thing, or I wouldn't be experiencing this right now.

I return the favor, unzipping her top inch by inch. She doesn't stop me. She's only got a black sports bra underneath, which is sexy as hell against her creamy skin. *That* I can see in the darkness, and it's enough to make me reconsider the whole having sex against a tree thing. My hands slide around her back, and I push her back to the tree again. I use the little sounds she's making as my roadmap for how far I can take this, which isn't nearly far enough.

She breaks away a few minutes later to catch her breath. "We've still got eight miles to go."

I don't know what to say to that. I couldn't care less about those miles. I'd stay out here all night if she'd let me.

"Do you want to keep going?" My voice is low, barely above a whisper, filled with lust, and her body shudders.

"Yes," she says. "To both."

She doesn't have to clarify. She wants to keep going with me and she wants to finish the race.

It nearly kills me, but I zip her jacket up, take her hand in mine, and walk her back to the dirt road. "How's your head?" I ask, trying to distract myself from the roughly one thousand non-race related thoughts that are coursing through my brain.

Not that I don't care. I do care. It's just parts of me are having trouble focusing on anything other than parts of her.

"I'm much better." She turns on her headlamp and shoots me a cheeky grin that makes my insides flip. "Let's run. My adrenaline is pumping. Would you happen to know anything about that?"

What I want to say is *there's blood pumping in places that aren't going to feel awesome while running.* But I suck it up and give her a sardonic wink because right now I would chase this woman anywhere, raging case of blue balls or not.

Now that my mind has crossed that line between thinking about Raven sexually as prohibited and thinking about sex with Raven as a possibility, I can't stop thinking about it. Is she ready for that? Am I? *Yes. I am.* But does she know I am? Should I say something? Invite her to my room tonight? Wait until we get back to Texas tomorrow? She has to drive home, so I won't actually be able to see her until Monday. I can wait as long as she wants, but I don't want to wait. I want her now. Hell, I wanted her ten minutes ago. Actually, let's be honest, I wanted her months ago.

These questions bounce around in my head, driving me mad. By the time we make it to the finish line, I don't know the appropriate move to make. It's been so long since I've been with someone, and I've only ever slept with one woman in my life. Jaci was my first, who I thought would be my only, but now I want Raven to be my next, maybe my last. I feel completely insane even thinking about it. I steal a glance at her crossing the finish, a big smile illuminated under that cheesy headlamp. What I wouldn't give to know what thoughts are coursing through her adrenaline-filled head right now.

I'm pretty sure, based on her physical response at mile five, that an invitation to her hotel room isn't off the table, but sex, though very appealing at the moment, isn't what I want from her. I want more. I want the new love that those damned tarot cards said I could have. *If* I see things with a new perspective––translation: if I don't mess things up.

SOMEWHERE BETWEEN THE HUGGING, sweating crowds of finishers and the car ride back to the hotel, I decide to handle things in true Briggs' fashion. I get weird and distant. When I fake a yawn and excuse myself to my room without the slightest hint of what transpired between us, I catch Leonard and Raven giving each other the look. The look that says, *He's back*.

The truth is, I want this too badly to let hormones and a serious dry spell dictate where things end up. If Raven and I were to wake up next to one another in the morning, there are only two possible outcomes. One, the heavens open and Barry White starts writing new bedroom anthems in our honor. Or two, I flip out, schedule an emergency session with Dr. Thomas, possibly sweat through the hotel sheets, and scare Raven into celibacy.

The thing is, both options feel equally viable.

I try to fall asleep, but I can't stop thinking about the feel of her skin against my lips and the promise that it will happen again and again and again, just as soon as I get my shit together.

A soft knock sounds on my door and I don't have to guess who it is. For a moment, I feel a little stuck––if I let her in, what will happen between us? Will I disappoint her? But if I don't let her in, I'll definitely disappoint her, and that's the last thing I want to do.

I open the door.

She's standing there in an oversized hoodie and pajama shorts, her hair wet from the shower, and looking as adorable as usual.

"Hi," she says carefully. "I wanted to check on you. Can I come in?" Her cheeks go pink.

"Of course." I open the door wider and seeing her in my hotel room with the unmade bed only steps away from us, becomes a test in self-control.

She tucks a strand of that wet hair behind her ear and gazes up at me. "I just wanted to say that if tonight was a mistake and you only want to be friends, just friends, I'll understand, and I won't hold it against you."

She worries her bottom lip between her teeth and her pretty eyes go wide as she searches mine. I'm not sure what she sees in them. Does she regret what happened? Does she want to only be friends?

"But personally," she continues, "I don't regret it. I'm glad we kissed, and I'd like to do it again."

This woman.

I wanted her before, but now? Now, I need her. Taking her hand and squeezing, I whisper her last name like it's a confession. "Oliver . . . " I drop a soft kiss to her mouth before forcing myself to pull away. "I don't regret it either. I can't believe I'm saying this, but I'd like to take it slow."

She nods and the smile that brightens her face is so radiant it puts the sun to shame. "Just because I'm a triathlete doesn't mean I can't go slow, you know." She kisses me again. Quick. Just a peck. As if to prove her point. "I can definitely go slow. In fact, I love slow. Slow is great."

My smile mirrors hers. "Slow is great," I say. "But not too slow . . . What are you doing Monday night?"

Chapter Forty-Two

RAVEN

It has been one month since I officially jumped on the roller coaster that is Briggs Lawson. Metaphorically that is. We still haven't sealed the deal, and I'm beginning to wonder if he got bit by some kind of desire-busting reptile out in the desert and refuses to come clean about his new pious lifestyle. I mean, I know he wants to go slow and all, but so far we've only kissed, and never as passionately as our first kiss. Is something wrong with me? Or maybe his definition of slow and mine are two different things.

"I have tried all the things to seduce this man."

"All the things?" asks Remi. Her eyebrow quirks up suggestively, and I glance around the teacher's lounge to make sure no one is in earshot before answering.

"The other night I purposely wore no underwear and exited his truck like early days Brittany."

She covers her mouth to keep from spewing egg salad sandwich across the table.

"Nothing. No reaction. It was like he was vagina immune."

"Surely this is not attempt number one."

"Ha, not even close. At this point, I'm running out of tactics."

Remi shakes her head in disbelief. "You know what it takes to make my husband want to have sex?"

I both want to know and do not want to know. Seeing as how her husband is someone I see on a fairly regular basis and imagine has a very hairy back.

"I'll take any and all advice."

Remi sighs. "Anything. It takes anything. We have sex like once a month because I'm so exhausted at the end of the day. I could tell him I have a horribly debilitating disease that is spread by sex, and sex alone, and the man would be like, that's okay, let's risk it. He's so deprived."

I can feel my face falling into a pout without my permission.

Remi slides a hand across the table and rests it on my forearm just before my head hits the table. A few good bashes feel like the right answer.

"Briggs isn't me. I strongly doubt the man does not want to have sex with you. There has to be more to it. You two wouldn't be on this six-month slow burn if he didn't ultimately want you." She lowers her voice to a whisper when third-grade teacher Mr. Simmons comes crashing into the room in search of his customary mid-morning easy mac. Remi squeezes my arm. "All of you."

I know she's right, but I feel defeated each and every time one of our dates ends with a chaste kiss goodnight.

"So no more looking sad. Back to the war path." She straightens her spine and narrows her eyes. "What's your next move?"

I feel ridiculous saying it out loud, but I do, in fact, have a plan for the evening.

"I went to one of those weird passion parties and bought this pheromone perfume that is supposed to render men helpless. Love potion style, but for sexy time."

"And how did that work out?"

"I'll tell you Monday. We're having Sunday dinner with my parents, and I'm going drenched in the stuff."

She snorts. She actually snorts. "Dinner with your parents is your aphrodisiac?"

Maybe she has a point.

"So, Briggs," my mother says over her meal. "Tell us about yourself. What do you do for work? Where do you live? What's your family like?"

It's a total farce. I'm certain my parents googled Briggs and formed a strong opinion the second I told them I wanted to introduce them to my boyfriend.

Lawson, like Lawson Construction Enterprises?

Yes, that Lawson.

How very capitalist . . .

We're sitting around the dinner table, and I can hardly touch the lasagna because I'm so nervous that Briggs isn't going to like them. Most people would be nervous that it would be the other way around, but I already don't care what my parents think of Briggs. They're impossible to please. They don't like me all that much, and I'm their own child.

Their only child.

The way I see it, Briggs is the one with the amazing family. Anyone would be lucky to be brought into a family like that. In my case, family is more of a detriment to what I have to offer than an asset. It's like that line in *Pride and Prejudice* where Elizabeth overhears Darcy slamming her poor connections and embarrassing family. I mean, sure, it's a dick thing to do, but he voiced what everyone was already thinking. What I need is cool siblings to help soften the blow, but it's like my parents realized they sucked at the job and stopped with me. I can't blame them for that. At least I have great friends. There's always that. Briggs loves my friends.

As Briggs describes himself, I study my parents' expressions. Nobody can read them like I can, and while dad may look interested, he's judging, and though Mom appears friendly, she's actually bored. This is how they are. Unless you're intellectually able to discuss highbrow topics, you're not on their level. Simple as that.

"Very impressive," my father says evenly when Briggs finishes explaining his position as CEO. "And what do you think of the Colorado River restoration project? Do you approve, or would you have rather seen something else done?"

It's a trick question, I'm sure of it, but before I can intervene, Briggs jumps into a detailed explanation as to why the river needs to be preserved in a certain way. Whatever judgment my parents harbored for him dissolves, and the three get into a lively discussion about water preservation laws. My nerves dampen enough to eat, and it's just as I'm finishing my plate when things take a turn.

"Maybe you can talk to Raven for us about pursuing her master's degree," Mom says, as if she just had a novel idea, "get some of that career ambition to rub off on her."

Briggs sets down his fork with a soft clatter. "I'm sorry?"

Dad follows Mom's lead. "For years we've been telling her she's wasted as an elementary school teacher. She's an excellent teacher, no doubt, but she ought to come over to the land of academia, follow in her parents' footsteps and really put that brain to work."

My cheeks flame and I glare at my parents. This isn't a new conversation. I'm so used to this wound between us that I've forgotten to care that it never stops bleeding.

It's not familiar territory to Briggs, though, and whatever show he was putting on for my parents moments ago vanishes with the remainder of my lasagna. The silence is thick. Briggs slides his chair out and stands, then he helps me up as well. He doesn't say a word. Mom and Dad stare up at us, confused, though I can't say why. Shouldn't they know they're being assholes? You'd think they would, but they truly think they're pushing me to a better life for myself instead of accepting that I'm happy where I am.

Mom jumps up. "Let me grab dessert."

"That won't be necessary," Briggs says gruffly. "We're leaving now. But let me be clear, if this were my house, I'd be asking you to leave."

My parents exchange haughty looks, as if to say:

Oh yes, his true colors.

He's a controlling asshole.

No good for our daughter.

Lord, how they love to be right, even when no one else in the room seems to share the same view.

He takes my hand into his and squeezes once as if asking for permission, or maybe for forgiveness, because what he says next rocks me to the core. "How can you not be proud of Raven and all she's accomplished?"

Dad stands as well. "Well, now, hold up. You've known her for a matter of months. I hardly think you're in a position to tell us how to raise her."

Briggs laughs cagily. "Raise her? She's already been raised, and look at her now, she's incredible. She's the best kindergarten teacher at her school." He turns to lock eyes with me. "Possibly on the planet."

I can't keep the blush from filling my cheeks. Am I the best kindergarten teacher on the planet? Probably not, but does that statement make me feel like royalty coming from Briggs' mouth? That's a hard yes.

"And I'll have you know," he says, "that's just as important as teaching at a stuffy university. Maybe more so. I'm sure with all of your combined years of education, I don't have to be the one to tell you that the first five years of brain development have a larger impact than the rest of a human's life."

My parents look taken aback, and I'm dying to burst into applause, sitcom style, but I keep it together because the man is not finished and I'm ready and willing to lap up every intelligent, sexy, thing he has to say.

"And what's more," his voice rises, "she's an amazing triathlete and coach. She's built something most people could never even dream of, and she does it with grace and tenacity and hard work."

I know that I should say something to end this conversation. Let Briggs off the hook and lower the tension, but I can't think straight anymore. Something painful unlocks inside my heart, pain at the way my parents have judged my life choices over and over and over again. They don't even really know me and haven't tried. Conforming to their beliefs about my life was all they wanted of me, and never once did they try to view things my way. I have spent years acting okay with it. Countless dinners spent playing the part and excusing their comments and lack of affection as par for the course. But witnessing Briggs' reaction shakes me. Can everyone see how wrong it is that they don't acknowledge who I am and only who they want me to be?

Mom wrings the cloth napkin between her hands. Her knuckles going white from the tension. "We're very proud of our daughter, but we know her better than anyone and we want the best for her."

"You don't know me better than I know myself." It takes every ounce of courage I have to get the words out. "I love what I do. I love teaching young children, I love children in general, *and* I love coaching."

Mom waves her hand. "You could still do triathlons. What you *need to do* is drop the coaching hobby and focus on your teaching career."

Drop the coaching *hobby*. She says it like I'm sixteen and choosing my garage band over college.

"No." My voice razor-sharp, maybe for the first time in my life. "I'm done hearing your opinion on this. Not only have I not asked you for your opinion, but you haven't earned the right to give it. Maybe if you'd come to my teaching events or my races, supported me in this even once, I would be open to listening." I glare at them both and my vision blurs with hot tears. "But you haven't even tried to see *why* I love what I do. What do you know about my coaching career or my teaching career?"

Dad bristles. "We know that you can barely afford that apartment, and Austin isn't getting any cheaper. What happens when they raise your rent again?"

I could scream. My parents have dedicated their entire lives to academia, and it's not like they are rolling in money as a result. They may not know me, that's painfully obvious, but I've understood my parents my whole life and this conversation is going nowhere.

"If you can't support me, so be it. You two are welcome to spend the rest of the evening judging me, but you can do it alone. We're not sticking around to listen." I squeeze Briggs' hand back this time. "Let's go."

Chapter Forty-Three

BRIGGS

I don't know what I thought would happen at dinner. Jaci's parents met me as a nervous, sweaty kid. Back then I kept my mouth shut and responded to everything with "yes, sir," and "thank you, ma'am." And they loved me from day one. It was different with Raven's parents. Not just because I am older, but because they didn't behave like parents should. Not the kind of parents I had anyway. Dad might disagree with some of our choices, but you would never hear him tear one of us down to a stranger. He'd sure as hell never try to coerce us into a direction we didn't want to go.

Probably, what I was supposed to do was show them respect and try to back out of the conversation without drawing a line in the sand, but keeping my mouth shut isn't my strongest skill these days. Besides, I find it physically impossible not to stand up for Raven. I've seen first-hand the impact she's made both in the classroom and in the coaching world. Taking her from either of those would be a disservice to the people who need her. Me included.

I wait until the two of us are inside my truck, the doors closed and the windows rolled up, before I apologize.

"I'm so sorry, but I don't think your dad and I will be golfing buddies."

Raven snorts. "My dad will tell you that sports are for those who can't think."

I can feel my blood boiling under the surface. Of course, he thinks that way. The pair of them are so one-dimensional it's depressing. You would think with a daughter who absolutely slaughtered the college track world, they would see that excelling physically wasn't a sign of mental weakness.

"I meant to make a better impression."

She scoots closer to me, buckling into the center seat and resting her head on my shoulder as I pull out of the driveway. Normally, this would stress me out, and that tinge of familiar fear slips into the space between us, but there is also a warmness, an excitement that builds at wanting to be close to someone again. Raven takes all of my worries and fears and transforms them. She's the free version of therapy. The feel-good version, where the hurt and the struggle are worth it every time. I want to tell her this a thousand times a day, but instead, I keep it to myself, wondering how long I can stop something this beautiful from shattering into a million pieces.

The Austin sky is changing from the last deep purple of sunset to the beginning of complete darkness. The stars are too far off to see as we turn on to her street, but I remember the way it felt standing beneath them in the Arizona desert, the night of our first kiss.

It was my plan to drop her off and drive home tonight, but the feel of her cheek on my shoulder and the warmth of her side pressed up against mine have me thinking of other things. I don't want to assume that I can drive us to my apartment instead, that she'll come upstairs with me, though I'm certain she will. The thought alone makes me want to jerk the wheel to the right and take her home where my bed is waiting with clean sheets and anticipation.

I don't though. It's been a tough night, and I don't know how to read her yet. Maybe she can put the argument with her parents behind her, but maybe she can't? I don't want to be the guy who tries to make a vulnerable moment into something it isn't, so I pull up to her apartment instead. Then I walk up the stairs to her doorway to kiss her goodnight. This has been our routine these last few weeks. We hang out, go on dates, text throughout the day, but it always stops at kissing. Just kissing.

"Goodnight," I say before I'm ready.

She stares at me for a long moment, unmoving, those dark eyes of hers searching for something in me. Just when I fear I lack whatever she's looking for, she draws me back to her. This kiss could never be described as *just* anything. This kiss is hungry, it's heady and needy--it's a confession.

And I return her confession with one of my own, pressing her body hard against the doorframe. Her hands drop from my shoulders down to my waist, cool fingers tracking the skin underneath my shirt like she's mapping my body.

I want her hands everywhere.

I want *my* hands everywhere.

"Sleep over," she whispers into my mouth.

This is the moment that I should pull away, where I should say I'm not ready, but that would be a lie. I'm ready in every way a man can be. It doesn't mean I deserve her. I don't, I never will, but if she wants me, I'm here. And I want to be here. Now. With her.

"Are you sure?" I ask gruffly.

She breathes out a firm yes, and the way she says that word makes it impossible to stop my body from responding to the feel of her pressed up against me.

My hands become greedy as they move over her body, taking more than they should, but not taking nearly enough. She breaks away only to unlock her door and then we're inside her dark living room, bodies pressed up on the backside of her front door--*I've never loved a door so much.*

Our eyes catch in the shadowed darkness, the light from the streetlamp out back casting a soft orange glow over everything. Excitement passes between us, and I reach up to yank off my shirt. Raven stops me, grabbing the soft hem of my t-shirt with both hands and dragging it up over my head.

With the cloth still covering my face, she teases, "Oh no, buddy. These are the parts I get to do."

If she thinks I'm going to argue, she's crazy. She tears the shirt back and removes her own. She's beautiful in her black bra and jeans, beautiful and distracting in the best way. I almost don't want to move. Almost.

"Fine, then I get to do this." I kneel as I unbutton her pants, sliding them inch by inch over her perfect ass, trailing kisses across her warm skin as I go. She lifts her leg as I tug the pants off completely. I kiss behind her lifted knee and have the sudden urge to hitch it over my shoulder and remove her underwear with my teeth. She drops her leg before I can, and takes my hand, leading me toward her bedroom instead.

"You get the lead right now, Raven," I say in the hallway. "But once we walk into that bedroom, I'm taking over."

She stops and looks back at me, her eyes round and shining with surprise. Lust softens her beautiful face.

"There you are," she whispers hoarsely. "I wondered when you'd show up."

"There's no going back after this, not for me. I'm a one-woman man." It's a cliché thing to say, but it's the truth.

She smiles and squeezes my hand, her action alone telling me what I need to know, but I want her to say it, to hear that this is what she wants, that I'm who she wants. Flaws and all. Because she's about to know me in a way nobody ever has, know the hurt and the pain and the passion and the fire too. Jaci knew the Briggs I was, but I'm a different man now, a changed person.

"There's not going to be room for two women in my bed," I say, wanting her to understand the gravity of this for me. Her eyes widen with something unreadable, something I want to beg her to explain, but she's silent as I finish. "I'm not someone who sleeps around. I've only been with one person. Most men would be embarrassed about that, but I'm not. I'm proud of it."

"And you should be––"

"I want you and I can't share you."

"And I don't want to share you either." There's more vulnerability wrapped up in her voice than I've ever heard from her before. "I know I'll never replace Jaci, and I wouldn't want to, but I do want to be your future, Briggs. I want . . . I feel . . . "

I know what she's thinking, what she wants to say–– those four little letters.

Love.

It would be so easy. I could say it first. Get it out there. Make this more. But I don't, and I can't let myself think about that without feeling like a total jackass, so I nod toward the bedroom door instead. She opens it and that's the end of talking.

Chapter Forty-Four

RAVEN

There are the things you know will happen, the frantic removing of clothes, the obvious physical response, the anticipation building, the attraction pulling at every piece of you until you feel like you'll explode if you don't just pull the other person in and consume them whole, but it's the things I don't see coming that have my head in a spiral.

He didn't have to say that the two of us together meant saying goodbye to Jaci in yet another way, but he did, and somehow it works like a cheat code on me. My nerves disappear, and I'm no longer with Briggs, the widower, I'm with Briggs, the man who knows what he wants and says it, eyes locked on yours, no room for interpretation.

I've seen him in various states of undress a dozen

times. In the pool and on those long hot runs when he tears his shirt off and tucks it into the waistband of his shorts. I was sure he was teasing me then, but it's nothing like now. I can't get over the feel of his skin beneath my hands, his mouth at the base of my neck.

We could go on like this indefinitely.

Our bodies are like a human playground with infinite features for the other to explore. We've waited long enough, though, and in one swift movement Briggs scoops his hands around my thighs and lifts me up. My legs wrap around his waist, and my lips find his as we stumble toward the bed. He's gentle when he sets me down, and I scoot back until my head rests on the crisp white pillowcase.

Briggs hovers over me, our faces so close I can feel his breath warm on my cheek as he inches the lace waistband of my underwear down and over my legs. For a moment he hesitates, frozen above me despite the heat in the room. I worry for one agonizing second that he isn't ready. That he'll pull back, apologize, and leave me in this room wondering when, if ever, he will really be ready to let go and lean in. But then his eyes find mine and whatever turmoil he's facing inside clears like a break in the clouds when you think the gray of the storm will never leave.

"There are condoms in the nightstand," I breathe, and he's quick to take care of the contraception.

He lowers himself to me and when I feel him there, ready to press forward, I catch a tear sliding from the corner of his eye. For him, this is both an ending and a beginning. For me it's a prayer, because I know now, more than ever before, that I want all of him, always.

He takes me all at once, stretching and filling me up so entirely that I can't discern what belongs to him and what is mine. Our bodies, our hearts, our breath—it's all one. Our movements are frantic and hurried. It's like we're a couple of teenagers, like we can't believe this is happening and want to take everything we can.

"You're incredible. You're—I'm not going to last long."

Like he can't help himself.

Like I'm the prize.

There's no more going slowly after that, no more tears, no hesitation. Our hands are everywhere, palms sliding against skin, fingertips digging and teasing. He's rough, but I am too.

A cry rips through me and his movements speed. I couldn't stop myself from coming even if I wanted to, and I don't want to. Wave after cresting wave courses through me, and for a second, I think this is what it's like to really be loved, for a man to know your body so well that sex feels like the summit, and not the hike.

He's quick to follow, his breath hitching, and his eyes locked on mine the entire time.

When his heartbeat slows, he kisses my forehead and collapses next to me, pulling me into his arms. "You have no idea how long I've been wanting to do that to you."

His words muffle in the soft skin of my shoulder.

. . .

LATER THAT NIGHT, I toss and turn, listening to the sound of his breathing beside me. There are times when he moans, clenches his teeth. Sometimes he looks peaceful, sometimes angry. I can't begin to guess what he is dreaming about, but I hope this isn't his subconscious way of making him feel guilty for last night.

I can't imagine regretting anything that happened, but while some people come with a touch of emotional baggage, Briggs carries a three-piece set of the most expensive type: self-loathing, regret, and guilt.

I think about his confession. How he wasn't afraid to tell me that our first time might not be a long time. It might just be the hottest thing I've ever heard. Maybe not what other women want to hear in bed, surely not what it'll be like the next time we do this, but right now thinking about his words makes me feel like the sexiest woman alive.

He stirs beside me, and I squeeze my eyes tight, pretending to be Sleeping Beauty and not the chick with bags under her eyes.

When his arms wrap around my waist and his chin comes to rest on top of my head, I feel like I can breathe again. We lie like that for a moment, soaking in the newness of being able to be so close without guilt and desire battling it out between us. But we're naked, and we can only be lying against each other like this for so long before we have to do something about it.

When we finally do get out of bed, it's only to make our way to the couch where the two of us order coffee and bagels for delivery, then commit to doing absolutely nothing until ten a.m. when I'm due to meet with Remi, and Briggs has some mystery appointment he won't elaborate on, but I strongly suspect is therapy.

I want to tell him to wear it like a badge of honor. Every woman wants a man who is willing to pay someone else to tell him what needs fixing, but I keep my mouth shut, because if I've learned anything in the last seven months, it is that communication takes time. Especially with this man.

I would like to say that I left the house looking like a sexed-up goddess, but Remi takes one look at me and asks if I spent the night crying. When I tell her I spent the night worrying that Briggs would regret having sex with me, she bursts out laughing.

"You deserve this guilt."

My jaw drops. "Excuse me?"

Remi wiggles her eyebrows. "You messed with witchcraft and now you are questioning whether he likes the real you or just your tricky love potion."

That's when I remember the pheromones.

"I'll have you know that I didn't need the pheromones. I used the sheer power of my hotness to seal the deal. That, and Briggs got into a heated argument with my parents, and it was kind of hot."

The two of us are seated at an outdoor breakfast bistro, iced coffee in front of me and a full-scale breakfast in front of her. Remi nearly chokes on the sausage link she's just bitten into.

"You have got to be kidding me. Your parents seriously ended up making this happen? That is wrong on so many levels." I can't help but agree with her.

"Truthfully though, you know my parents, they did the whole *Raven needs to go back to school and get a real academic job* thing and Briggs wasn't having it." I lean in over the table like what I'm about to say is a big secret and not just adorable. "He quoted early brain development statistics for why kindergarten is so important."

Remi picks up her napkin and pretends to fan herself.

"Okay, I get you. I'd bang him too."

"There was one thing though . . ."

I'm not even sure if I should mention it. I don't want to sound ungrateful.

"Out with it." Remi raises a forkful of scrambled eggs at me. "Was it awful?"

"No, it was the best sex of my life." My cheeks prickle and I stare at my iced coffee for this part. "But . . . I almost told him I love him."

"Well, that's okay," Remi says. "There's still plenty of time for that."

I nod and meet her eyes. "It's just that he knew what I was about to say, it was obvious, and he stopped me."

She sets down her fork and leans forward, her features softening. "He must not be ready to say it back. That's all."

"So does that mean he doesn't love me? Or does that mean he's still falling? Or what if I'm the woman he's using to get over his dead wife, and he's never going to love me like I love him?"

Because I love him, I do. There's no denying it after last night. I want to tell him, and I would if I wasn't afraid it would scare him away. It sounds harsh saying that he might be using me because Briggs doesn't seem like the type, and he said himself that he's a one-woman man, but my insecurities are not playing fair today. This is the complicated part of relationships. Two people showing up to a private party, not sure how much the other one actually wants to be there.

"All it means is that he's not ready to say it," Remi says. "That's all. It doesn't mean he doesn't feel it, or that he's not going to profess undying love to you tomorrow. You're going to drive yourself crazy speculating on this, but I understand why you are." She knows my history. "I know you want all the answers now, but Briggs can't explain what he doesn't understand himself, and he definitely can't read your mind to know how badly you need to hear it." Remi sips her mimosa and pauses for a moment. "Sometimes you need to let go of the wheel and take a backseat."

I have no idea what she means, and my facial expression must show it because Remi's serious expression cracks into a wide grin.

"Let him say it first, Raven. Let him start the difficult conversations and trust he cares enough to do so, in his own time."

My heart gives a little tug. "I just can't come in second place, not for this."

I've never felt good enough to be first in anyone's heart, not with my own parents and not with any boyfriends. And Briggs? I'm not sure I can face possible rejection. It's not as if I'm going to run out and break it off with him. If anything, I want to try harder, to be more patient, to help him open up until I get all of him. But what happens to us if I can't wait? If I tell Briggs I love him and he can't say it back?

Chapter Forty-Five

BRIGGS

I've spent the better part of our hour-long session explaining my relationship to Dr. Thomas. The way I see it, I can move on with Raven and give us both a good life. We can live in whatever kind of home she prefers, travel the world for races, and do anything she wants. No guarantees, but I'd even consider children.

"But I can't love her," I tell him, my voice dejected but firm.

"You can't love her, or you won't love her?"

Has he not been my therapist for three years? Does he not have firsthand knowledge of everything I've been through?

I scoff. "I can't. It's not like I don't want to."

"And what does love mean, from your perspective?"

I hate the question, and still the answer comes blaring into my head like a song you've heard but hate. You can hate the melody, but the lyrics still slip from your lips. Love means being happy in the fullest possible way and then having that happiness ripped out at the roots and shredded into pieces. I've learned both sides of love first-hand, and I can't undo that knowledge. To simply forget what happened or change who it made me isn't possible.

"I know what love is, that's not the issue here. The issue is that I can't give it to Raven."

"If the love you gave Jaci is different from the love you can give Raven, is it still not love?"

That gives me pause, because I don't know the answer to that question, and I wish I did. All I do know is that as much as I want Raven, as much as she inspires me and challenges me––my heart is already broken. And it always will be.

"I can't make Jaci come back. That's a fact. And I'll never be able to love again because I'm a broken person. Also a fact."

Dr. Thomas's bushy eyebrows furrow and a line deepens between them. "And you don't believe broken people can love?"

I shrug. "Broken hearts don't work the same way anymore."

He's usually pretty good at staying neutral, but pity fills his eyes, and it makes me squirm. I hate pity. I don't deserve it. I don't deserve Raven either, not when she could find someone with a whole heart instead of a broken one, not when she's so amazing and could live a full life without grief shadowing her partner, but I'm selfish enough to hope she keeps me anyway. Even if I'm in pieces, I want to be her pieces.

WE DON'T TALK about love for the next couple of weeks that follow, even though it hangs between us like a ticking time bomb. I'm terrified that when I tell her the truth, she'll be hurt. She can leave me, and I wouldn't blame her, but I don't want to cause her any pain. I don't want Raven to become the collateral damage of my problems.

So we don't talk about love in all the moments we should––on the doorsteps, on the phone, and especially in bed. It's there for her, and it's not for me, and that's my fault. If I don't tell her soon, she's going to think something is wrong with her, and that's the last thing I would want her to think.

Today we are headed to the teacher appreciation picnic at Charlie's school. It's the first real group thing we've done as a couple that wasn't with the tri club, and I'm not sure how I fit in. It's been eons since I played the role of boyfriend, and today is important because today Raven gets the recognition she deserves. The recognition her parents are too blind to offer.

I wanted to do something special for her, so this morning while her hair was still fanned out over my pillow, I snuck out of the condo and made a detour to the one-hour photo. The first time I really saw Raven as more than the woman I wasn't supposed to fall for was the day I dressed as Santa for the *Polar Express* celebration. I had her classroom aide take a photo of us together, her in her conductor hat, me as Saint Nick, and the kids circling around us, each of them holding a silver bell. She's probably created a dozen special memories for her students this year, but I like to think that one stands out, and I can't wait to see her face when she unwraps the framed photograph.

I've tucked the photograph in our picnic basket, just under the two deli sandwiches we picked up on the way. Together we enter the courtyard and I lace my fingers through hers as we pass that nasty woman who runs the PTO.

Raven leans in and whispers in my ear, "You did that just to piss her off."

She's right, except I also did it to show off, because I'm pretty sure every man here today wishes he had a woman like Raven on his arm.

Every man, including Turner, who catches sight of us just as Charlie does. Before I know it, I have to let go of Raven's hand because Charlie is bounding into my arms, his cotton candy wand sticking to the back of my shirt as he clings around my neck like a baby sloth.

"Dad didn't know you were coming," cries Charlie. "He said the S word."

Raven reaches her hand up to cover her mouth, and I know without a doubt that she's forcing herself to stifle a laugh before Charlie catches his kindergarten teacher laughing at a swear word.

As if summoned, Turner makes his way across the grass. His hands are shoved deep in his pockets, clenched into fists if I had to guess.

I give him the standard man wave, a tilt of the chin. "Turner."

"Briggs."

Then the two of us stand there staring at each other like idiots until Raven intervenes by taking Charlie's hand.

"Come on, Charlie, you and I are going to get something to drink while your dad and uncle apologize to each other and start acting like grownups."

If Charlie is curious why we need to apologize, he's more curious about the soda selection because he doesn't hesitate to follow Raven and leave us to duke it out.

I should be the one to apologize. I know it, but it's not any easier than when we were kids. I still have that urge to roll around on the ground and get it over with, with fists instead of words, so I procrastinate.

"Charlie says you didn't expect to see me."

"I bet that's not all Charlie said." Turner shakes his head, and a frown brings out the creases between his eyebrows. "Samantha is going to give me so much crap for swearing in front of him."

"How's that all going?" I ask, feeling more than just a little shitty that I've been so distant lately that he has to explain it to me at his child's school picnic rather than over a beer after work.

"Well, let's see. She'd like the house, a solid chunk of my income, oh and Charlie."

I know they didn't have a prenup, but my stomach drops anyway. "Charlie? She can't be serious. You're his dad."

"Apparently that's a duty that can be managed every other weekend."

Turner is an every day kind of dad, and going to fifty/fifty split time will be hard enough, but every other weekend would kill him. I've never particularly disliked Samantha, but at the moment I'm pissed enough to wish her a long, head-first dive into a shallow pool.

"I don't know what to say."

Turner sighs. "Say you're done avoiding me like the plague. I've lost my wife. I'm being told when and for how long I can interact with my son. I don't need you to hate me too."

"You're giving me an easy out here."

A smile ticks at the corner of Turner's mouth. "Did you think I was going to hold out for an apology? There are things you haven't apologized for from grade school."

He is one hundred percent right. Still, I feel like an asshole just pretending nothing happened and letting him be the bigger person.

"Well, for this one, I do apologize. I shouldn't have been so hard on you. I can't expect everyone to turn into a work robot when life gets hard, and I don't know what it's like to be in your position, especially with a child in the mix." My throat catches on the word child and I have to look away.

Turner pats me on the back. "Already forgiven. And I'm sorry too. I shouldn't have said those things to you."

"You said them because they were true, and I needed to hear it." My mind returns to Turner telling me that I wasn't pursuing Raven because I liked being miserable. He thought I was using Jaci's death to keep myself off the hook from dating and getting hurt. At the time, I'd wanted to wring his neck, but I realize now that he was right. Sure, he could've delivered that kind of blow a little softer, but he was still right.

Turner whistles. "How hard was that for you to admit?"

"You have no idea." I give him a hard stare. "But it was easier to say now that things are getting better at work."

Because I had also been right––Turner was slacking too much, and the company was suffering as a result. He'd since turned things around, not going back to his regular way of doing things, but doing even better. I'd never seen him show up the way he has been lately.

"You're such a competitive son of a bitch." Turner laughs.

Charlie comes bounding over, tugging Raven along with him, and plops down in my lap. "Uncle Briggs, are you going to marry my teacher?"

Raven's face goes pink. "I'm going to grab a lemonade," she squeaks, hurrying away before I can offer to get the drink myself.

"Nice one, kid," I say, rubbing the top of Charlie's head.

"Well, are you?" Turner gives me a questioning look. It's a big question, one I never thought I'd be asking myself again.

"We'll just have to wait and see." I leave it at that, because right now I can't think about marriage and love and the kind of happily ever after that my nephew is imagining. Those things aren't guaranteed, nothing is. All I can guarantee is the here and now, and right now, my sole purpose is to make sure Raven has a great day.

Seeing as how Charlie has already embarrassed the pants off both Raven and me once today, I set up our picnic away from Turner and Charlie and wait for Raven to join me, two cups of bright-yellow lemonade in her hands. As we eat, the PTO joins the principal on a stage to hand out teacher awards. Raven grows nervous the longer her name isn't called, and when she's announced "Educator of the Year" for the entire school, tears spring to her eyes, and I help her stand on shaky legs.

Students cheer and several surround her in hugs and congratulations as she goes to collect her trophy--a crystalline apple with her name engraved across the front. I smile the entire time.

She's way too good for me.

I'm the millionaire CEO of one of the most lucrative construction companies in the state. That should make me a catch. Only, I'm also broken, widowed, and being an asshole comes as naturally to me as breathing. Raven is pure sunshine, gorgeous inside and out, and not only does she train adults to push through their physical limits, she's making a difference in the lives of young children.

We're not even in the same league.

When she returns to our blanket and the awards finish, I consider wussing out and not giving her my gift. Maybe I should bow out of the relationship so she can find someone worthy of her heart. What would Dr. Thomas say to that? He'd probably tell me to remember my mantra, that I am deserving of forgiveness and joy.

"I have something for you," I say, retrieving the framed photograph and handing it to her.

For the second time, her eyes brim with tears. "Thank you." Her voice is soft. "I love it." Then she stares up at me, her eyes open and vulnerable and so damn beautiful. "I love you, Briggs."

Those words. Those three little words--they mean everything to me. And they mean everything to her too because her expression is locked in a question. She's dying to know if I can say it back, and once again, I'm reminded just how not good enough for her I am.

My own heart tugs with hope and pain. This is it. This is the moment where I either lie and say it back, or I break her heart. I'll have to explain the deep feelings I have and hope she'll understand why love isn't one of them, that I want to love her, but I can't make myself capable of feeling something I lost forever. This isn't a game of lost and found--death just doesn't work like that.

But I do neither of those things. Instead, I freeze, saying nothing, and her face crumbles.

"Raven, listen——" I start, desperate to redeem myself, but we're interrupted by a gaggle of students and parents coming up to congratulate her.

We don't talk about love again.

Chapter Forty-Six

RAVEN

Lately I have been thinking about our first run together. That September morning it had been hard to imagine Briggs crossing any type of finish line. He was so clearly a mess. I didn't know why, but I knew he had light years to go before he had the mental or physical stamina to challenge himself the way today's triathlon will. And here we are now, standing in line to check in and get our monitors, every doubt replaced by total confidence.

He's done the work, and he's about to reap the benefits.

"You don't regret your decision to run this one without a pacing group?"

Briggs smiles, but when he reaches up to rub the back

of his neck, I know he's more nervous than he will ever admit. It's a tell he has, focusing on some random part of his body, and letting his eyes stray any way but toward mine.

"You'll be on the course."

"I'll be miles ahead of you. No offense."

The corner of his lip lifts. "I'm mildly offended."

But I know he's not, not even a little. Yesterday, when the club came to register, set up our bikes, and look over the course, he couldn't get that shit-eating grin off his face. The man was all kinds of excited, as he should be.

We reach the front of the line, and Briggs gives his name and birthdate to a tall man with bushy eyebrows and an equally bushy mustache. The guy grabs Briggs by the bicep and scribbles the number 206 on his upper arm in thick, dark ink.

"This is waterproof right? In case I drown in the first leg, and they need to identify my body?"

Swimming is still Briggs' weakest event. He's joking, but it won't be easy. I've seen people choke in the water before, especially if the weather is questionable or the temperature is too warm for the race officials to allow wetsuits but still cold enough to feel like you're going to cramp up. It isn't pretty, and it's a massive waste of a race fee.

"You won't drown. I mean, probably not anyway. Highly unlikely."

I can't help it. I start imagining Briggs sinking to the

bottom of the lake. If he does struggle, there will be nothing I can do. I likely won't even know about it until hours later when I can finally get my phone back and check his monitor on the app. All I can hope is that if something goes south, the volunteers see him go down. I've been avoiding asking, but I can't avoid the question today, not when I'm starting to feel more nervous than some of these athletes look.

"Your shoulder good?"

Briggs rotates his arm in a circle and pounds his fist into his rotator cuff like a monkey beating his chest.

"I've been doing all the exercises Leonard prescribes. My doctor cleared me to go just last week, and you've seen me in the pool, Raven." A crease forms between his eyebrows. "I'm starting to think *you* don't think I can do it."

"It's not that I don't think you can, more like, I feel responsible as your coach. If today goes poorly . . . "

"Do you always feel this way when a client races for the first time?"

I can't help it, the question makes me laugh. Not once have I worried about a client's safety. Have I had my doubts? Definitely, and usually I'm right to have them. I've told clients they aren't ready before, only to have them disregard my professional opinion and learn the hard way. The problem is that everything is different with Briggs. He's been clouding my judgment since day one, and now that we are seeing each other for real, I am less and less confident that I can evaluate him the way I would evaluate any other client. All bets are off with Briggs, and he knows it.

"My clients aren't usually my boyfriend."

And this isn't some measly race. It's over seventy miles of swimming, biking, and running. The average time to finish this particular course is six hours--far further and longer than anything Briggs has attempted before, even with our long training days.

A buzzer rips through the air above us before either of us has time to argue what I've just said.

"Well, Coach, suck it up, because in a few hours I'm going to be running through that finish line, and I expect to hear you cheering embarrassingly loudly."

"Not just her," says a familiar voice. Turner has snuck up behind us and he's not alone. "I brought everyone." Turner then points to the spectators' area where, in true Lawson fashion, everyone has gathered to celebrate.

Briggs' face goes stark white. "You invited the board?"

A laugh escapes me, and instinctively, my hand flies up to cover my nose. I've never met the board of Lawson Construction, but I'm willing to bet my itty-bitty savings that the four men and women in three-piece suits sitting behind Mr. and Mrs. Lawson are to whom he is referring.

"They are going to bake in this sun. Did you tell them how long this thing is?" Briggs asks.

I snort because they're going to lose sight of Briggs within minutes of his start time. Then they'll have to travel around the course to watch him travel by for all of thirty seconds, that's if they can even make him out in the hordes of people he'll be racing with. At least the finish line will be a fun moment to look forward to––in six or seven hours.

"Oh, I didn't tell them anything," says Turner with a smirk. "You can thank your father for inviting them. He thinks it demonstrates how well you are doing."

Briggs' hands ball into fists at his sides. "Was there ever any doubt? Am I not killing it at work?"

Turner pats Briggs on the shoulder. "Calm down, buddy. They mean well. It's a family business, remember?"

The color is returning to Briggs' face, only now there is a little too much of it.

"Okay," I say. "Visiting time is over. Coach's orders."

Turner wraps Briggs in a hug before he can protest. "Seriously, man, we're excited for you. You got this."

"I hope so," mutters Briggs, and it's like I can see his confidence deflating like a balloon with the tiniest of holes in it.

There is no time for a pep talk, so instead I grab him by the neck and pull his forehead down to mine.

"I'll be waiting at the finish line. Promise me you'll be there."

Briggs tilts his head and answers with a kiss. The feel of his lips on mine is still a novelty, and despite the fact that there are hordes of people surrounding the two of us, including members of my own tri club who hoot and holler, I lean into the kiss like it's just he and I hiding behind that tree in the Sedona desert.

But in the back of my mind, a little voice is telling me that he doesn't love me like I love him. Hell, he can't even say it back to me. Like always, I tell that little voice to shut up, even though I know that eventually that voice is going to get too loud to ignore. Eventually it's going to be screaming.

"Are you sure I can't pace with you?" I whisper as the two of us finally break free. "I could see you through this every step of the way."

The race official blows another warning horn for Briggs' group, and we turn and walk toward the start line. My group starts fifteen minutes after him, but I'll probably pass him in the water and likely won't even see him out there. "Not because you need me, but because I want to be there when you meet your goal."

I'd do it––I'd wait for him after the swim, take longer with my transition than necessary, and then we could bike together and run. I don't care that I'd have to slow down, that I'd probably end with one of my slowest times. I don't care what the tri club will think or if it would potentially hurt my business. All I care about right now is him.

Briggs grins and steps back toward the starting line. "You're going to rock it out there today, baby. I can't be the guy to slow you down." I want to argue, but he gives me a knowing look. "This one I have to do on my own."

And I know he is right, but I hate it all the same. With one final wave, I duck off to stand back with my clients who haven't had their start times yet. The professionals started over an hour ago, Allen is already in the water, and the rest of us will be out there within the hour. Together we watch as a flare gun shoots into the sky, and the next wave of people make their way toward the water, Briggs' broad shoulders bouncing up and down with the rest.

Chapter Forty-Seven

BRIGGS

The water hits me like a blaring five a.m. alarm you forgot you set the night before. I don't want to think. I want those hours of training to take over, transforming me into a swimming/biking/running machine. I'd pay an ungodly amount of money to be able to mentally check out and let my body do the work today, but it doesn't work that way for me. Not for the swim part anyway, and I doubt the biking or running will be much better, because after a minute of being in the lake, face down in the murky water, turning from side to side to catch my breath and hopefully not another hand or foot to the face, doubt creeps in.

Can I really do this?

I'm not so sure. The other races were child's play compared to this one.

But I press on, because whether or not I can do it isn't the point anymore. How many times have I been faced with something I thought I couldn't do and lived through it? Too many times. This will have to be another one of those times, no matter how shitty it gets. I committed to be here and I'm not going to quit. Still, I promise myself that if I hate triathlons by the end of the race, I never have to sign up for another one. It's not like being committed to Raven means being committed to her tri club. She'll love me either way.

She'll love me either way––that thought is like oxygen right now. It's everything. It's also brutal, because the thing about Raven is that she'll go all in even when I can't. Is that really fair to her?

Of course not.

Do I want to keep her anyway?

Absolutely.

And that's the crux of it. Now that I have her, I'm terrified to lose her, but I also know she deserves better than a sorry widower who will always be broken. Eventually, she's going to realize it, same as I have.

A mouthful of water pours into my mouth, and I come up coughing, lungs burning. I look around at the other swimmers gliding past me, although gliding probably isn't the best word for most of them. Water is splashing everywhere, and everyone is a yellow monochrome blur from behind my tight goggles. It looks wild out here, nothing like the swimming pool. Is Raven in the water by now? Her start time wasn't far after mine, but she's so much faster that she'll leave me behind in short order. As much as I want to look for her, I couldn't find her out here if I tried. There's just too many of us.

I gaze over at the shoreline instead, at the distant spectators standing there, at the race officials floating on paddle boards throughout the water to assist anyone who needs it, and at the people already climbing out to transition to their bikes. I better get my head in the game. The last thing I need is to waste any time. I'm going to be lucky to finish by my six-hour goal time––it'll be more like seven, but Raven wanted me to make a push goal anyway.

By the time I drag myself up the shoreline to change out of the wetsuit and jump onto my bike, my muscles are burning and my skin is covered in gooseflesh. The damn wetsuit is a bitch to get off and the zipper sticks as I try to pull it down my back. Everyone is being so quick in their transitions, and I feel like a giant toddler trying to get this stupid thing off. If Turner and the rest of them are watching me right now, I'm going to kill him later. This shit is embarrassing. When I'm done hobbling toward the finish line, I have every intention of letting Raven know that transitions need at *least* one dedicated club meeting. And honestly, having Raven teach me how to shuck a wetsuit in record time does not sound like such a bad way to spend an hour.

A cold hand pats me on the back just as I get the zipper down. I turn to find bright honey eyes gazing up at me.

Raven is beaming, and even her eyes rimmed from where the goggles had made indents against her skin don't make her look any less gorgeous.

"You okay?" she asks.

My eyebrows raise, and I'm sure I look just as silly with my own goggle indents. "I'm fine. Now get your pretty ass on that bike, woman."

She laughs. "It's okay to let someone help you every once in a while, Briggs."

"And it's okay to leave me in the dust. Now go!"

I'm talking about the triathlon, of course, but it occurs to me that leaving me behind in this race might not be the only area it's best for her to pull away. If she left me today, I wouldn't blame her.

Her face falters for a moment, but then she winks and sprints off to where her bike is stationed. I hope I don't see her until the finish line. I meant it when I told her I didn't want to slow her down, but I think she understands that, because she's pulling on her helmet and speeding away before I've even strapped my shoes into my own bike.

Fifty-six miles.

Thank God Texas is flat.

I take off and find the cycling to be much easier than the swimming. And thanks to Raven's coaching, I know exactly when to fuel myself and how often, how to read my fitness tracker, when to push my body and when to slow it down. I'm not looking forward to the gooey protein packets or the water mixed with a ridiculous amount of fake-berry flavored electrolytes, but if her coaching keeps me from cramping up or spending an hour in one of the porta potties, then so be it.

The sky is a clear, crystalline blue and the sun's warmth, combined with the wind at my back, dries me out in no time. Before long, I'm sweating buckets, and it's still early in the day. I check my fitness watch often, but phones aren't allowed in this race, so I don't know if or when I'll see Turner and the others on the sidelines. I wouldn't mind them watching me speed by on my bike like an athlete. That would be much better than the toddler fumbling with his zipper back at the shoreline.

The miles are tough at first, but then they get easier.

The course switches directions as the wind picks up, pushing against us now, and my strength begins to whither, as does my speed.

And the sun? It only beats down harder, merciless and mocking.

We already knew it was going to be a hotter day than we would've wanted. May in Texas is like July in northern states, and the high is expected to reach into the nineties. The sooner I can get this over with, the better, because if I'm not careful, I'm going to be out running in the heat of the day. And then not only will I be finishing in seven *or more* hours, but I'll be wanting to die too.

Several of the cyclists I've been keeping up with so far have disappeared from view, and more are passing me. There are still ten more miles left on the bike, and I'm falling further and further behind. Is that because my body is too tired, because the wind is too strong, the sun is too hot––or because my self-talk is total crap? Because it sure as hell looks like everyone's tired out here. We're all facing the same environment, but most of these people are handling things far better than I am.

Toughen up, Briggs.

Finishing out the bike leg takes longer than I expected. I knew there wasn't a prayer of me hitting the finish line in six hours, but I'm starting to worry that seven is a stretch. The good news is the transition between the bike and the final leg of the race is nothing like the first one. Raven's bike selection was top-notch, and as a result, I have no trouble tossing mine into place where all the other bikes are waiting.

A quick scan of the line reveals several open spots in the corral. At least I'm not in last place. That's my actual worst fear. Not, not finishing or getting injured, but crossing the finish line dead last. I know it's petty, but I need to do more than finish. I need to finish well.

The first mile is ugly, but I'm prepared for that. It doesn't seem to matter how long you train for or how much you improve, mile one always feels like horse shit. I swear it's a mental game, my brain's way of begging me to give up. *Take this and multiply it by thirteen, sound fun?* I've learned to ignore that voice over the last few months, but it's screaming in my ear, and that combined with the sun is making me want to listen instead of pushing it aside the way I usually do.

For the first time since plunging into the water, I regret not taking Raven up on her offer to pace me. She'd be full of bubbly bullshit to keep me motivated right now. Instead, every dark thought I have seems to float to the surface. By mile three, my legs feel like lead and my attitude has soured so much that I feel sorry for the volunteers at the water station. I'm pretty sure one of them flinched when I crushed my minuscule cup of water in one hand and tossed it dangerously close to his head.

It's mile seven though, that I find myself hunched over the side of the road, puking into the ditch and regretting my existence. I can't do it. I can't finish the race. There are still six point one miles between me and this goal, and I don't see it happening. I don't see any part of my body making it over the finish line. Not my three-hundred-pound legs, not my head, which now feels like someone is playing a bass drum upside my skull, and certainly not my spirit, because that part is crushed, obliterated, a pile of dust on the pavement.

I wipe my mouth with the lip of my shirt and plant myself on the curb. I don't care about what other racers think. Dipping my head between my knees and checking out for a moment doesn't embarrass me in the slightest. Only when I lower my head, it's not relief that I feel--it's blood rushing in my ears, little dots swimming before my eyes and an overwhelming desire to puke again.

I'm not sure how long I'm sitting like this before I feel a familiar tap on my shoulder. I shield my eyes from the sun and look up. That's when I know I'm dead--I'm the first member of the tri club to bomb so hard that they actually croaked--because standing over me, backlit by the sun, blond hair hanging loose around her shoulders, is Jaci.

Chapter Forty-Eight

RAVEN

I hear the finish line before I see it. The dinging of those cheap metal bells the sponsors hand out like candy combined with the hollering of the spectators and the rumble of the announcers over the speakers can't be missed. The noise echoes for nearly a mile in every direction. It gets louder as I approach, spurring me on. There are a lot of racers who will finish around the same time, and some are from my club--they also keep me going.

I don't even think about slowing down anymore, but it helps that I'm in great shape. My muscles always burn like hell by this point, and my joints either go numb or throb like someone's jammed nail files into them, but luckily, it's a numb joints day today. That numbness won't last long--by tonight I'll be lying in an ice bath, the high having worn off. And the next week will be tough, recovery always is. A smile busts across my face, and if I wasn't concentrating so hard on finishing, I'm sure I'd be hunched over laughing on the side of the road. Recovery will be rough for me, but recovery is going to murder Briggs.

I round the last corner and the arched finish line rises ahead, the black carpets laid out for us, and even more spectators cram against the barriers. It's not a championship event, so it's not nearly as crowded as I've seen it, but this is one of the more popular races on the triathlon circuit, and there are loads of people out today.

I usually try not to look at the crowd because I'll lose focus and a few seconds of time. Keeping my gaze ahead, I let the people fly by in a blur, that is until I hear my name being screamed by an entire group of people. I catch sight of Turner and several members of the Lawson family. I only have two seconds to wave and smile back at them before they're behind me, and I fly through the finish line, my name and time being announced.

I smile for the cameras between gasps of air and then hightail it into the recovery tent, scanning the sea of athletes for my club members. The tent is one big open coed space, and several people are sprawled down in the grass, arms outstretched. The race organizers have set up tables piled high with boxes of pizza, sodas, and water bottles. On the opposite side of the tent are outdoor showers, more porta-potties, and a few curtained-off changing areas. There's already a line at those, because sometimes athletes, usually the men, will pee in their suits, unwilling to take the time to stop at the bathrooms along the route. Personally, I'm unwilling to risk the chafing. Well, that, and being drenched in my own urine.

I sit down on my own plot of grass and stretch out my muscles for a good ten minutes, then I hit the bathrooms and one of the outdoor showers. It's so hot today that I don't mind getting soaked by the stream of cold hose water. After toweling off, I grab a pepperoni pizza and guzzle some more water. Then I find the members of my club who've already finished to discuss our times and see where everyone else is on the course.

"Do you have your phone yet?" Allen asks halfway through our conversation about his race today.

He sits next to Kate and Damien, who are busy devouring the pizza I plopped down between us. The fragrant smell of cheese and tomato sauce is so wonderful I could cry, but the taste is even better.

I swallow my bite. "No, not yet." Phones aren't allowed during the race, and I haven't gone to my locker to retrieve mine. "How's everyone else doing?"

"Here." He shoves his into my hand, the triathlon app already pulled up so I can see where everyone else is currently at on the course. Before we start, everyone is given waterproof trackers that we're required to wear for the duration of the race. Sometimes the trackers are unreliable. They might fall off or stop working, but nine times out of ten they're helpful.

I scroll through the list of familiar names, noting that

everyone in the club is about where I expect them to be by now. Except for one person . . . Briggs.

"Do you think his monitor broke?" Allen asks.

"I wish I knew the answer to that." But I don't, and it makes me uneasy.

I worry about my athletes all the time, but this is different. This is Briggs. I would go out there, go make sure he's okay, but his monitor location isn't very accessible. I'd have to take the shuttle to my car, then drive to the closest neighborhood, find parking, go try to find him, and by then he'd already be gone. If he's hurt somewhere, the race staff will help him, and if his monitor is faulty, then he's still running.

"Go talk to his family," Kate says. "They probably don't know what's going on."

I usually stay in the tent for a good hour after finishing, and once we're all done, the team sits near the podium and waits for announcements and awards while we discuss how things went. It's our ritual, and I don't want to disappoint any of my paying customers by spending my time with my boyfriend's family instead.

"I know what you're thinking." Allen raises his eyebrows. "But guess what? We all love that you have a boyfriend that pays you by the hour. It's a serious upgrade from the last few."

"Hardy har, har," I say, but I have to admit, he's right. Briggs is easily my best boyfriend in the past decade, and the man does technically pay to be around me.

Damien and Kate nod. "Go hang out with his folks for a while. We've got it handled over here."

Giving them each a quick hug, I retrieve my things from my locker and then hobble over to the Lawsons. They're still standing by the metal barriers, cheering on the nearly constant stream of finishers, though I note that the people in suits have all gone home by now. Their faces are flushed from the sun and much of their earlier enthusiasm has been diminished by hours of standing around.

"You were incredible." Turner sees me first, going in for a hug around my middle, little Charlie going in for one around my knees.

I try to stop them. "You're all wet," Charlie squeals, stepping back from our embrace. His face screws up in confusion and I feel like I should probably explain to him that I just got out of the shower, that I'm not just soaked in sweat, but in true five-year-old fashion he's already wiggling his way through the crowd bells in each hand, his energy renewed as he searches the finish line for the first glimpse of Briggs.

"Thank you for what you've done for our son." Mr. Lawson pats me on the back. "And great job out there today. You're very impressive."

My cheeks warm as I nod, then clear my throat. "Are you tracking him on the app?"

"There's an app?" Turner throws his hands up. "I swear, I'm going to kill my brother. That would've made things a lot easier today. Do you know how hard it was to find him out there on the course? I'll tell you how hard––impossible. It was impossible."

I grimace and explain what the app is and how it works while they download it, but then Briggs' icon hasn't moved, so I also have to explain that the app is probably showing him stuck in the same spot because his monitor fell off or stopped working.

"But I'm sure he's fine," I add. "Technology isn't perfect. He'll probably be finishing in another hour."

Mrs. Lawson's face creases with worry, and she tugs me away from the group. We find a tree with an empty park bench away from the noise so we can talk. "You really think he's okay?" she asks. "You can tell me if you don't."

"I can't say for sure, but the staff knows how to handle things if someone gets injured. If he's not fit to finish, they'll help him, and they'll call his emergency contacts."

"And if he quits?" She doesn't say it like she'd be disappointed in him if he did, she says it like she'd be disappointed *for* him.

As a coach and an athlete, that's something I understand more than anyone. He's worked hard to get to this day, but sometimes things don't go as planned.

"If that happens, he'll take a shuttle back here or one of the volunteers will let him use a phone to contact someone to come pick him up." Even as I say it, I know that's not what she's really asking. If Briggs quits this race, it's going to erase so much of the progress he has made these last few months. He needs that finish line moment to break through years of grief and guilt.

She squeezes my hand. "He loves you, do you know that? I want to make sure you know that."

My throat grows dry and I look away. I wish I knew his feelings for certain, but I don't. "He hasn't said so."

"I know my son. I've only seen him in love twice in his life. With Jaci, and now with you. Just because he hasn't said it yet doesn't make it not true."

I wish I could believe her. My heart does. But my head? My head isn't so sure. "He's been through so much." My voice cracks. "He thinks he's broken."

She pats my hand and I look at her again. Tears rim her eyes. And gratitude. And faith and trust. All those things I need to cling to right now. I wish I could borrow some of hers, because honestly, I'm not sure how much longer I can be with a man who can't tell me he loves me. I haven't been through what he's been through, not even close, but I've been through enough to know what I'm worth.

"Look at him now," she says. "He's out there, doing this incredibly difficult race. He's *trying*. Is that what a broken person does?"

I shake my head slowly. "I don't think he's broken. I think he's perfect. If that matters. . . "

Maybe he's right and he did break when Jaci died, but does that mean he's always going to be that way? I don't think so. God, I really hope not.

"And if he is broken," I say, my voice hitched with tears. "Then I'm into broken."

"You're the thing that's putting him back together." Her spine straightens as she pulls herself together one vertebrae at a time. "He's stronger for it. *You* did that for him, Raven. Not his therapist, not running an unholy amount of miles in tiny shorts. It was you." She casts her eyes toward the finish line where Charlie and Turner are still ringing their ridiculous bells. "You did that for our whole family."

She wraps me in a tight hug, and for a moment, the two of us are just a blob of tears and sniffling. We both know that whatever happens next between Briggs and me is up to him. I love him and I don't want to give him up, but he's got to love himself too. He's never going to be able to love me if he can't do that, and I'm not going to be able to stay with someone who can't love me the way I deserve. There's not much left to say after that, so the two of us head back to the group.

Along the way, I'm stopped by a pat on the back. "Great job out there, honey."

I turn, astonished, to find my parents grinning at me. Dad's got a bell in one hand and his camera in the other, and Mom's got a poster-board with my name on it and "that's my daughter" written across the front in boxy black lettering.

"I got some amazing pictures of you." Dad holds up the camera. "You look so focused and professional."

Mom pulls me into a hug. I'm still stunned and can barely lift my hands up to hug her back. "I'm going to show all our friends the pictures. They're going to be so impressed."

"Uh--Mom, Dad," I stumble through my words, "this is Mrs. Lawson, Briggs' mother."

"It's nice to meet you. Would you like to come join us? We've got room," says Mrs. Lawson.

Dad gives me a little wink, and that's how we end up all standing together, watching the racers come through the finish line, one after another. My joints stay numb through it all. In fact, I think my whole body stays numb because I can hardly believe it. This is the first event my parents have attended since my college days, and I didn't even tell them I was competing in it. They must have done their own research. This means they're trying. Actually trying. *Finally trying.* It's only a start, but sometimes a start is all you need.

Chapter Forty-Nine

BRIGGS

Jaci sits beside me on the curb. She's wearing her old running shoes, the ones so bald and tattered that you can barely make out the Nike swoosh along each arch. Instinctively, I straighten my spine. Hobbled, with my head in my hands, is not how I want her to see me, even if she is just a figment of my imagination.

With shaky hands, I pull a gel from the waistband of my shorts and pop the foul squishy substance into my mouth. I should have listened when Raven said to fuel even when you feel like you don't need it. Seeing your dead wife has got to be a symptom of low blood sugar. Otherwise, it's a symptom of me losing it.

"She couldn't get you in a unitard?" she asks, nudging me in the side with her elbow.

Twenty yards out, a runner slows to a jog and looks my way. I wave to let him know I'm alright and wait until he rounds the corner to turn back to Jaci. Raven has got to be worrying about me by now, tracking me on that damn app that lets everyone know when you're in failure mode. The last thing I need is someone at the finish line reporting that I'm half dead on the side of the road. It's true, but still.

"What are you doing here?" I'm past the point of caring that I'm essentially talking out loud to myself.

Jaci feigns insult. "I'm motivating you, duh."

I want to pull her into my arms, lock her hand in mine, and keep her at my side until I die of old age. If she thinks she's motivating me to finish this race, she's as far gone as I am.

"You're doing a bad job," I say, and she rolls her eyes.

For just a second, an old familiar annoyance creeps up on me. How many times did an eye roll result in an argument? She knows it drives me crazy. *Knew.* She *knew* it drove me crazy. But I'd put up with a million eye rolls if they could be the real thing.

But I can't, so I close my eyes and count to five instead.

"Still here."

I shake my head. "This isn't real."

"Does it matter?"

I open my eyes.

In truth, it doesn't. I'll take Jaci in whatever manner I can get her. Dreams, psychotic episodes . . .

"Get off your ass." Her voice rocks me out of my stupor, and I have to stop for a second to remember why I stopped moving in the first place. Maybe the gel is doing its thing or maybe what I needed was a swift kick to the ego, but I no longer feel like I'm going to hurl or pass out or pass out hurling.

I pull a water bottle from my fuel belt and drink slowly, despite the urge to chug it like I've just spotted an oasis among miles and miles of blistering sand.

"See, you do know what to do."

I rise to my feet and wait for another runner to pass before scowling at her.

"Your motivational speaking sounds a lot like bullying."

"It's tough love, baby. And you need it."

The sun is no longer directly over us, and I'm beginning to feel like myself again. Stronger, focused.

She'll be gone soon and we both know it.

Or I guess I'm the only one who knows it, considering she's not really here.

"Ah, but maybe I am really here," she says.

"Stop that."

She's half serious, half joking. "I'll always be here."

"I know, but––" I shake my head. "That's not fair to you."

"Death isn't either and neither is life, but you're here to live, Briggs, so get moving."

I'm either sweating or crying or both, because I can't make sense of the salt in my mouth. It's too much. *This* is too much.

"I mean it. Don't make me haunt you."

As if she hasn't already . . .

My feet move with a mind of their own, first a hobble, then a walk, slow jog, smooth gait. Before long, I'm running again, and the finish line no longer feels impossible. Beside me, Jaci's footsteps grow more muffled with each stride. I rack my brain for something to say that matters before she's gone. But there's nothing. I can't apologize anymore, and even if I did, I get the sense it was never what she needed anyway.

"I'm fine, you know. It's you who is a mess." Her smile is like water to a dying man. "It's okay to be messy, so long as you don't stop."

I want to laugh, because ghost Jaci is no nonsense and a bit of a pain in the ass, but I feel a tear slipping down my cheek instead. Okay, so the salt isn't just sweat, but that's okay. I'm okay. I think about Dr. Thomas and his silly mantra. *I am open to forgiveness and joy.*

It's not so silly to me anymore. It's the truth.

The miraculous, gut-wrenching, beautiful truth.

I turn to my right, ready to tell her that I may be a mess, but I'm a work in progress, a therapy-going, girl-friend-having, triathlete of a mess, only her footsteps have been replaced by another runner closing in on me from behind. This guy is at least sixty. He's hairy and sweaty and sporting a pot belly that tells me exactly how far behind I have fallen.

I kick it into high gear, leaving him and his labored

breathing behind me as I pass the second-to-last mile marker. I don't see Jaci again, not in the stretches where there are other runners, not even in the stretches where I am alone. I get the feeling her *you're a mess* pep talk is the last I will hear from her, but it pushes me forward, drives me to prove her wrong. I was a mess before Raven, a disaster before Dr. Thomas, but I don't have to live that way anymore. I have no intention of it. What matters now is that I don't stop.

Don't stop running.

Don't stop living.

Don't stop loving.

Bells clang in the distance. The metallic noise starts quiet and grows louder as the yards fall away beneath my feet. Somewhere among the din is my family, my mother with her heart on her sleeve and my father trying desperately to hide his own. And Raven, she'll have that glow about her, all those endorphins coursing through her, putting that adorable pink in her cheeks. I'm spent, but the thought of finding her in the crowd has my feet moving faster. My arms pump at my sides, and I no longer care that my whole body hurts and most of my breakfast is on the side of the road several miles back.

I'm doing this––I'm finishing the race.

When I arrive at the final stretch, the carpet laid out before me, the crowd ecstatic, my family cheering me on among them, a moment of clarity settles over me. I may be glad to finish this God-awful race, but I'm also so damn grateful I did it. It's not despite the pain of putting my body through what I just did, but it's *because* of the pain that accomplishment washes over me in great waves.

Life is like that too.

Sometimes we coast downhill and sometimes we're lying on the side of the road convincing ourselves not to give up, but what matters is that we keep moving forward. My life has been a beautiful shattering. I can't put the broken pieces back together the way they were before. I'll never be able to do that, but I can clean up the mess and turn it into something new. Something equally beautiful.

I expected to stumble through the finish line, but I don't. I finish strong, and on the other side I see her. She's waiting for me with her arms outstretched and the biggest smile, a smile that isn't water--it's oxygen.

"Raven," I breathe into her mouth the second I meet her, wrapping her into my arms and kissing her like she's the prize. Because she is the prize. Whether I deserve her or not, somehow, she wants me anyway. Somehow, I'm her prize too.

I don't care who could be watching or that I stink or that it's hot or that my legs are Jello. Kissing her outweighs the rest of the world. For a long moment we stay like that, our mouths confessing all the things we've held back, without actually saying a single word. The cheering around us grows louder, but I don't stop to check if it's for the finishers or for us.

She finally pulls away, her hands squeezing mine. "You did it. Congratulations, Briggs. I knew you could do it."

I chuckle hoarsely. "You were the only one who did."

Her smile lifts. "Deep down you knew it, too, or you wouldn't be here."

I guess she's right. "You're so smart." I press another kiss to her lips, quicker this time. "And beautiful."

"Right back atcha."

She means it, and if that woman thinks I'm beautiful right now, when I've just been through hell and back, then she's even more special than I thought, because Lord knows I look like I just swam, biked, and ran seventy miles in the blazing sun for the first time.

"Come on, we've got to celebrate. Everyone's waiting."

She turns to tug me after her, but I hang on tight and pull her right back. "They can wait. This can't."

I kiss her for a third time and then I inch back just enough to look into her eyes, just enough to make sure she can see exactly how certain I am about her.

"I love you," I say. It's not a confession this time, it's a declaration.

Her mouth pops open and her eyes go crinkly around the edges.

"I love you," I say it again because I can't not say it again. "I've loved you for months, and I'm so sorry I didn't tell you sooner." I trace her lips with my thumb, forcing myself not to kiss her. Again. "I didn't know how to accept my feelings. I thought loving you was betraying her."

Tears break free from her perfect autumn day eyes, and I wipe them away. "Please don't cry. I'm sorry I hurt you getting here."

"I'm not crying for me. I'm crying for you," she says. "And for her. It's not fair I get you and she doesn't, that they don't."

"Life and death aren't fair," I repeat the words Jaci told me back there on the road. "But it's what happened, and while I can't say I wouldn't change their death, because I would, I also wouldn't change loving you."

Her eyebrows furrow and I want to make sure I do this the right way.

"She taught me how to love," I say. "But you taught me not only how to love again, but also how to finally love myself. Jaci will always be a part of me. Our unborn baby will always be a tragedy. But they're a part of my past. I can't claim to know the future. I know better than anyone that it can all be taken away, regardless of your plans, but I do know that the future I want is the one with you." I swallow hard. "If you'll have me."

Her head is shaking so hard that the tears spilling over her cheeks take flight. She wipes them away with the sleeves of her shirt and crushes her mouth to mine. "I'll have you," she repeats those three words over and over between her tearful kisses. "I'll have you. I'll have you. I'll have you."

And then, when she says the three words that matter the most, when she whispers, "I love you," it's almost like hearing it for the first time.

Almost. I finally understand that moving forward and letting go don't depend on one another. The I love you's of the past can stay there or come along, and either choice will be okay, because there's more than enough room in my heart. And there's enough room for my future. From now on, I'm taking Jaci's advice.

I'm moving forward.

Thank You

Thank you for reading *Beautiful Shattering*. This is our third book together writing as Grace but our first book that made us shed tears. Briggs and Raven's story took us in a direction we've never written in before—a love story centered around shattering grief and the beauty of forgiveness. We hope you love this book as much as we do, and if you do, please consider leaving reviews and recommending this book to your friends. And of course, many thanks goes out to our editor, cover designer, early readers, family, and team.

Love, Grace

Also by Grace Costello

Twinfluence

Your economics teacher twin calls in one last swap.

Ivy League Liars

Your rival challenges you to find a better wedding date.

About the Author

Grace Costello is the pen name for Nina Walker and M. F. Lorson. If Grace were a person, we'd take our best traits and make her a wacky librarian with a soft spot for cats. Unfortunately, Nina isn't cool enough to be a librarian and M.F. foolishly hates cats. We'll leave Grace up to your creation and hope she's fun enough to invite to your girls' nights, sophisticated enough to trust for dating advice, and compassionate enough to invite over for a late night pseudo-therapy sesh complete with Godiva chocolate and tarot cards.

www.ingramcontent.com/pod-product-compliance
Lightning Source LLC
Chambersburg PA
CBHW060221030726

47499CB00004B/1140